The Chronicles of Tiny Tim
3000 Christmas Candles

Liam Mac an Ghoill

Copyright © 2014 Liam Mac an Ghoill

ISBN:0956907141
ISBN-13: 978-0956907141

ALSO, BY LIAM MAC AN GHOILL

The Moss Wall
Among The Shadows of Men
Face2Face

DEDICATION

Dear Mr. Dickens

It is sometimes said that a gifted blind man could see a good opportunity long before it blooms on the horizon. For children, reality is often put on hold so that we might live our visions, and when we become old enough to know the difference, all that remains is a breathing apparition.

The Chronicles of Tiny Tim could be best described as a living ghost, a resurrection of solid determination, held together by the rivets of the soul. Others may describe it as a desecration of a literary grave or a tactical blending of capital ingredients.

Whatever opinions the philosophical minds of society wish to bequeath to this respectful undertaking, only the coming years can be turned back to make way for the judgement of history. An amnesty given for a first mistake is a fair prerogative but does not apply when we only get the one chance. The Chronicles of Tiny Tim will cross my mind once, and within that small instance, be forever engraved on a vast and endless wall of time.

I offer no apologies nor seek no laurels and in the silence within myself, I will whisper only to those that cannot hear. From the seeds that you have sown so many years ago, humanity now feasts on a great bounty of words and within your shadow, I only hope that I can smudge the surface of your monumental greatness.

Sincerely

Liam Mac an Ghoill

Liam Mac an Ghoill

For Dita

CHAPTER 1

Scrooge was as dead as a doornail, his father was deader than a doornail and scrooge's grandfather, without reservation, was as dead as the nail in any old door. What will become of this story depends on the reader recognizing that dead as a doornail is not something to be taken lightly.

Gabriel Shivers plunged his dark wood fountain pen into the old inkwell and proceeded to etch the epitaphs of fallen souls onto the thick paper ledger before him. Letter after letter, word after word cruelly stood side by side to blindly gorge upon a never-ending harvest of misery and agony. He had entered the employment of The War Office the week before with expectations far exceeding his humble station, only to be tossed into the depths of an ocean of tears. The electric desk light flickered in unison with every motor vehicle or horse drawn cart that passed within a few feet of his window. The confines of his small office stank with the mustiness and dampness of its years, and corridors on the other side of his heavy woodworm door echoed to the shuffles of personnel going about other people's business.

To register the war deaths had no special meaning to

Gabriel, other than to do a job he would rather have avoided. The 1st of November 1914 was the day; month and year he had reached twenty-one years old, and even that joyous day of the coming of age had given him little cause to be excited. The grey smog filled streets of London were a far cry from the peaceful and scenic hometown of Pickering in Yorkshire. Yet Gabriel still clung to the hope that somehow, somewhere, something would arrive to ferry him away from the dreary emptiness of his non-existent life. Three loud knocks strained the oak door and momentary awoke Gabriel from his bed of thoughts. The tall darkly dressed lady swamped his table once again with more deathly lists. No word of 'hello' escaped from the thin pale bloodless lips, protruding from an ashen colored face. No 'Goodbye' as she closed the door quickly behind her and hurried off to the place of a hundred hurried feet. Gabriel threw a quick glance at his silver pocket watch and bowed his head once again to his solemn task. It did not flock to his attention that the countless names added to the list were only eighteen, nor did the absence of next of kin throw any bureaucratic shadows across the walls of his mind. Gabriel continued to plunge and write, plunge, and write the ever-increasing names of those who would dream no more.

"READ ALL ABOUT IT, GERMAN FORCES CAPTURE MESSINES". Gabriel reached for the newspaper from the shouting boy and after paying; he made his way past St Michael's Church and walked briskly the half mile to his room. At the entrance to the main building, Gabriel reached to apply the large gothic-style door knocker, in the hope that someone would assist him. He had frequently left his key behind, owing to its oversize and weight. And it was only when he stood before the door helpless and shivering with cold, that he regretted this action. But Gabriel would certainly forget it the next day, and the day after that, and the many weeks to follow, or until pockets were made large enough for such an annoying object. And day after day, the disapproving expression on the moon-faced caretaker would continue to greet him disapprovingly.

Evenings were all cloned in their own unique dull, grey bastions of boredom. Gabriel would boil the water on top of the black iron stove and make a pot of tea. He would sit at the table in front of the window that leered out onto the street below. After finishing his bread and Jam, Gabriel would spread out the daily newspaper before him like a ship's sail and read until it was time for bed. He would read the engagement announcements, the weddings, and almost every announcement that caught his attention. The only publication that Gabriel did not see, were those of war and death. He chose to darken these words out because he had lived enough of death during his working hours, now he wanted to read about life.

At first the shadow that suddenly appeared on the wall, did not cause Gabriel any concern. The light hovering above his head had often cast large shadows from the slightest movement of his arm or leg. It was only when the shadow remained unchanged as Gabriel moved his arm from side to side, that his curiosity began to take hold of his senses. He quickly rose to his feet and approached the walls where the shadowy vision had appeared. He placed his hand on the wall and to his amazement, it disappeared. Gabriel rubbed the top of his head with the palm of his hand and shrugged the discrepancy on the wall off as probably a change in the light or his eyes tired from reading. He decided that as bedtime was upon him, he would better get his rest in anticipation of the hard day ahead.

More lists of names were piled high on his desk as Gabriel entered his office, more than the day before, and the day before that. And to Gabriel's surprise, the first folder that he lifted to record, all the casualties were eighteen years old. All the deaths recorded on one folder were all the same age, no date of birth, just eighteen. Every time Gabriel filled in a name on the death register, the age of eighteen jumped up at him like a hare hiding in the long grass. He once saw a three-legged calf being born and even had the pleasure of watching someone jump over a six-foot fence. So, the more he thought about strange things happening, the more he began to dismiss the age of eighteen as nothing other than strange but believable. He continued until the bell rang somewhere in the corridor, reminding everyone it was time for lunch.

Gabriel left his office and made his way up the corridor and out onto the street. At the eating house on the corner of Cheap Street, he took his seat at the table nearest the door and ordered the usual lunch of the day. Two tables across from him a young couple sat together eating and talking in an almost quiet manner. The young man was dressed in a soldier's uniform, and Gabriel could not help wondering if this would be the last time they would sit down together. As much as Gabriel wanted to forget the war ever existed, both in his work and the streets around him, the grim reality was never too far away. He hungrily began to eat the food the waiter left down before him, trying not to look at the two young soldiers who had just arrived into the room. It was not Gabriel's intention to put faces to the lists of names he wrote out daily, but the more he walked and the more he turned; those very names were beginning to come to life.

He returned to his office and quickly sat down again to write the list of lists. From the moment he entered this morning and up until now, Gabriel noticed that the fountain pen began to feel heavier between his fingers. His hand was now slower and the air around him began to reek of doom. He tried hard to concentrate, to brush aside certainty and deny all facts about the present world he was living in. But the best he could do was struggle to keep his hand from faltering, and promptly wish the hours away until he could shut his room door behind the tingling of his conscience.

"READ ALL ABOUT IT, READ ALL ABOUT IT, RUSSIA DECLARES WAR ON TURKEY".

Gabriel stopped momentarily to purchase the daily newspaper and then commenced his journey back to his room. After knocking the front door, he didn't wait to thank the moon-faced caretaker for his services, but hurriedly made his way up the stairway and into his creaky and damp lodgings. He sat down heavily on a brown leather armchair and breathed a sigh of relief. He didn't want to get caught up in the great net of war and death. He never asked to be reeled into the floating vessel of other men's principles. Nor did he ever want to live too close to the mordant shore, that he might be drowned in the tides of hidden compassion. All Gabriel ever wanted was to live inside a bubble of his own creation and float off into a reality of his own choosing. But somehow, the pictures of the last few days were beginning to flow freely down the clear cool stream of life and reveal the riddle of his imagination.

Gabriel awoke from his nap on the armchair and sensed that another presence was already accompanying him inside the room. He arose from the chair and scanned the four corners of the room for some physical part of what he was now feeling. He walked into the bedroom and searched up and down, side by side, but nothing jumped out at him from any part of his two-room accommodation. He walked back to the armchair and on sitting his bewildered self-back down, he knew that someone was there. He knew this as a fact, because his senses had told him so some minutes earlier and he knew it also by the strangely dressed man smiling at him from the doorway.

"Good evening young man, may I come in"? He asked.

Gabriel fought to keep the nervousness in his voice from revealing the terror that was trying to take precedence over the proceedings and replied,

"Yoo you aare already in".

The man seemed a little surprised by this revelation and after looking around the room, said,

"Oh, so I am, I never can get used to the way this place has changed".

Gabriel picked himself up from the sudden shock of finding someone in the room, and asked,

"Who are you and what do you want?"

"May I sit down first?" asked the stranger.

"You may", answered Gabriel.

The man proceeded to look around for somewhere to sit, and to Gabriel's astonishment, he sat down neatly on a chair that wasn't there.

"Who are you?" asked Gabriel.

"Ask me who I was" replied the stranger.

"Who were you then?" asked Gabriel, trying to keep both annoyance and fear from his voice.

"In life my fine fellow, my name was Ebenezer Scrooge", answered the stranger.

Gabriel took a while to digest what the old gentleman had just announced and wondered if the man now staring at him had just escaped from the lunatic asylum. The clothes the man wore were strange to say the least, but Gabriel was flabbergasted by how the man was able to get in through the heavily barred door. He had heard of lunatics who claimed they were King George, or Napoleon Bonaparte, but a character straight out of a Charles Dickens novel, was a nut too far.

"Tell me Mr. Scrooge," asked Gabriel, "How did you get through my door without making a noise?"

"Goodness gracious", replied Scrooge, "I made enough noise to awaken the dead".

"Well I didn't hear you, so you must know another way of getting into these rooms", said Gabriel.

"Before we enter into the interrogation process young man, why don't you begin by asking me why I am here", said Scrooge, at the same time directing a wide grin in Gabriel's direction.

Gabriel stared at the old man, and could sense no badness in the way he looked and smiled. He had been caught completely by surprise, and had only a short time to access the situation that now lay plainly before him.

"Where did you learn to do that trick?" asked Gabriel.

"What trick?" replied Scrooge.

"The trick with the chair, there is no chair there, yet you're leaning back as if relaxed", answered Gabriel.

"But I am relaxed", replied Scrooge, "and there is a

chair here, I'm sitting on it".

"You are not", said Gabriel boldly.

"Oh dear, I'm sorry you are right as far as being a mortal, but where I am sitting, trust me, the chair is definitely there", answered Scrooge.

Gabriel began to analyze the words he had just heard and began to plan ways of getting rid of the mad man who continued to taunt him with his madness. What this old man was stating, was that he was living in some other dimension, and Gabriel was in no doubt that the same dimension was inhabited by people clothed in freshly starched long white coats.

"You claim to be Ebenezer Scrooge", asked Gabriel, "but the last time I heard that name mentioned, it was in a work of fiction".

"I am sure there are many works of fiction that bear similar names to those who exist", answered Scrooge, I once knew a man by the name of Mr. Wilkins Micawber who owed money to half the businesses in London, and who was always a firm believer that something will turn up", answered Scrooge.

"And where did this Mr. Micawber end up", asked Gabriel in mild amusement, "a lunatic asylum?"

"No, no," answered Scrooge, he and his family went to Australia and I believe he became a magistrate or something of a similar situation".

"I think it's time you went home", said Gabriel, "I'm extremely tired and I would like to go to bed".

"I am home, my fine fellow", replied Scrooge.

"No you are not", answered Gabriel, "I live in these rooms".

"I know you do young man, but I live in this house and to spare you any embarrassment, I will leave you with a message", said Scrooge.

"And what might that message be?" asked Gabriel.

"You will be visited by one ghost", replied Scrooge, "expect it when the bell tolls three".

"Now you have really surprised me, where may I ask are the other two?" asked Gabriel mockingly.

"I will leave you now in your mortal world", said Scrooge.

"On your way out", asked Gabriel, "could you show me how you got through those two bars and heavy metal lock?"

"Certainly, my good man", answered Scrooge.

Gabriel watched Scrooge rise to his feet and make his way silently towards the door. He turned to Gabriel and said,

"Goodnight".

And before Gabriel could get his wits together, Scrooge walked through the door.

Gabriel stared at the door first in momentary amazement, and then in complete shock. He rubbed both his eyes with the palms of his hands and tried to regain some remaining fragments of his sanity. He walked to the armchair and once again sat heavily down upon its age stained leather. He began to blame his job and the countless names of deceased soldiers for the illusion that he had just witnessed. He blamed the newspaper seller for shouting out doomed headlines, and even blamed the thick smog escaping from the passing motor vehicles. He accused everyone but himself and concluded that he had been dreaming. Gabriel arose from the armchair and after first extinguishing the light; he made his way to bed.

Sometime later Gabriel was awoken by three chimes from somewhere outside his window. The chimes of clocks didn't normally wake him up, while he was fast asleep, but the cause of being awoken at this early in the morning had given him cause for thought. Gabriel lifted himself up from his bed and stared at the tall figure dressed in black now taking residence at the corner of his room. The figure frightened him so much that he began to shake and prayed inwardly that the night would go away.

"Whaa waa do you wa want of me?" asked Gabriel, trying to keep some stability to his sanity, "if you don't leave I will call for the police".

"It is not what I want from you, but more like what you want from me", replied the ghost.

"I don't wa wa want anything from you, get out", said Gabriel as he added some bravado to the shivering tone of his voice.

"Why do you doubt your own judgement?" asked the ghost.

"I don't doubt anything", replied Gabriel, "I have an uninvited guest in ma my room, whom I would like to see leave".

"A guest I am indeed", returned the ghost, "uninvited I am not".

"Who invited you here, for it most certainly was not me", asked Gabriel as his voice hovered on the edge of anger.

"Let me first accompany you on a journey and then you will see who invited me here", replied the ghost.

"If you la le leave it until morning, I might give it a try, but definitely not at this hour", answered Gabriel.

"What I have to show you can only be seen at this hour", said the ghost.

Gabriel now climbed out of bed and stood upright on the floor a few feet away from the ghost. He was feeling tired and drowsy and had no wish to tramp the streets of London at this small hour, yet somehow he knew that the night would never go away unless he did.

"I guess all I have to do now is touch your hand and be transported back in time", said Gabriel sarcastically.

"No, no", replied the ghost, "I am the ghost of the future and I certainly would not expect you to go out at this time of year dressed only in your night shirt".

Gabriel slowly started to get dressed, occasionally glancing towards the ghost to make sure he was still there. He knew that what he was doing was sheer madness, especially going out so early with someone who calls himself a ghost. Yet the day had ended in madness for Gabriel and insanity was something he could not escape from. No sooner had he buttoned the last button on his coat, when he noticed he was no longer in his room.

"Everyone must play their part and should not have to be reminded of their duty to King and country", said the headmaster, "serve your country well and your country will serve you well".

"Where am I?" asked Gabriel, as he stood confused before the sight before him.

"You are in a school room", replied the ghost, "but these children have all something in common".

"What do they have in common?" asked Gabriel.

"They are all orphans", answered the ghost, "all with no one to love and be loved by no one".

"If you are a ghost of the future, then tell me how far into the future we are seeing now", asked Gabriel.

"It may be a day, a week or a month," replied the ghost, "but these are shadows that will be".

Before Gabriel could ask another question, he found himself in another room.

"But Kitchener needs more men, if we are ever to

win this war, we need more soldiers", said an aged gentlemen dressed in an officer's uniform.

"You mean more fodder for the German machine guns to feast upon, I tell you it's all madness", replied a small bald headed man rubbing his forehead with a handkerchief.

Gabriel now stood before a barren scorched black land and viewed the desolation that lay before him like a scene from hell. All across the gorge of furrowed mud, trenches twisted and curled like some never ending serpent, and within these tracks of ruin, dirt covered soldiers awaited the coming of man's terrifying rage.

"What is this place?" asked Gabriel, now hardly able to find his voice.

"This is the mortal hell that frightens the very devil himself", replied the ghost, "this is the place where heartless men wash their petty differences with the blood of poor men's children".

"Why have you taken me here, lead me from this place now", shouted Gabriel.

Gabriel now stood at the side of an unfamiliar country road and watched cart loads of dead soldiers pass him by. When he forced himself to stare at one of the dead soldiers, he noticed something familiar.

"That is one of the orphans we saw in the school room", said Gabriel surprised, "but, but he doesn't look a day older".

"A day older perhaps, but old he is not", answered the ghost.

"Then why is he in a uniform, without a parent's consent I thought you had to be at least eighteen", said Gabriel in astonishment.

"Without a parent, a child is no longer a child",

replied the ghost.

"I want out of here now", shouted Gabriel as he tried to control his emotions.

"Just one more shadow", replied the ghost.

Gabriel found himself staring at someone dressed in a straitjacket with his face turned away. The man was muttering something that Gabriel could not make out.

"What's he saying?" asked Gabriel.

"He is repenting", answered the ghost.

"What is he repenting about?" asked Gabriel.

"Why don't you ask him?" replied the ghost.

The person turned around to face Gabriel, with his eyes plainly missing from his sockets. Gabriel could hear the words eighteen, eighteen, being repeated over and over again. He knew the face, and even without eyes, Gabriel could feel that person's very soulless stare. He knew the creature before him so well, because Gabriel was looking at himself.

CHAPTER 2

A full moon shone through Gabriel's window, lighting up the room and casting stray shadows across the wall. He sat up on his bed and began to contemplate what had just happened to him. From somewhere beyond his window, a distant clock struck four notes and signaled to Gabriel that one hour had passed since the ghost had entered his room. Gabriel was frightened, not only by the things he saw, but he knew that two ghosts in one night meant that something was expected of him. He became aware that his life was about to change, and that no longer could he be expected to bury his head in the sand. Exhausted both mentally and physically, Gabriel put his head back down on the pillow and drifted off to sleep the remaining three hours he had left until another day at The War Office would eventually arrive.

Another large pile of lists greeted Gabriel as he entered his office, and he was not the least bit surprised to discover the folders were higher than the day before. Gabriel's thoughts were suddenly interrupted by three soft knocks on the door and just as he was about to call out to come in, he noticed an envelope being slipped under the door. Gabriel walked to the door and picked the envelope up, before opening it he looked out onto the corridor to see if he could get a glimpse of the person who delivered it. To Gabriel's surprise, no one could be seen, so he closed the door and moved back to the chair before his desk. Gabriel opened the letter with the small silver letter opener that permanently rested on the desk, and read the note inside,

FIND TINY TIM.

As he stared at the writing for what seemed eternity, he could not fathom why someone would ask him to find someone with no surname. Gabriel put the note into his waistcoat pocket and decided to let it rest until the day's work had finished. He lifted a list of names at the top of the pile before him and commenced the chore of adding them to the register. Suddenly Gabriel dropped the folder on the desk and began to stare deep into the lines of ink stretched out across the page. His heart began to thump violently within the pit of his chest and the words eighteen leapt up at him like a frenzied wild animal. He turned the page and there before him were lists of name, rank, number and no date of birth, just long lists of eighteen, eighteen and eighteen again and again.

Gabriel needed air to breathe; he needed to rid himself of the madness that now lay out before him on the desk. If only for a few minutes, to look at something different, to see the faces of normality, to hide from the responsibility that now crawled into his life like a poison spider.

"Would you watch where you are going mister", shouted a young lady.

"I, ah ah am so sorry", replied Gabriel, as he helped the young lady gather the various papers from the cobbled street.

"Do you always push your way through women?" asked the young lady, as she took the papers from Gabriel and added them to the ones she gathered herself.

"I'm so sorry, I apologize a thousand times", replied Gabriel.

"Ok then", said the young lady.

"Ok what?" asked Gabriel.

"I'm waiting for you to apologize one thousand times", answered the young lady.

"It was only a figure of speech", answered Gabriel, "like what you say when you are truly sorry".

"But you're not truly sorry; I don't believe you are in the least bit sorry", said the young lady.

"I truly am, I promise", said Gabriel.

"If you were genuinely sorry for barging into me like a male chauvinist pi..., you would have stuck to your word and said it a thousand times", replied the young lady.

"I am not a chauvinist, and just because I don't stand like a halfwit repeating myself a thousand times, does not mean I am not sorry", said Gabriel.

"I bet you think I should be at home now, married with a child and another one on the way, bare foot and pregnant, is that what most men think?" asked the young lady as she looked Gabriel straight in the eye.

Gabriel was unable to deal with the situation before him, yet had no intention of walking away defeated. He had jumped straight from the paradoxical flames of his closed in office and if he could at all help it, he had no intention of leaping into the frying pan.

"Perhaps as a way of expressing the sincerity of my one thousand apologies, I could buy you a cup of tea", said Gabriel, trying to defuse the situation.

"You men, you always think that all problems can be resolved by buying a lady a cup of tea", answered the young lady.

"Ok I give up", said Gabriel as he lifted his hands up into the air in mock frustration.

"Oh don't give up yet", replied the young lady as she flashed a smile across her face, "throw in a chicken sandwich and a custard tart and you have a deal".

The tearoom was almost empty save for an old man reading a book and a couple chatting about the weather. Gabriel pulled a chair out from the table to allow the young lady to sit down, and after doing so he took a chair facing her.

"You're quite the gentleman when you're not trying to knock people down", said the young lady as she lifted a menu from the table.

Gabriel began to assess the situation that had only just invited itself into his already overburdened state of mind. He knew they wouldn't miss him from the little room at The War Office for half an hour at the very least and he also knew that the young lady now sitting across from him was very pretty. Gabriel also discovered while he was collecting some of her papers from the cold cobbled street, that she was either a supporter of suffragettes, or a full grown member.

"A pot of tea please for two, two chicken breast sandwiches and two custard tarts", ordered the young lady as the waitress came to take their order.

"Forgive me", said Gabriel, "but I couldn't help noticing that you are a supporter of women's rights".

"A militant supporter if you must know, only the war has suspended our activities", replied the young lady.

"There are those who believe that the war will play a great part in achieving those aims", said Gabriel, "a great many supporters of the suffragettes are contributing substantially to the war effort".

"Indeed", replied the young lady, "let's hope this war will end soon and those aims are realized".

"Without coming across as bad mannered", said Gabriel mockingly, "but may I ask you your name?"

"What do you want to know my name for?" asked the young lady.

"Well it would be nice to know at least a little of the person who tried to knock me down", answered Gabriel.

"What's your name?" asked the young lady as she began to pour the tea for both Gabriel and herself.

"Gabriel Shivers", replied Gabriel as he took the cap of tea offered and thanked the young lady.

"And where do you work?" asked the young lady.

"I am employed as a register at The War Office just around the corner, in fact that is where I was coming from when you crashed into me", answered Gabriel.

"My God!" muttered the young lady.

"I know", replied Gabriel, "it's a job I wish I had never taken".

"Is it true what they are saying, that thousands of our soldiers are getting killed?" asked the young lady in a low voice.

"I am not supposed to say, but yes there are far too many deaths", replied Gabriel.

"Do you live around this area?" asked the young lady, changing the subject.

"I have taken rooms about half a mile from St Michael's", answered Gabriel.

"You don't surely live in that huge house with the big gothic door knocker?" asked the young lady.

"The very place", replied Gabriel in surprise.

"That's where I saw you before", said the young lady excitedly, "you were knocking the door and waiting for frog face to let you in".

"Well I thought his face looked more like a moon to be honest", replied Gabriel.

"How long have you been living at Tim Cratchit's place?" asked the young lady.

"Just over a week, hold on a minute", said Gabriel in sudden surprise, "who did you say owned the place?"

"Tim Cratchit", replied the young lady as she paused from eating her sandwich, "my grandmother told me once he inherited the place from a very rich uncle or someone".

"Do you know the uncle's name?" asked Gabriel.

"She died before I got old enough to be interested", answered the young lady, "but I think Tim Cratchit's nickname was Tiny Tim".

The young lady finished her chicken sandwich and started to take small dignified bites from her custard tart. Gabriel never noticed, she could have been on top of the table dancing and singing aloud and he would have observed nothing. His pounding heart was pumping blood so quick around his body, he thought his ears were about to explode. The note told him to find Tiny Tim and now within a short space of time, he knew who he was and where he lives. Gabriel took a generous gulp from his tea cup and began to once more play a part in the present proceedings.

"Are you ok?" asked the young lady, "you turned very pale all of a sudden".

"The pressures of work have been getting me down recently ", replied Gabriel.

"I bet they are, I also bet you that those young men in the trenches would swap you jobs any day of the week", said the young lady.

Gabriel excused himself and arose from the table, after putting three shillings on a small plate to pay the bill, he said to the young lady,

"Excuse me, but they are going to miss me at work, it was very nice to meet you and thank you for your wonderful company".

Gabriel made his way out through the tea room door and as quickly as he could, he returned to his office and closed the door firmly behind him. He continued to do what he was paid to do while wishing the day whole heartily away. Name after name were copied onto the register and name after name were also copied onto a blank piece of paper that Gabriel had laid out before him. All the eighteen's lay facing him on the table like pieces of some dark and mysterious puzzle. Line after line, page after page were mirrored in order to set Gabriel off on a journey of which he knew not where. All he wanted now was to see the day end and when he returned back to his rooms, he would seek out the owner of the big house, Tiny Tim.

As Gabriel approached the door of the big house, almost automatically, the door slowly opened to reveal the character of moon face in all his boring glory.

"Good evening", said Gabriel politely, "is the owner of this property at home?"

Moon face just shook his head from side to side, but didn't say a word.

"Could you tell me when he will be home?" asked Gabriel.

Again moon face indicated with his head movement that he did not know the answer to Gabriel's question.

"Where can I find this Mr. Cratchit?" asked Gabriel, trying not to show his annoyance at Moon face's absence of speech and of the whereabouts of Tiny Tim.

And again, Moon face signaled that he could not accommodate Gabriel in any of his requests.

"Ok", said Gabriel as he proceeded to make his way up to his rooms, "I'll just have to find out from someone who does".

Gabriel made his way up the stairway and on arriving at the top of the stairs; he turned the key on his room door and entered the cold musty enclosure. He quickly poked the spent coals of the small black stove and commenced to light a fire. No sooner had Gabriel added a flaming match to the kindling, when the door of his room vibrated to the sound of three loud knocks. Gabriel rubbed his hands on a moth eaten cloth hanging over the grate, and when he had finished cleaning his hands as best he could, he walked over to the door and opened it wide.

"Good evening Mr. Shivers, or may I call you Gabriel", said the young lady as she offered Gabriel a wide grin.

Gabriel was taken aback by the site of the lady he had tea with a few hours earlier and all he could muster in the form of a reply was,

"Hello, ahh would you like to come in?"

"I thought you would never ask", replied the young lady, "it's freezing out on that corridor, in second thoughts", she joked as she entered the room, "I think it's warmer outside".

Gabriel offered her a chair beside the kindling stove, when the young lady sat down, Gabriel sat down on a chair next to her.

"If you don't mind, I'll keep my coat on", said the young lady as she stared at the stove as if to mock its uselessness.

"Give it five or ten minutes", said Gabriel as he shoveled on some coal and closed the stove door, "I only got back a few minutes before you".

"Did you enjoy your day?" asked the young lady.

"If you are implying that recording death is an enjoyment, then I was elated", said Gabriel sarcastically.

"Well, I was going to mention our little tea party that came to an end so suddenly", replied the young lady.

"Oh sorry Miss, or is it Mrs.?" asked Gabriel.

"What do you think", asked the young lady as she turned to look Gabriel in the eye, "do I look like a Miss or a Mrs.?"

"You look like a Miss", answered Gabriel, after quickly looking at her hands for any sign of a wedding ring.

"Ok then now we have that settled, I suppose you are wondering why I am here", said the young lady.

"As a matter of fact, I was thinking that very thing", replied Gabriel.

"Well there are two reasons why I came here to see you", said the young lady, "the first was to thank you for buying me tea, but since you ran out on me half way through it, I have decided not to bother. The second one was to tell you my name, which if you had of had the manners to stay a little longer in the tea room, you would have known by now and saved me the bother of tramping up those flight of stairs".

"I am so sorry", replied Gabriel, "I had to get back to work, and well, a few other things I would rather not talk about have been bothering me recently".

"Did you see any ghosts yet?" asked the young lady.

"Why do you ask that?" asked Gabriel while

searching her eyes for any sign of familiarity with his prior ghostly encounters.

"They say all these old houses are haunted", replied the young lady in mild amusement.

"Sorry to change the subject", said Gabriel, "but you did mention something about your name".

"Oh, so I did, how silly of me", replied the young lady.

For a few minutes the room slipped into silence as Gabriel waited for the young lady to reveal her name.

"I'm waiting", said Gabriel fainting impatience.

"My mother once told me that Ebenezer Scrooge haunts this place", replied the young lady.

"Who is Ebenezer Scrooge?" asked Gabriel.

"Charlotte Starr", said the young lady as she held her hands out to the now awakening stove.

"You're winding me up", said Gabriel.

"So you think my name is funny, what about Shivers, I bet they call you Shivers because you can never get this stove to work", replied Charlotte as she slightly raised her voice.

Gabriel prepared himself to ask Charlotte for forgiveness, but before he could get the words to flow from his mouth, she began to laugh. Gabriel remembered how the other children used to laugh at him at school when they heard his surname, a laughter which ended with a bloody nose. He now watched Charlotte do the same, and his only reply was to join her.

"How's the stars tonight my dear?" asked Gabriel as he shook with laughter.

"This room is giving me the shivers", replied Charlotte as she slapped Gabriel playfully on the back.

As Gabriel watched Charlotte laughing before him,

he was glad she came to call. He needed cheering up and what better way than to laugh in unison at their unconventional surnames. When she mentioned Ebenezer Scrooge, Gabriel thought for a brief moment that she had somehow known more than she was at first letting on. But he soon concluded, that as Mr. Scrooge once lived here, then so must the haunting rumors.

"I asked Moon face on the way in if he knew where Mr. Cratchit was", said Gabriel as he finished laughing, "but all I got was movements of the head".

"The reason why you got head movements instead of words", replied Charlotte, "is because he cannot speak".

"That says it all", replied Gabriel, "I thought he was being rude or perhaps trying to hide something".

"If you really must find him, then I will ask around for you", said Charlotte.

"Thank you that would be greatly appreciated", replied Gabriel.

"But it will cost you", said Charlotte.

"I hope it's not going to cost me an arm and a leg", replied Gabriel as he reached to put some more coal in the stove.

"It will cost you both your legs and an arm to hold on to", said Charlotte, "I want you to accompany me for a walk in the park tomorrow during your lunch hour, I hate walking alone".

"Ok, if you are outside The War Office around 1.00pm I'll be there with lead and all", replied Gabriel.

"We'll see who has the lead", said Charlotte in a tone of defiant amusement.

Gabriel didn't care who had the lead, as long as he had her company to look forward to. As he followed

Charlotte to the door and watched her descend the stairwell, Gabriel felt for the first time in his life a hollow emptiness within the pit of his stomach. He made tea and the usual jam sandwiches, but still the emptiness remained. He read the newspaper, trying to avoid all violent stories and notices of casualties. He thought of home and how those who he went to school with would be joining up to feed the jaws of hate. He heard a dog bark from somewhere in the distance, and the loud screech of an interrupted cat. In the street down below, motor vehicles and horse drawn carts were still going about their business. Laughter could be heard from one of the rooms inside the building, followed by silence and then laughter again. Many times before Gabriel heard all the same noises of life inside the belly of a busy city and many times before he would imagine the lives of others and weigh them against his own. But now Gabriel would not exchange his life with anyone else in the whole wide world, and his tomorrow would be priceless.

CHAPTER 3

"Where's your lead?" asked Gabriel as he greeted Charlotte precisely at the hour of 1.00pm.

"My lead is invisible," she replied, "so bear with me Mr. Gabriel and you will feel it sooner or later".

"It's actually Mr. Shivers", said Gabriel as he allowed Charlotte to place her arm around his.

"I prefer Gabriel", she replied, "the other has a certain wintery feeling to it".

Gabriel decided not to respond to Charlotte's playful taunts, but instead, wallowed in her company as they breathed in the crisp cold November air.

"I made some sandwiches", said Charlotte, "let's sit here beside the pond and taunt the ducks".

Charlotte and Gabriel sat down on an old stone wall and watched a little boy throw large amounts of bread into the pond. No sooner had the bread hit the water, when the ducks dived upon the feast and devoured it almost in an instant.

"I made lettuce sandwiches", said Charlotte, "in case you turned your nose up at them, and they could still be fed to the ducks".

"You couldn't be more wrong", answered Gabriel,

"I hate lettuce but I will be damned if I let the ducks eat them".

If Charlotte's sandwiches had have contained paper, Gabriel would have still ate them. Partly because he was so hungry and mostly he did not want to disappoint her. All around the park people walked and talked, some fed the ducks while children played.

"I have found out some news about your friend Mr. Cratchit", said Charlotte as she interrupted Gabriel's thoughts.

"I wouldn't say friend", replied Gabriel, "I haven't even met the man".

"Would you like to meet him?" asked Charlotte as she shared some of her sandwich with a ravenous looking duck.

"That in itself goes without saying", replied Gabriel.

"What do you want him for?" asked Charlotte before turning around to face Gabriel.

"I would like to discuss a private matter with him", answered Gabriel.

"If you don't tell me what it's about I shall consider the subject closed", said Charlotte still holding Gabriel's stare.

"What do you mean by closed?" asked Gabriel.

"I mean closed, our meeting yesterday did not happen and you will never see me again", replied Charlotte defiantly.

"That is what most people would call blackmail", said Gabriel as he tried to hide the emotion that was now beginning to build up inside him.

"Call it what you will", replied Charlotte, "but if you don't tell me within the next ten seconds I'm walking". Gabriel could hardly believe what he was hearing; the moment he was so looking forward to was going to be destroyed forever. He could not understand Charlotte's curiosity, nor could he fathom her sudden change.

"Ok then", said Charlotte as she tossed the remainder of her sandwiches into the pond, "it has indeed been a pleasure to have never have known you".

Charlotte turned from Gabriel and began walking away in the direction they had first arrived. Gabriel's heart was pounding, he tried to reach within himself for some strength, but all he could muster was weakness. He wanted to shout, to yell from the top of his voice, to surrender the last few remaining fragments of his character. But now Charlotte was gone, forever lost in the caverns of his memory, never again to be found. He gathered himself up from the stone seat and slowly made his way back to work. He told himself he was both a fool not to have told her and an idiot to have let her go. He felt that hollow emptiness that he felt the day before begin to swell and crush his body like some great grip of torture.

As he sat behind his desk, Gabriel realized that the pain he felt now was only a crumb compared to those who had lost loved ones in the war. For the short time he had known her, Charlotte has projected a glimmer of light into the darkness of his world. Now he was back within the blackness again and Gabriel could see no more light at the end of an endless tunnel. He would sit in this dismal office day after day, week after week, adding to the blackness with his black ink. Night after night he would sit in his room and weekend after weekend he would bathe in the depths of his own stupidity.

Gabriel did not hear what the paper boy was shouting as he grabbed the evening paper and quickly paid for it. He made his way through the large open door of the big house and ascended the wide stairway to his room of a hundred thousand boredoms. He opened the door and barred it safely behind him, before hanging his overcoat on the wall hanger beside the door. As he made his way into the room he did not notice at first, the two people sitting at the table. It was only when one of them spoke, that Gabriel got both the scare and surprise of his life.

"Hello Gabriel", said Charlotte, "I would like you to meet Mr. Tim Cratchit".

Gabriel was taken aback and the surprise at finding the two people sitting before him was plainly written across his face.

"Good evening young man", said Tim as he reached over to shake Gabriel's hand, "I've heard a rumor recently that you were looking to see me".

Gabriel shook Tim's hand and sat down on a chair beside the already burning stove. Charlotte proceeded to make herself at home by gathering some cups and saucers together in preparation for the kettle she had put on to boil some time earlier.

"Has the cat eaten your tongue young man?" asked Tim.

"I am sorry", replied Gabriel, "I just didn't expect to find anyone here when I got in".

"Well I am sorry to have surprised you this way, but let's all have a cup of tea and discuss what you wanted to see me about", said Tim.

Gabriel eyed the character of Tiny Tim before him and decided that he may have to call the fashion police immediately. The old man before him was dressed in a long navy blue trench coat, a yellow shirt, a long shoelace black tie and a pair of brown trousers that must have been given to him by his mother on his tenth birthday. Tiny Tim was someone who could be easily recognized in a crowd and Gabriel decided on dress sense alone, Mr. Cratchit was someone who plainly had his own mixed up mind. Charlotte offered Gabriel a cup of tea, which he accepted gladly.

"Now young man", said Tim as he sipped noisily on his tea, "you have met my granddaughter Charlotte I hear".

"I have met her sir", replied Gabriel, "and as I have discovered, she is not short of a few surprises".

"Well young man, I am not short of surprises myself, let's say she is a chip off the old block", said Tim as he continued to employ the method of sucking from his cup, instead of drinking from it.

"A few strange things have been happening lately", said Gabriel, "and one of them was a note slipped under my door at work".

"What did the note say?" asked Tim.

"All it said was FIND TINY TIM", replied Gabriel.

"You mentioned other things?" asked Tim.

"Well", replied Gabriel feeling embarrassed, "I would rather not say".

"Listen young man", said Tim as he continued to remove the last few drops of tea with his tongue, "how am I supposed to know what the note meant, if you don't fill me in on the other details".

Gabriel looked at Charlotte and noticed she had a thinly veiled smile appearing on her face. He would have rather talked to Tim on his own, but one half of him was glad that she was there.

"Well", said Gabriel after first clearing his throat, "I might have seen a ghost or maybe two in this very room".

"You might have seen them, or you didn't, did you see a ghost or not? asked Tim.

"Well, the first one claimed to be Ebenezer Scrooge", answered Gabriel.

Tim suddenly stopped from trying to retrieve any more tea from his cup and placed it along with the saucer on the table. Gabriel noticed that Charlotte no longer wore the smile she so skillfully tried to hide, and both were now staring at him attentively.

"What did he say to you?" asked Tim.

"After some light hearted talk, he told me that the ghost of the future would be calling with me when the bell tolls three", answered Gabriel.

Gabriel looked at the two souls before him and waited for any sign of them preparing to make a speedy exit towards the door. He looked for any signal of disbelief, but all he could find were two sets of eyes zooming in before him, showing no signs of skepticism.

"What did the ghost of the future show you?" asked Tim in an urgent tone of voice.

"He showed me a school with boys being taught the lessons of being loyal to King and Country", replied Gabriel, "I then saw what looked like trenches and young boys dressed as soldiers. This was followed by cart loads of these same young boys dead".

At the closing of Gabriel's revelation, both Tim and Charlotte slowly looked at each other, showing signs of distress. Suddenly Tim arose from his chair, placed two fingers into his right ear and began to pace back and forward across the room floor. Gabriel looked directly at Charlotte, and noticed two small tears rolling down her cheeks. He wanted to reach over and hold her, to tell her that everything would be ok, but he didn't know how.

"Have you noticed anything else happening recently, that might be related in some way to what you saw?" asked Tim as he continued to march back and forth.

Gabriel reached inside his pocket and produced the list of names he copied from the register.

"Take a look at this", said Gabriel, handing the list to Tim.

Tim stopped and stared at the list that Gabriel handed him, after a short while he passed the list to Charlotte.

"Have you noticed anything strange about the list?" asked Tim as he turned back to look at Gabriel.

"Yes I have, they are all eighteen, and unlike the other lists, there are no dates of birth", replied Gabriel.

"What does that tell us?" asked Tim.

"It tells us that someone is forging names in order to recruit underage boys for the army", answered Gabriel.

"It also tells us that first, the culprit or culprits are confident of no repercussions, second no repercussions equal no one to inquire and third, if there is no one to inquire then they must be orphans", said Tim.

"My God", gasped Charlotte, "those poor children".

"Poor indeed, children most definitely", said Tim, "but it is up to us to stop it".

"Gabriel", said Charlotte "is there any way you can find out more information, does The War Office hold any records regarding where they came from?"

"So far all I have seen are these lists, but I will try and do some digging tomorrow", replied Gabriel.

"Try and find out anything you can", said Tim, "we will meet here tomorrow evening around the same time".

"I have a friend who may know something about

orphanages in the area, I will pay her a visit tomorrow", said Charlotte as she rose to follow Tim towards the door.

"Until tomorrow my young friend", said Tim as he opened the door and made his way towards the stairs.

"Goodnight", said Charlotte as she reached to lightly squeeze Gabriel's hand, before following Tiny Tim down the stairs.

As Gabriel lay down to sleep he felt as if a great weight had been lifted off his shoulders. He was no longer alone to face the mordant tasks that destiny had set out before him and he felt confident in the knowledge that Tiny Tim believed without question, his ghostly revelations. Whatever dangers or whatever trials that would arrive to face him, Gabriel contented himself in the fact, that not only did he get to see Charlotte again, she called him by his first name.

Gabriel spent the next day searching every file he could reach, without causing suspicion. He convinced a young lady in the records department he had got some of the lists mixed up and needed to check the originals. He managed to flick through folders on other staff members' desks, when they rallied to the call of nature. And at lunch time he stayed behind and rummaged through various offices in the hope of finding one tiny lead that would point him in the right direction. At the closing of the working day, Gabriel had to start out on his way home none the wiser than he first began.

As he entered the room, he could feel the heat of the stove and the noise of someone busy inside. Charlotte stood over the table, and by some culinary miracle, laid out a plate of meat stew before Gabriel.

"Eat that up, you can't live on jam sandwiches", she

said as she sat down at the table across from Gabriel.

"Thank you", replied Gabriel as he obeyed her request, "you shouldn't have went to all this trouble".

"No trouble", replied Charlotte as she threw a smile in Gabriel's direction, "just some of last month's stew I was throwing out to the dogs, so I decided it would probably make the poor dogs sick".

"Wouldn't want to make the dogs ill, would we", said Gabriel humorously.

"Did you find out anything today?" asked Charlotte as she delicately spooned some of the stew into her mouth.

"Nothing", replied Gabriel, "I turned the place upside down but to no avail".

"Grandfather wasn't expecting you to find anything else, he thinks it was prepared by someone before it reached The War Office", said Charlotte.

"I thought he was to be here this evening", said Gabriel.

"He said he is following a lead, so he will let us know if he finds anything", replied Charlotte.

"You didn't tell me he was your grandfather", said Gabriel.

"You never asked, and come to think of it you didn't say what you wanted him for at the park", replied Charlotte.

"I didn't want to tell you what I saw, in fear you got me committed to the lunatic asylum", said Gabriel apologetically.

"I'm glad you didn't tell me", said Charlotte as she lifted her head to stare into Gabriel's eyes, "if you had have told me, I could never have trusted you".

"You said you had a friend who might know something", asked Gabriel, "had you any luck?"

"Whenever we finish dinner, we have a fund raising appointment to attend", replied Charlotte, "that friend I was talking about said we need to watch out for a man with jet black hair and who wears a monocle".

As soon as Charlotte and Gabriel finished dinner, they both made their way to the bottom of the stairs and out through the front door.

"Where are we going? asked Gabriel as he buttoned the top button of his coat to keep out the cold.

"Let's link arms and I will show you the way", replied Charlotte as she finished putting on her gloves.
Gabriel noticed that the streets of London looked and felt a lot different when it was dark. Gas lights threw shadows of giants across the gables of tenements and all around, the hustle and bustle of faceless people, filling their lings with cold November air.

"Here we are", said Charlotte, as they approached an old church hall.

Charlotte and Gabriel made their way through the door and into a wide room, filled with tables covered with various things for sale. As they approached a table that sold bread and cakes, Charlotte caught the eye of a young lady finishing serving an elderly couple.

"Is he here?" asked Charlotte, as she tried to keep her voice low.

The young lady looked sideways at the corner of the room and on turning without revealing the obvious, Charlotte and Gabriel watched the very man talking to a soldier while nodding his head in agreement with something only they knew.

"We need to find out that man's name", Charlotte whispered to Gabriel.

"Does anyone here know who he is?" asked Gabriel in a low voice.

"No one knows his name, he goes by the name of Jimbo, but that could be a nickname", whispered Charlotte.

"So what do you suggest, do we call out every name we can think of in the hope he will answer to one of them, or do we just ask him?" Muttered Gabriel.

"If things were not as serious as they are, that would be funny", answered Charlotte.

As soon as the soldier wished Jimbo goodnight and parted company, Charlotte nudged Gabriel and said,

"I have a plan, let's go".

Charlotte and Gabriel made their way through the various assortments of tables, stopping occasionally to feint a false interest in their contents.

"My God", said Charlotte, as they stopped beside Jimbo, "it's James; I haven't seen you since I was a little girl".

Jimbo looked at Charlotte and expressed a look of confusion,

"My dear, forgive me, but to whom have I the pleasure of addressing?" asked Jimbo.

"Oh, I haven't changed that much", replied Charlotte, "it's Martha Dywer, you must remember me?"

"Please forgive me once again my dear, but I really don't have the foggiest who you are", said Jimbo.

"Did father put you up to this, he did, I know he did, he is always up to his old tricks", said Charlotte as she threw Jimbo a smile.

"I'm sorry dear, but I have never heard of a Martha Dywer, or any Dwyer's as a matter of fact", replied Jimbo.

"Do you still live in Camden Town?" asked Charlotte, "oh please do send Maisy my regards, I used to love her strawberry jam tarts".

"Now there my good lady", replied Jimbo, "I live on Holborn Road and I don't know anyone by the name of Maisy".

Charlotte looked at Jimbo for a short while and said in a softer more balanced tone of voice,

"James Maybin I presume?"

"James Burnhouse at your service my dear", replied Jimbo now thankful that he was not losing his memory.

"I am so, so sorry", said Charlotte as she held the palm of her hand up to her forehead, "I could have sworn you were someone else".

"My dear", replied Jimbo, "I have been mistaken by various classes of people for someone else, but never by one as pretty as you, good night".

Jimbo walked away from Charlotte and Gabriel and without looking back, made his way through the main exit of the hall.

"My dear", said Gabriel in mock humor, "you should consider a career in the theatre, for that was the greatest display of acting I have ever seen".

"My dear", answered Charlotte as she ushered Gabriel towards the exit, "how do you know I am not playing you along in the same way".

As Charlotte and Gabriel walked out onto the night air, a full moon had now arrived to offer a cleaner view of the street before them.

"Tomorrow being Saturday, we will have a little walk over to Holborn and see if we can find out anything else about our Mr. Burnhouse", said Charlotte as she shivered in the night air before hooking on to Gabriel's left arm.

"Let me walk you home", said Gabriel as they made their way down the street.

"Ok", replied Charlotte.

"Just show me the way, you don't expect me to be telepathic", said Gabriel as they turned the corner and headed in the direction of Gabriel's room.

"I will", replied Charlotte.

To some confusion in Gabriel's part, they arrived before the great door of Gabriel's rooms.

"You are not walking home on your own", said Gabriel protesting.

"I am not walking home on my own", replied Charlotte as she made her way through the half open door.

"Ok, so you want to come up for a cup of tea", said Gabriel.

"Not tonight my dear", replied Charlotte trying to hide the amusement in her voice.

"Then what are we doing here?" asked Gabriel.

"Thank you for walking me home", replied Charlotte as she opened a door at the bottom of the stairs and wished Gabriel "good night".

CHAPTER 4

Gabriel was awoken the next morning by the sound of someone gently tapping his door. At first he thought he was dreaming, or a mouse had decided as there was nothing to eat in the house, something hard to chew on would be a suitable revenge. Gabriel arose from the bed and covered his night shirt with his overcoat. He then walked to the door and on opening it; he was surprised to see Charlotte with a sleepless look upon her face.

"Grandfather hasn't returned home in two days", said Charlotte as she walked into the room.

"Well he is a grown man", replied Gabriel as he closed the door after her.

"There is something wrong, don't ask me how I know", said Charlotte as she took a chair beside the table.

Gabriel looked at Charlotte and noticed she had a genuine look of worry written all over her face.

"Don't be troubling yourself half to death", said Gabriel in a comforting tone of voice, "he is probably wrapped up somewhere in bed".

"No he is not", replied Charlotte, "something is wrong".

Gabriel looked at the pocket watch that he removed from his coat, and the time read 7.14. For Charlotte to awaken him so early on a Saturday morning caused Gabriel to allow more thought to the seriousness of the situation.

"Did he ever disappear like this before?" asked Gabriel.

"Yes, but he always let me know where he was going or where he was by messenger", answered Charlotte.

"Do you trust your instincts?" asked Gabriel as he contemplated the best way to deal with the crises before them.

"My instincts are the same as yours, following your night of ghosts", answered Charlotte as she looked worryingly into Gabriel's eyes.

Gabriel's heart began to gather pace as he realized that Charlotte had just been visited by some immortal spirit. He knew that by some unknown fate, they had been thrown together to fulfil a humanitarian quest and where that may lead them, only the future knew the answer.

"Give me ten minutes to get dressed", said Gabriel as he made his way into the bedroom.

"Have you any idea where we might start looking?" asked Gabriel as he returned from his bedroom fully clothed.

"I have no idea", replied Charlotte, "grandfather was a very private person and if he had friends outside our family he never told me about it".

"Ok", said Gabriel as he buttoned the top buttons of his coat, "let's have a look around Holborn Road".

The morning was quiet as Charlotte and Gabriel

made their way in the direction of Holborn Road. A tired looking bobby, who was just finishing his shift, greeted them as they turned the corner and crossed to the other side of the road. A young boy on a bicycle stopped occasionally to push a morning newspaper through a letter plate, and then hurriedly moved to the next one.

"Did you ever think about joining the army?" asked Charlotte as they crossed another street and onto Holborn Road.

"I actually wanted to be an officer", replied Gabriel as he indicated to Charlotte to walk slowly, "but my working class background prohibited it, so I am stuck at The War Office pushing pens".

"What do you expect to find here?" asked Charlotte.

"I have no idea", replied Gabriel, "but what else are we to do?"

Charlotte and Gabriel walked down Holborn Road and when they reached the end they walked back up it again.

"We can't keep doing this all morning, it's going to look suspicious", said Charlotte.

"I agree", replied Gabriel, "we need to find your grandfather first and I don't think Mr. Burnhouse has him locked up somewhere on Holborn Road".

"Let's have a cup of tea at those tearooms we passed", suggested Charlotte.

A few minutes later Charlotte and Gabriel sat at the table and ordered a pot of tea.

"There must be someone who knows where he disappeared to", said Gabriel.

"I have twisted my brain a thousand different directions", replied Charlotte, "and I can't think of one person or idea, oh Gabriel, what are we to do?"

"Just calm down, by the looks of you, you didn't get much sleep", said Gabriel as he looked into Charlotte's tired face.

"I think you already know the answer to that", replied Charlotte as she began to sip her cup of tea.

"Is there anyone you can think of who may have come into contact with him", asked Gabriel.

"No one I can think of", replied Charlotte in a tired tone of voice, Ah maybe the little shop on Cheap Street where he buys his newspapers."

"It's worth a try", said Gabriel, "hope can come from the most unusual places".

As Charlotte and Gabriel walked through the door of the little shop, a bell rang to alert the shop keeper of their presence.

"Good morning", said Charlotte politely, "I am looking for my grandfather Tim Cratchit, have you seen him recently?"

"No my dear, he usually comes in every morning for his newspaper, but haven't laid eyes on him these last two mornings", replied the female shop keeper.

"Did he mention to you that he was going anywhere, or give you any hint that he was leaving?" asked Gabriel.

"No, nah, nothing that springs to mind, I do hope he's ok", replied the shop keeper, "he's a good soul and always has a cheerful word to say".

"I do hope so", said Charlotte as she turned to leave the shop, "thank you".

"Oh by the way my dear, if you do see him will you tell him I have that book he ordered", said the shop keeper.

"I will take it for him", said Charlotte as she turned to pay the shop keeper for the book, "how much is it?"

"Five shillings my dear, why anyone of his age would want to learn a foreign language is beyond me", said the shop keeper.

Charlotte handed the shop keeper the five shillings and thanked her for the book. As she walked out onto the crisp cold air, she signaled for Gabriel to quickly follow her down a narrow alleyway.

"My God", said Charlotte as she took the book out of the brown paper wrapping, "he's gone to France".

Gabriel knew that this time Charlotte was right, for the title on the book read, A BEGINNERS GUIDE TO SPEAKING FRENCH.

As Charlotte and Gabriel made their way back home, Gabriel tossed the news they had just heard around in his head and tried in vain to come up with a reason why Tim suddenly decided to go off to France. From his short encounter with Tim, he found him to be both a little bit eccentric, with above average intelligence. He knew if Tim was to get up suddenly and rush off to a foreign country without first saying where he was going, then he had a very good reason to do so.

"Would you like to come up for a cup of tea?" asked Gabriel as they approached the front door.

"I suppose", replied Charlotte, "two heads are better than one and I'm damned if I can think of any reason that would take him over there, especially during a war".

Gabriel turned the key on his room door and carried out the usual ritual of hanging his coat on the hanger before entering the sitting room. He did not notice any change on his way through the door, it was only when he walked into the main room that he noticed the strangers facing him from across the room.

"Good afternoon Miss Martha Dywer, or do I call

you Charlotte Starr instead", said Jimbo as he leered across the room at the surprised looks on both Charlotte and Gabriel's faces.

"How did you get in here?" asked Gabriel as his tone now changed from one of surprise to that of anger.

"You shouldn't go about leaving your doors unlocked", replied Jimbo, still sporting a wide grin.

"The door was not left unlocked", said Gabriel,
"you're trespassing or did you break in to steal something?"

"Now my good man, let's be reasonable", replied Jimbo as his grin disappeared, "I only called in to inquire about your health and to ask that you return that item you removed from my residence sometime in the early hours of this morning".

"What are you talking about?" asked Charlotte, "we took nothing from you".

"But my dear, you were both seen loitering outside my house a few hours ago", replied Jimbo.

"We were to meet a friend there", said Charlotte in pretense, "she didn't turn up so we carried out a few errands and came back home".

"Did anyone ever tell you to go for a career on the stage, that one is as tall as Miss Martha Dwyer", replied Jimbo.

"Get out of this house or I will call the police", said Gabriel angrily.

To Charlotte and Gabriel's sudden shock the long shadowy figure of a man who stood beside Jimbo silently, produced a walking stick with a blade protruding from the base.

"Hand it over or I will be forced to allow my loyal friend here to extract the information of its whereabouts without mercy", said Jimbo as he flashed another smile.

Gabriel knew within that small second of making a decision, he must carry it through. He reached for the long iron poker perched on top of the stove and with a firm grip he brought it down hard on the walking stick. As the walking stick hit the ground, Gabriel caught sight of Charlotte flinging a foot stool in the direction of the surprised Jimbo. Jimbo's shadowy friend recovered quickly from Gabriel's attack and counter attacked with a heavy kick to Gabriel's shin with all the ferocity of an angry man. Gabriel wanted to scream out in pain but knew to do so would offer the enemy the satisfaction of a victory. He swiped the poker across the knee of Jimbo's shadowy companion, and watched triumphantly as he crashed into the side of the table and then fell heavily to the floor. Gabriel once again watched Jimbo's face change from one of surprise, to a look of shock. He turned to Charlotte but noticed it was not her who had caused the change in Jimbo and turned to see Tiny Tim standing behind them with a flintlock pistol pointed in the direction of the frightened Jimbo.

"One more move from you or your friend Mr. Burnhouse and someone is going to get a nasty surprise", said Tim.

"Oh Mr. Cratchit sir, you really do not want to be discharging that thing in a closed in space", replied Jimbo in a quivering voice.

"Pick your friend up and get out of here", said Tim, still pointing the antique firearm.

Jimbo reached down and helped his shadowy friend up from the floor. Gabriel noticed the man was crying like a child and heard him mutter words between sobs, that he wanted his mother.

"Ok", said Tiny Tim as he followed the pair with his flintlock pistol, "now would be a good time to leave before I forget my benevolent disposition".

Jimbo hurriedly left the room followed by the sight of Tim's pistol. Whenever the door was closed firmly behind them, Tim lowered the pistol and was soon smothered by Charlotte's loving embrace.

"Now, now my child", said Tim, "I've only been away two days".

Gabriel lifted the stool that Charlotte had flung in Jimbo's direction and placed it back in its rightful place. He then sat down on a chair beside the table and cried inwardly for the pain in his shin. He did not notice the leg of his trousers being lifted up until he felt a stabbing pain followed by Charlotte's voice.

"My God, he could have broken your leg".

"It's ok", lied Gabriel.

"Grandfather", said Charlotte as she rose to light the stove, "you and Gabriel were extremely brave, I could face any danger if I knew you were both by my side".

"You didn't do too bad yourself", said Gabriel still trying to hide the agony that was flowing through his leg.

As Charlotte worked on the stove, Tim sat down across the table from Gabriel and placed the pistol down before them.

"Where in God's name did you get that contraption?" asked Gabriel, "you could have killed everyone in the room if that had of went off".

"I'll have you know young man that this is a fine piece of hardware", he replied, "it has served faithfully two generations and still continues to do so".

As the stove began to come alive, Charlotte put the kettle on to boil and busied herself with the essentials of making tea.

"What were they looking for?" asked Gabriel.

"I don't know", replied Charlotte, "they seemed to think we stole something belonging to them".

"And did you?" asked Tim as he tapped his fingers lightly on the table.

"No we did not", replied Charlotte, "we didn't even know which house he lived in".

"But you did know what street he lived on my dear", said Tim, "how did you manage to discover that I wonder".

"Charlotte worked her magic", replied Gabriel.

"That's my dear", said Tim proudly, "that girl should be an actress".

"How many times am I going to listen to both friend and foe dictating what I should or should not be", said Charlotte, "I will be what I want to be, and no one, especially a man will tell me otherwise".

"That's my dear", said Tim for the second time.
Gabriel noticed that whenever Tiny Tim called Charlotte her dear, there never was any form of protest offered in response. The way Charlotte flung her arms around Tim when she discovered he was safe and well, told Gabriel that an unbreakable bond existed between the two and as she put his tea before him, he wished that someday he would become part of the unbreakable.

"Ok grandfather", said Charlotte as she joined Gabriel and Tim at the table, "where did you disappear to?"

"I went to visit a dear old friend", answered Tim as he began the sucking process with his cup of tea.

"And this dear old friend, do they speak French?" asked Charlotte.

"My God, you really are a chip off the old block", answered Tim, "how in God's name did you discover that?"

"I got this from your book shop", answered Charlotte as she put the book on the table before Tim's eyes.

"Humm!" said Tim, "I could have been doing with that earlier".

"Now are you going to tell me why you went to France?" asked Charlotte.

"You need to ask him something else as well", said Gabriel butting in.

"And what would that be my good man?" asked Tim as he finished cleaning the inside of his teacup with his tongue.

"What you took out of Jimbo's house in the early hours of the morning", answered Gabriel.

"My young man", said Tim as he turned to look at Gabriel with admiration, "are you sure you are not related to me in one way or the other?"

"Not that I know of sir", replied Gabriel.

"Grandfather", said Charlotte, "tell us please, have you got something that Jimbo was after?"

"Children", said Tim as he examined his cup for any minute drops of tea, you both did well on your quest for answers, but I myself have been several steps ahead of you".

"We would be grateful if you could enlighten us sir", said Gabriel.

"Before I burden you with my findings", said Tim as he turned to look at Gabriel, "you young man will have to stop calling me sir, it makes me feel old".

"Ok Mr. Cratchit", replied Gabriel humorously.

"No, my friends call me by my first name, you can

call me Tim", said Tim.

Despite the amusement in the discovery that Tim cannot accept that age has caught up with him, Gabriel was happy that he was now added to Tim's list of friends. Despite his strange habits, Gabriel liked the old gentleman very much and his granddaughter a lot more. He was confident that Tim was no thief and whatever forced him to burgle someone's house, Gabriel knew that it could be nothing less than very important.

"I have in my pocket", said Tim, "a list of names and dates of births of a battalion of soldiers who will attack German machine gun positions on Christmas day".

"Why is that list of names so important?" asked Charlotte

"Why do you ask indeed my dear", replied Tim, "I will tell you why, because Christmas day is not only a day when we should celebrate the birth of Christ, it is a day when peace and goodwill and love and compassion should be exercised. It is a time when children sing carols and await the opening of gifts while their little innocent hearts burst with joy. But on this Christmas day instead of enjoying the God given and moral rights of childhood, this battalion of children will be entering the pits of hell".

"Dear God", said Charlotte as she placed her hand on her heart, "we have got to try and stop this".

"Yes my dear, we must try and stop it", replied Tim as he turned to look at Gabriel, "and you my young friend must fulfil your destiny".

"How are we going to stop this?" asked Gabriel.

"I will return to France and figure out a way of preventing the slaughter of these children", said Tim, "and you two must find someone in authority and

49

present this evidence to them".

"But who do we go to?" asked Gabriel, "there must be someone at the top who is involved in this evil".

"Tread careful my young friend and protect my dear granddaughter, for if she is harmed then my heart will die and along with it a generation of ingenuous souls".

"Will Jimbo try to stop us?" asked Gabriel.

"He will try everything in his power to get his hands on that list", replied Tim, "prepare yourself to make a stand against the blackness of iniquity".

"When will you leave for France?" asked Charlotte.

"Soon my dear, soon", replied Tim, "but now we will chat around another pot of tea and talk of bygone days, did I ever mention to you that as a child I used to walk with a crutch?"

CHAPTER 5

"Grandfather has left, I believe to France", said Charlotte after she greeted Gabriel with a smile outside the tearoom.

"So, it begins", replied Gabriel as he followed Charlotte inside and sat down at the small table by the window.

"I did some searching this morning", said Gabriel, "asking around in a tip toe sort of way, but it seems that anyone who may be trust worthily at the top, are beyond reach".

"Nothing is beyond reach", replied Charlotte as she finished ordering, "we have got to find a way or grandfather will be on his own and in possible danger".

Gabriel stared out the window at the various movements of life passing by and could only yearn inwardly at what humanity had become. He had thought of ways of reaching someone who could be trusted, but had been beaten back by the simple reality that he was just a clerk, a drop of moisture in a very large ocean.

"There is a notice up on the wall at work, requesting volunteers to go to France", said Gabriel.

"Don't they know there is a war going on there", replied Charlotte.

"Precisely", said Gabriel, "they want people to take notes and forward those same writings back to The War Office for analysis".

"You have enough on your plate without poking your nose in to see what others have on theirs", replied Charlotte as she poured them a cup of tea.

"I was thinking if I volunteered I might get closer to those who can help us", said Gabriel, "Tim is going to need all the help he can get".

"Don't you dare Mr. Gabriel", replied Charlotte as she give Gabriel a piercing look.

"I have already dared", said Gabriel as he tried to escape Charlotte's optical wraith.

"My God, are you stupid, people are getting killed over there", replied Charlotte.

"I have no other choice", said Gabriel, "if this mess is to be stopped, I need to find out who can do it".

"You can do that here, I could make a few inquiries, something will turn up", replied Charlotte as she tried to hide the emotion in her voice.

"Listen Charlotte, I know this is the only thing left to do, and I feel strongly that it is the right thing to do", said Gabriel.

"Ok then Mr. Gabriel", said Charlotte in defiance, "I'm coming with you".

"I am sorry to have to insult your belief in equal rights, but females are not permitted", replied Gabriel.

"How dare them, there will come a time sooner rather than later, they will have to give in to the God given right of equality", said Charlotte as she tried not to raise her voice.

"Let's not get into that argument", replied Gabriel,

"at least not until we have put this to rest one way or the other".

"One thing for sure", said Charlotte.

"And what might that be?" asked Gabriel.

"I will get to France by fair means or foul", replied Charlotte.

"I'm worried about Jimbo when I am gone", said Gabriel as he threw Charlotte a worried look.

"Then you will have to stay behind and be my protector like grandfather said", replied Charlotte before she took a bite of her hot buttered scone.

Gabriel knew that Charlotte was right, Tiny Tim had entrusted him with her safety and now he found himself in a difficult situation. He had no alternative but to accept the job in France, as staying where he was would most certainly reap a harvest of nothing. If he chose to find some way of Charlotte joining him in France, then her welfare would be equally in danger. He would have to devise a plan that would keep Jimbo at bay, at least until Tim and he returned.

"Charlotte", said Gabriel as he finished the last of his tea, "will you meet me outside work this evening?"

"If it makes you happy then anything to oblige", replied Charlotte.

Gabriel waited for Charlotte to finish her tea and after paying and thanking the waitress, they made their way outside.

"Now listen to me please", said Gabriel, "go back home and stay out of sight, I will meet you later".

"Have you got something up your shirt sleeve my dear", replied Charlotte as she flashed Gabriel one of her all-knowing smiles.

"My dear indeed", said Gabriel, "take care".

When Gabriel returned to the office he was met with

another bundle of assorted forms to fill in, including another more detailed version of the official secrets act. He filled them in neatly and upon completion, placed the papers inside a large brown envelope and wrote a name on the front. When finished, Gabriel proceeded to fill in the names of the dead, and silently prayed for each and every one.

"You did come after all", said Gabriel playfully as he met Charlotte after work.

"How could I resist a request by a charming man like you", replied Charlotte as she hooked on to Gabriel's arm.

"I hope you are up for another display of your fine acting skills", said Gabriel.

"Indeed sir, I am but an umble wench", replied Charlotte playfully.

"Let's pay a visit to Mr. Jimbo at Holborn Road", said Gabriel as the proceeded to walk in that direction.

"What have you up your sleeve mister?" asked Charlotte.

"First we need to find out what house he lives in, and then I want you to deliver this envelope through the letter plate on his door", said Gabriel.

"Are you going to tell me what's in the envelope?" asked Charlotte

"It's best you don't know at this time, but I will fill you in later", replied Gabriel.

Charlotte and Gabriel continued to walk the short distance to Holborn Road, pausing occasionally to find their way through the dim glare of the street lights.

"I need you to knock on any door you want", said Gabriel, "and use every ounce of your fine breeding to get directed to Mr. Burnhouse's place of residence".
Charlotte walked across the road carrying the brown

envelope that Gabriel had given her, and knocked on the first door she saw.

"Good afternoon", said an old gentleman as he opened the door.

"Oh good afternoon sir", replied Charlotte, "I was given this envelope by a Mr. James Burnhouse to drop off, and I have forgotten which number he said".

"It's two doors down, number seven", said the old gentleman.

"Oh thank you sir, I am so sorry for having to trouble you", replied Charlotte.

"It's ok dear", said the old gentleman as he closed the door.

Charlotte walked the two doors down to number seven and pushed the envelope through the letter plate on Jimbo's door. She casually began to walk back to Gabriel who was waiting out of sight around the corner.

"Good girl", said Gabriel as both Charlotte and he commenced their retreat.

"I'm not a good girl", replied Charlotte, "I have a feeling that I have just instigated something dreadful on a poor unsuspecting Mr. Burnhouse".

"If everything goes to plan, you will have freed yourself of any danger from Jimbo, now and in the foreseeable future", said Gabriel.

"I still don't like being labelled a good girl", replied Charlotte as she tightened her grip on Gabriel's arm, "it's sounds immature".

"How about a brave girl then?" said Gabriel playfully.

"How about a fine lady", replied Charlotte as they turned a corner and headed straight for home.

"I can't find them anywhere", said Gabriel as he looked all around the office.

"When did you last see them?" asked the policeman as he watched Gabriel looking under the table.

"I left them on my desk yesterday evening and when I arrived this morning, they were gone", answered Gabriel.

"What is that you're holding up to look at?" asked the policeman as he looked at Gabriel suspiciously.

"It's an address written down on a piece of paper, it's not my address or anyone I know" answered Gabriel as he handed the piece of paper to the policeman.

"Deliver to 7 Holborn Road, London and you will be generously rewarded", said the policemen as he read the address aloud.

"What does it mean?" asked Gabriel.

"It means whoever took your papers have unintentionally left us a calling card", replied the policeman with a triumphant look on his face.

"My God, they really have been stolen", said Gabriel as he feinted surprise.

"Stolen to order by the look of things", replied the policeman, "good day sir, I'm off to catch a criminal".

As soon as the policeman left the office, Gabriel continued with his scribbling of names. He had little doubt that his plan would work and by tonight, Jimbo would no longer be a threat to Charlotte and hopefully for a long time to come.

"You didn't?" asked Charlotte as Gabriel filled her in on the story.

"I had no other choice", replied Gabriel, "I promised your grandfather I would keep you from harm and that was the only way I knew how".

"So you're still going ahead with this madness?" asked Charlotte.

"Indeed my dear", replied Gabriel, "one person's madman is another person's hero".

"I'll pass on the hero for now if you don't mind", said Charlotte.

"Any word from Tim?" asked Gabriel as he poured some milk into the cup of tea before him.

"Nothing", replied Charlotte as she poked the stove before sitting down at the table beside Gabriel.

"I don't know whether in this case, that no news is good news", said Gabriel.

"Trust me", replied Charlotte, "no news from grandfather is not something you need to throw a party for".

"At the very least when I get over there, I can write to you and keep you up to date", said Gabriel as he sipped on his tea.

"That's if you live long enough", replied Charlotte.

"Don't worry", said Gabriel trying to add some humor to the conversation, "if you want me to, I will come back in one piece".

"And if I don't?" asked Charlotte as she lifted her head to look into Gabriel's eyes.

"Then with no one to care for me, I will no doubt be left to a similar fate as those children we are trying to save", replied Gabriel as he tried to bar Charlotte from seeing through the window of his inner feelings.

"What happens if grandfather is back before you leave?" asked Charlotte as she turned to stare in the direction of the stove.

"Then I hope he has his antique pistol with him, so that he can shoot me on the foot", replied Gabriel,

"No doubt I will have to have my whole leg

amputated if he sets that thing off".

"Do you believe the story he told us about the crutch?" asked Charlotte.

"Well I'm not really sure; he certainly is one of the liveliest on their feet characters I have ever known", replied Gabriel.

"He said that his family were very poor and he himself would have died if it hadn't have been for one Christmas day long ago", said Charlotte.

"What happened on that Christmas day?" asked Gabriel.

"I am not really sure, from what I heard my great grandfather's employer who was a hard wretched old miser, changed on Christmas day", replied Charlotte. "At first everyone thought he had gone mad, but after a few weeks they realized that he was as sane as everyone else, and that something had really happened that changed the way he looked upon life".

"How did he save your grandfather's life?" asked Gabriel.

"He paid for him to see all the best doctors in England and grandfather subsequently looked upon him as a second Father", replied Charlotte.

"It certainly is a very interesting story and four weeks ago I wouldn't have believed any of it, but as time passed I will now believe almost anything", said Gabriel as he rose to put some more coal into the stove.

"Where do you think Jimbo is now?" asked Charlotte.

"I have my strong suspicions that he is looking out through iron bars and trying to figure out how he managed to get there", replied Gabriel as he returned to sit down at the table.

"Will you do me a favor before we say our goodnights?" asked Charlotte as she arose from her chair beside the table.

"I will if it doesn't entail jumping off a very high building", replied Gabriel jokingly.

"Well, we will get to that another time", said Charlotte as she made her way to the door, "please try not to snore, you're keeping me awake downstairs".

As Gabriel lay in bed the events of the day flashed before him and he hoped within himself that all Christmas' before him would bring some good into people's lives. Shadows of the past, present and future were now entwined to form an unearthly alliance to fight an earthly cause. Tomorrow would most likely be his last day before he would catch the train to Dover and then a ship to France. Charlotte had arrived into his life by a collision on the footpath outside his place of work, and he now wished he had never had to leave. Before Gabriel could allow another thought to gush into his mind, a voice interrupted them from the enclosure of the dimly lit room.

"Have you seen my glasses, I can't find my glasses". Gabriel looked down at the foot of his bed, and before him was the old man who called himself Ebenezer Scrooge.

"Oh there they are", said Scrooge as he applied a pair of glasses to his head.

"What are you doing here?" asked Gabriel.

"You mean what was I doing here", replied Scrooge as he showed Gabriel a wide grin.

"You are standing before me now", said Gabriel as he propped himself up on one elbow on the bed.

"I was standing before you", replied Scrooge.

"For the sake of any argument", said Gabriel, "and contrary to the fact that I can live without sleep, may we please get this conversation over with".

"Ah, humm, now what was it I used to tell you", replied Scrooge.

"Don't tell me I'm to be visited by another spirit", said Gabriel despairingly, "look at all the trouble the last ghost caused me".

"No, no my good man, I just brought a letter for Tiny Tim", replied Scrooge as he reached into his side pocket and produced a letter sealed by wax.

"Why didn't you give it to Tim when he was here?" asked Gabriel.

"I tried", replied Scrooge, "but I kept missing him by a few years".

"Ok, if you must you can leave it on the wash table", said Gabriel as he was beginning to feel the tide of sleep drifting towards him.

"You mean the table that was, my young friend", replied Scrooge as he continued to look around the room.

Gabriel was trying very hard to fight off the impulse to get angry with the vision before him. For some reason knowing only to Scrooge, the furniture that now filled the room that Gabriel slept, had never filled the room that Scrooge knew.

"Ok then", said Gabriel as he tried to accommodate Mr. Scrooge, "leave it on the window sill".

"What a remarkable chap you are, an intelligent chap", replied Scrooge as he walked to the window sill and placed the letter firmly upon the white painted wood.

"Now will you please go", said Gabriel as he lay down flat on the bed, "I have a long day tomorrow".

"You will see that Tiny Tim gets that letter my good man", said Scrooge as he continued to walk around the room, "It was very important".

"You mean it is very important", replied Gabriel.

"It is for him, it was for me", said Scrooge as he turned to once again smile at Gabriel's tired figure stretched out on the bed.

"Ok whatever you say", replied Gabriel, "I promise you faithfully that Mr. Tiny Tim will receive the letter whether it be present tense or past.

"It might be better in the future tense as the present may be already past", said Scrooge as he applied his hand to scratching his head.

"When I see him I will give it to him, so please allow me the dignity of falling asleep", replied Gabriel in a groggy tone of voice.

"My young friend, no one is depriving you of sleep", replied Scrooge, "if you cannot sleep you may need to see a doctor".

"I may need to see a Psychiatrist", said Gabriel, "if anyone hears that I have been talking to someone who isn't there, my feet won't get touching the ground".

"Come now my good fellow", replied Scrooge, "surely you mean someone who wasn't there".

"Are you sure you don't need to see a doctor", said Gabriel as he drifted off to sleep.

"Certainly not my good friend", replied Scrooge, "or the undertaker either".

CHAPTER 6

At the train station Gabriel waited to say goodbye to Charlotte and embark on a journey that had a destination yet to be written. Throngs of soldiers and several sailors said their farewells to the loved and broken hearted. When the call rang out for everyone to board, Gabriel stepped onto the train with a heavy heart and an empty feeling in the pit of his stomach. As he took an empty seat by the window of the train, Gabriel sadly watched as the buildings began to move slowly, then gather pace as they moved off in the direction of Dover. It was difficult to hide his disappointment at not saying goodbye to Charlotte, for his reflection on the window glass told no tall tales.

"Is this seat taken dear", said the young nurse as she hovered beside Gabriel waiting for an answer.

When Gabriel turned around to tell her it was available, he didn't know whether to cry, scream or fly into a fit of temper.

"What in God's name have you done?" asked Gabriel.

"Did you think I was going to let you slip off to France and have all the fun, while I played the helpless female at home waiting for word whether you were living or dead", replied Charlotte as she sat down on the chair next to Gabriel.

"Why did you do it?" asked Gabriel now revealing the fear he had for Charlotte's safety in his voice.

"Do you like my uniform?" asked Charlotte, "my grandfather always said to keep one step ahead of everyone else and I would be sure to get there before them".

"How did you do it?" asked Gabriel as he stared at Charlotte in astonishment, "you are not a trained nurse".

"I joined the Voluntary Aid Detachment, you only need three months experience in hospitals, and I gained that experience alongside a Suffragette friend of mine", answered Charlotte.

"When this train stops at the next station", said Gabriel, "I want you off it and on the next one back to London".

"I can't do that", replied Charlotte as she threw a smile in Gabriel's direction, "I haven't got my grandfather's antique pistol to shoot myself on the foot".

The sight of Charlotte appearing before him unexpected, had filled Gabriel with a curious mixture of fear and happiness. Charlotte had her own mind and no one however meaningful in their intentions, would ever change it for her. Gabriel wasn't sure how she could be of help, and without calling in the services of the kettle calling the pot black, he also had no idea how he could be of any assistance either.

"Where will you be staying?" asked Gabriel as the surprise of Charlotte's disobedient presence began to subside.

"I might be staying in a luxury hotel with very large rooms, but in the other hand there might not be any roof on it", replied Charlotte.

"And where might your place of residence be?" asked Charlotte.

"Probably next door to you in the stables", replied Gabriel.

Gabriel didn't notice the two soldiers who sat down on the two seats opposite, until one of them began to speak.

"Couldn't find a uniform where you come from mate?" asked the young soldier with ginger colored hair.

"I bet they couldn't find one to fit him", said the other soldier with the bald head.

"I work for The War Office if you must know", replied Gabriel as he produced his identity card to show them.

"Oh, and what do you do for them, make cups of tea", said baldy as he looked at Ginger and smiled.

"As a matter of fact we both work for The War Office", said Charlotte.

"Don't tell me", said Ginger, "I bet you make the beds".

"Not quite", replied Charlotte as she moved closer to the soldiers, "you both are aware of the official secrets act".

"I should hope we are", replied Baldy.

"Well this must not go any further, the Captain and myself work behind enemy lines and this is our disguise", said Charlotte in a for your ears only tone of voice.

Both Baldy and Ginger turned slowly to look at each other as if someone had just presented them with some terrible news.

"Are you sure you are not trying to pull our leg?" asked Baldy.

"It's not that we don't believe", said Ginger.

"Scout's honor", replied Charlotte as she spoke in almost a whisper, "the captain here is going on his seventeenth mission.

"I am so sorry sir", said Ginger as he stared pleadingly at Gabriel, "we thought you were, well you know".

"Who is your Commanding Officer?" asked Gabriel.

"We haven't had our posting yet sir, we are truly sorry", replied Ginger.

"For all we know you could be spies", said Gabriel.

"No sir we promise, now if you excuse us, we have some urgent business to attend to further up the train", replied Ginger as he nudged Baldy out of his seat.

Gabriel and Charlotte watched as the two soldiers hurriedly moved to the upper end of the train, before bursting into laughter.

"You did it again my vixen", said Gabriel as he smiled at Charlotte.

"Am I really your vixen?" replied Charlotte as she suddenly stopped laughing.

"What do you mean?" asked Gabriel as he faced Charlotte's stare.

"Do they serve tea on this train?" asked Charlotte, "I'm dying for a cup of tea".

"Excuse me", said Gabriel as he caught the eye of a steward, "do you serve tea on this train?"

"Not unless you are royalty old son", replied the steward as he continued on his way.

"That's that ruled out", said Charlotte, "we will probably have to wait until we get to France".

"And even then tea is not guaranteed, I believe they drink coffee there", replied Gabriel.

"If that's what I'm to expect, then I think I will get off at the next station", said Charlotte jokingly.

As Gabriel turned to stare out the window at the passing telegraph poles and green fields, tea was the last thing that was going through his mind. The words "Am I really your vixen", floated before him like a magic Persian carpet waiting to hear those enchanted words, ordering it to fly away. Charlotte reminded him of a school friend who stood poised before a great jump, but just as everyone thought he was about to take it, he turned back. He knew the journey would be long, and he was happy to have Charlotte by his side, but how or where their journey together in life would end; only Charlotte held the answer and wasn't about to give it up without a push.

As Charlotte and Gabriel sat down at a small table on the deck of the ship, Gabriel once again stopped a Steward.

"Pardon me sir", said Gabriel, "may I be bold enough to inquire if tea is served aboard?"

"Yes sir, would a pot of tea for two be sufficient?" replied the Steward.

"Excellent, thank you very much", said Gabriel.

"Good, but not as good as", said Charlotte as the steward went off to fetch the tea.

"Good as who?" asked Gabriel.

"Yours truly, who else?" replied Charlotte as she scanned the surrounding docklands before her.

"I will not flatter you with an answer to that question", said Gabriel.

"That my dear is because you know me so well",

replied Charlotte.

Gabriel paid for the tea the steward delivered and included a generous tip. As the ship moved off and headed out onto the English Channel, Gabriel suddenly remembered the envelope sitting upon the window sill, and realized that he had forgot the letter for Tiny Tim.

"Gabriel Shivers reporting", said Gabriel as he handed the soldier behind the desk a number of papers.

"Just take a chair and someone will be with you shortly", said the young corporal behind the desk.

Gabriel looked around the room he had just entered and could picture nothing but disarray and unashamed clutter around him. The corporal behind the desk was busy doing nothing and stacks of newspapers and files lay scattered around the room.

"The colonel will see you now", said another much younger private.

Gabriel arose from his chair and followed the young private into another smaller room.

"Take a seat", said the colonel as the door closed firmly behind them.

"I see by this report you have only been a few weeks with The War Office", said the colonel as he stared at Gabriel's record.

"Yes sir", replied Gabriel as he took a seat before the aged colonel.

"It is my understanding that you volunteered for this assignment", said the colonel, still not lifting his eyes from the desk.

"I did sir", replied Gabriel, "I thought that I might do some good over here".

"You will take your orders from Lieutenant Fleming, who reports directly to me", said the colonel, "he will brief you and show you to your sleeping arrangements, do you understand?"

"Yes sir, replied Gabriel.

"And remember", said the colonel as he lifted his head and stared into Gabriel's eyes, "there are two types of reports we write here, what the public back home want to hear and what they should not hear".

"I will remember that sir", replied Gabriel.

"You can go now", said the colonel as he pointed towards the door.

"Thank you sir", replied Gabriel as he arose from his chair and made his way out through the door.

Gabriel followed the young soldier outside and down a gravel pathway between two wooden buildings. At the bottom of the gravel path, they entered into a long wide room with a few beds and tables scattered in confused arrangements.

"Straight through that door there", said the young soldier as he pointed straight ahead, "the lieutenant is expecting you".

Gabriel thanked the young soldier and followed his directions before knocking three times on the door.

"Come in the door is open", a voice shouted from the other side.

Gabriel walked through the door and after closing it behind him he stood before a young lieutenant about his own age who looked tired and extremely agitated.

"My name's Gabriel Shivers sir, straight from The War Office", said Gabriel as he introduced himself.

"I am really pleased to meet you", said the young lieutenant as he stood to shake Gabriel firmly on the hand, "please take a seat".

"Thank you, sir,", said Gabriel as he sat down on an old wood wormed chair.

"The colonel said I was to gently brief you", said the lieutenant as he applied a match to his pipe, "but that's not the way I do things, I like to fill you in on the realities, unlike the colonel's fairy stories".

"Fairy Stories sir?" asked Gabriel in surprise.

"According to the reports coming from the front, we are giving the Germans a damn good thrashing", said the lieutenant as he attempted to fire up his pipe once again, "but in all honesty, we are losing men by the thousands and the Germans are mowing them down faster than we can replace them".

"So, what you are telling me sir" said Gabriel, "is that the newspapers back home are lying".

"Lying would be putting it mildly", replied the lieutenant, "black propaganda of the vilest is what it is and we are here to make sure it happens".

"Why can't we report the truth?" asked Gabriel.
"Because if the truth ever got out, the streets of England would be thronging with protesters, which in turn would bring down parliament and hand victory to Germany on a plate", replied the lieutenant as he once again attempted the task of lighting his pipe.

"I wasn't sure what my job was", said Gabriel, "they told me at The War Office it was writing reports on how the war was progressing, which were then to be sent back to The War Office.".

"Indeed", replied the lieutenant, "but that was before you signed the official secrets act and all those assorted papers the colonel has on his desk".

Gabriel realized that he had been tricked into signing by false pretenses, and now he had no other choice but to obey. The short time he had known the young lieutenant give him hope that he could eventually trust him, and perhaps something good could still be pulled out of the catastrophic hat.

"Is there anyone else working with us sir?" asked Gabriel.

"There were three chaps sent from The War Office", replied the lieutenant as he give up on the idea of lighting his pipe, "one lost his head literally, and the other two lost their minds".

"When you say lost his head, what actually happened?" asked Gabriel as he felt the nerves pouncing around inside his stomach.

"He got too close to the front lines and a piece of shrapnel the size of a kettle took it clean off at the neck", replied the lieutenant, "speaking of kettles, be a good chap and make us a cup of tea, one sugar and just a dash of milk for me".

Gabriel arose from his chair and made his way out of the office and into the general living quarters. Gabriel noticed a stove already lit at the end of the room and commenced to bring together the ingredients of tea making.

"Just make yourself at home old chap", shouted the lieutenant, "take us as you find us, there are no airs here".

As Gabriel waited on the kettle boiling he began to think of Charlotte and wondered how she was getting on in her new situation. Somehow he knew that the road ahead would be paved with many bleeding thorns, and both Charlotte and he would be tested to the very limit of mental endurance. He needed to find Tiny Tim and tell him about the letter that was left behind, but above all he needed to stop the slaughter of innocent children. Where or when he would find Tim he could not tell and all he knew of the present situation was he needed to keep his head down and wait.

"You are going to have to wear a uniform", said the lieutenant as Gabriel handed him a cup of tea.

"Why?" asked Gabriel, "I never signed up for the army".

"If the Germans capture you in civilian clothes they will treat you as a spy and shoot you", replied the lieutenant as he sipped on his tea before thanking Gabriel.

"Well I am a spy in a way", said Gabriel.

"True", replied the lieutenant as he proceeded to once again battle with his pipe, "but you still don't want them to know that".

"May I ask you a question sir?" asked Gabriel.

"Feel free, I told you there are no airs here, or indeed formalities either", replied the lieutenant.

"I have a friend who I believe may be here in France", said Gabriel, "his name is Tim Cratchit".

"Is he a soldier?" asked the lieutenant.

"No sir, he is an old man who is looking for his son", replied Gabriel in deliberate pretense.

"I don't believe I have ever heard of him, but I will ask around in the officers mess", said the lieutenant.

"Thank you sir I would gratefully appreciate it", replied Gabriel.

"Take your pick of the beds inside", said the lieutenant as he pointed into the main part of the building, "and any desk you choose will not be disputed by their previous owner".

"Thank you sir", replied Gabriel as he picked up the two empty tea cups from the table, "If you don't mind I'll unpack and get settled in".

"Carry on", said the lieutenant, "and get a peaceful

night's sleep because you're off to the front early in the morning".

Gabriel selected a bed next to the window and placed his bag on top. He removed several items of clothing and fitted them neatly into the foot locker beside the bed. He collected his pens and pencils and placed them on top of the nearest desk, checking each drawer for any sign of the previous occupant's belongings. On satisfying himself that nothing remained, he deposited some of his own items into the top drawer and laid claim to the desk. From the distance Gabriel could hear a loud whistle, followed by an explosion and wondered whose life had ended as a result. His mind quickly returned to Charlotte, and began turning over ways and means in his mind to get to see her. Gabriel's thoughts were interrupted by the young soldier appearing beside him.

"I was told you needed a uniform, so I think this is about your size", said the soldier.

"I see the previous owner didn't need it for long", said Gabriel as he noticed holes on the front of the coat, now patched up.

"I'm not really sure", replied the soldier, "it was sent down from the stores".

"Thank you", said Gabriel as the soldier said goodbye.

Gabriel placed the uniform neatly on the bed and proceeded to first remove his shoes and then his trousers. He tried on the uniform trousers which fitted well, and the jacket fitted as if it was made for him. He noticed a mirror hanging on a wall to his right and on presenting himself before his own image; he knew that danger glowed from the very sight before him. It wasn't only the uniform that reeked of fear, or the holes that ended the existence of its previous owner. And Gabriel could safely say that the shells squealing in the distance, no longer brought whirlpools to the pit of his stomach. What Gabriel feared most at that moment in time, was the stranger reflecting from the mirror before him.

CHAPTER 7

The sight before him did not stray from the description the ghost of the future had shown him. Hell in its mud caked pitiless portrait stretched out before him as Gabriel made his way across the mud and into the belly of the trench.

"Could you point me in the direction of Captain Burke please?" asked Gabriel as he now stood facing a bunch of mud soaked and weary soldiers.

"Follow the trench for about two hundred yards and his shelter is on the right", replied the soldier.

Gabriel thanked the soldier and made his way down the trench as instructed, while every step took greater and greater effort. As he stood before a makeshift shelter forged into the side of the trench, a sign in chalk outside amusingly read The Ritz.

"Good morning", said Gabriel as he bent his neck to gain access to the crudely designed habitat, "I am looking for Captain Burke".

"You just may have found him", said a soldier who sat at a small table looking over some maps.

"Captain Burke sir", said Gabriel, "I was sent by Lieutenant Fleming and told to report to you".

"I know who you are", replied Captain Burke, "and next week or the week after if you are lucky to last that long, they'll send another one to take your place".

"Could you give me your assessment of the situation sir?" asked Gabriel as he produced a note pad and pencil from his pocket.

"You won't need that", said the captain as he lifted his head from the maps to look at Gabriel, "the situation hasn't changed from the last report and the one before that".

"And what's that sir?" asked Gabriel.

"That we are short of men, low on materials, and as quickly as we take any ground, the enemy is taking it back again".

"Is there anything positive to report that might cheer the public back home?" asked Gabriel as he returned his notebook back to the shoulder bag hanging by his side.

"Yes", replied the captain, "tell them it will soon be Christmas".

"I believe they already know that", said Gabriel.

"I'm jolly glad to hear that", replied the captain, "take a look around you and tell me if anyone in this hell hole will know if it's Christmas".

Gabriel was entirely conscious of the fact that the hell hole the captain had just mentioned, was a lot further away from the Christian message that Christmas was meant to express. He already felt lost and unwanted, and lieutenant Fleming's assessment of the grinding down of lies to make a false truth, was already clear before his very eyes.

"Excuse me, are you Gabriel Shivers?" asked a soldier standing just outside the makeshift shelter.

"Yes", replied Gabriel as he turned to face the

soldier.

"Major Short would like to see you", said the soldier.

"Where will I find him?" asked Gabriel as he excused himself and stepped outside the shelter.

"Follow the trench to the end and he will be waiting for you", replied the soldier, "you can't miss him".

Gabriel thanked the soldier and proceeded to laboriously push his way through the mud to reach Major Short. As he finally reached his destination he was surprised to see that there was no one there. As Gabriel contemplated the assumption that Major Short might have been called off on an emergency, and he should wait, the whistles of death arrived to herald the coming of German shells.

The earth shook violently as the shells fell on the ground before him, taking large bites of soil and stone like some ravenous monster. Gabriel dived to the bottom of the trench and covered his ears and head with both his arms, trying to escape the thunderous wraith that had arrived so suddenly to spit its anger on its undeserving victims. Gabriel prayed like he had never prayed before, he thought of home in Yorkshire and his rooms in London, and within his mind a picture of Charlotte trying to smile, yet her eyes could not hide the genuine concern that pointed in Gabriel's direction.

"He's coming around Sister", said a young nurse with black hair and deep piercing blue eyes.

"He's going to be fine", said the sister as she moved off to attend another patient.

"What am I going to do with you", said Charlotte as she applied a bandage to Gabriel's head, "if I leave you alone for a day or two, you nearly get yourself killed".

Gabriel could now recognize the face of Charlotte glowing before him like an angelic vision. He remembered the ferocity of the shelling, but couldn't recall what happened or how he ended up looking up at Charlotte.

"I bet you thought you died and went to heaven, and are now disappointed to discover that it's not an angel you're looking at, it's me", said Charlotte as she finished applying the bandage to Gabriel's head.

"Not in the least bit disappointed", replied Gabriel in a mumbling tone of voice, "I knew all along that there was an angel by my bedside".

Charlotte looked deep into Gabriel's eyes and proceeded to move her head closer to Gabriel's head. Gabriel could smell the familiar aroma of her perfume and see clearly the lipstick painted precisely across Charlotte's lips. He noticed the two dark bags gathering under her eyes, the small scar on the side of her nose and just as her mouth was almost touching his; she changed direction and whispered in Gabriel's ear.

"If you die on me I will hunt you down and kill you", whispered Charlotte before standing up straight again.

"Don't worry", mumbled Gabriel, "if I die I will hunt you for eternity".

"Well old bean", said Lieutenant Fleming as Gabriel walked into the office, "I see you have survived your baptism of fire ".

"Yes sir", replied Gabriel as he took a chair across from Lieutenant Fleming, "If I have nine lives like a cat then the first one's certainly gone".

"How did you manage to escape the worst of it?" asked the lieutenant as he proceeded to attempt to fire up his ill-fated pipe again.

"I was sent for by a Major Short and as soon as I reached our meeting point, the shelling started", replied Gabriel.

"You got a damned nasty knock on the head I see", said the lieutenant as he continued with his attempt to smoke his pipe.

"Never felt a thing at the time", replied Gabriel, "I just awoke in the hospital with a thumper of a headache".

"This Major Short", said the lieutenant, "did you see him?"

"No sir, when I arrived at the meeting point there wasn't any one there", replied Gabriel.

Gabriel watched as the lieutenant turned to look out the small window while choosing to remain silent for a few minutes.

"That Major Short you speak off", said the lieutenant as he turned back from the window, "he was my uncle".

"Your uncle?" asked Gabriel in surprise "Is he ok, did he get injured in the shelling?"

"My uncle was killed five weeks ago", replied the lieutenant.

Gabriel remained silent as he turned over in his mind what he had just heard. He was not mistaken that Major Short was the name mentioned by the soldier, and furthermore, when he arrived at the meeting point Major Short was nowhere to be seen.

"I would be grateful if you didn't mention this to anyone", said the lieutenant as he interrupted Gabriel's thoughts.

"As you wish sir", replied Gabriel, "I had a knock on the head, I may have been mistaken".

"Do you remember speaking to Captain Burke?" asked the lieutenant.

"Yes sir, he didn't seem interested in what I had to say", replied Gabriel.

"Well he certainly won't be interested in what you have to say now; his shelter took a direct hit", said the lieutenant as he once again abandoned his craven for a smoke.

"I don't know what to say sir, I only met him for a short time, but I am still saddened", replied Gabriel.

"My grandmother once told me", said the lieutenant as he turned to again stare out the window, "that opportunities and guides are placed before us in life, but as soon as we realize they are there, it's too late. Almost as if there are written directions to make it to an old age, if you learn nothing else in this life Gabriel, learn to read those directions".

"I believe I almost know what you are trying to say sir", replied Gabriel.

Gabriel watched the lieutenant stare once again out the window at something only the lieutenant knew. He needed to find someone to trust from within and he needed to find them fast. From what he had just witnessed and the way the lieutenant looked you in the eye when speaking, allowed Gabriel to come to the decision that he was a good man.

"Sir", said Gabriel.

"Yes", replied the lieutenant as he turned to look at Gabriel.

"I believe that a terrible crime is being committed by someone high up in The War Office", said Gabriel.

"Be careful what you say, if you accuse someone with influence you could end up in prison or worse, a firing squad", replied the lieutenant.

"Sir, please", said Gabriel, "there are children as young a twelve being recruited from orphanages to join the army".

The lieutenant arose from his chair and before closing the door to the office; he first looked around to make sure no prying ears were listening.

"Where did you hear that?" asked the lieutenant as he returned to his chair.

"I worked at the register of deaths and discovered a lot of discrepancies", replied Gabriel.

"And were some of these discrepancies relating to missing dates of birth?" asked the lieutenant as he now spoke in almost a whisper.

"Yes sir", replied Gabriel, "how did you know sir?"

"I too worked at The War Office and when I arrived here, I discovered something wasn't right", said the lieutenant.

"Did you discover anything during your time here?" asked Gabriel.

"No", replied the lieutenant, "I was a coward; I didn't want to step on toes in case it disrupted any promotion. But it has been eating at my soul night after night, day after day until I can no longer think straight".

"I don't believe for a minute that you are a coward sir", said Gabriel, "for cowards do not lose sleep".

"Perhaps", replied the lieutenant, "but I no longer care whether I get promotion or not, I just want this damn war to go away".

"We all do sir, but until it does, we must face whatever demons that are sent to confront us and survive this war as men, rather than monsters", said Gabriel.

"Is that why you are here?" asked the lieutenant, "to save those children".

"Yes sir, I volunteered for that purpose", replied Gabriel.

"My God", said the lieutenant, "I really thought no one else noticed this other than me".

"Will you help me sir?" asked Gabriel.

"I will", replied the lieutenant after a short pause, "by God man I will".

"A General Wilson will be paying us a visit", said the colonel as he walked into Lieutenant Fleming's office.

"I take it we need to spruce the old place up a bit", replied the lieutenant.

"The new chap here can start on the beds and desks to make things a little presentable", said the colonel.

"On it right away", replied Gabriel as he left the office and proceeded to carry out the colonel's orders.

The Room where Gabriel slept reflected an image of confusion and disarray. Gabriel looked at the sight before him and started putting the desks into some sort of orderly fashion. Everywhere there were discarded newspapers and letters, empty tin cups with the dried remnants of tea still clearly visible. He brushed the floors and dusted the desks and when he thought that there was no more life he could breathe into the room, he began dressing for the highlight of the day, the general inspection.

"Make sure your top button is fastened", said the lieutenant, "these type tend to treat soldiers with their top button unfastened worse than the enemy.

As Gabriel started to fasten his top button a soldier put his head around the side of the door and whispered loud enough for both of them to hear.

"General is on his way".

The lieutenant and Gabriel stood upright as they heard

a commotion in the next room and heard heavy footsteps approaching.

"Good evening gentlemen", said the colonel as he entered the room ahead of the general, "may I introduce General Wilson".

It was some time before Gabriel realized the sight standing before him was real beyond any shadow of a doubt. Behind the clean cut and finely tailored uniform was a sight, if one didn't know too well, of a pure specimen of military refinement. Gabriel didn't know whether to laugh out loud or allow the tears to run freely down his face. He didn't know whether to salute or pat him heartily on the back or invite him for a cup of tea out of one of the old tin cups he spent the last ten minutes trying to clean. And Gabriel didn't know how he ever was going to tell him he forgot the letter he promised to deliver.

"Good evening general", said the lieutenant, "I trust you had a pleasant trip".

"Rather a bit rough if I may say so", replied Tiny Tim, "I can never get used to those motor car things".

"Would you like a cup of tea sir?" asked Gabriel as he recovered from the shock.

"And who might this young-looking rascal be?" asked Tim as he responded to Gabriel's question.

"A new lad over from The War Office sir", answered the lieutenant.

"I have just travelled all this way on a smoke filled automobile contraption and he offers me a cup of tea", said Tim.

"I have a little brandy in my office general", said the colonel.

"I don't want brandy by Joe I want tea like the good fellow suggested", replied Tim, "keep your eye on this one colonel, with perception like that we'll win this war in a few months".

As Gabriel began to prepare the tea things, the two officers and Tim sat down at a table Gabriel had so neatly prepared beforehand. The vision of Tim walking through the door dressed as a general was still clearly etched on Gabriel's disbelief. He had some idea of what lengths Tim would go to save the children, but never would this act of impersonation ever have crossed his mind. He made up his mind to withhold Tim's true identity from the lieutenant, until he witnessed some kind of act that would cement his loyalty.

"Now I would like to have a word with this young man", said Tim as he finished his tea and biscuits, "need to catch up on a few peaceful things across the channel".

"Ok sir", said the colonel, "if you need me you'll find me in my office".

"I will take my leave also", said the lieutenant, "I have a few errands to see to".

As soon as both the colonel and the lieutenant left, Tim folded his arms over his lap and waited for Gabriel's barrage of questions.

"How did you pull this off?" asked Gabriel.

"I won this uniform in a game of cards, I do believe that the real General Wilson is, may I say, preoccupied", replied Tim.

"You know that in time of war you could be shot for impersonating an officer", said Gabriel.

"A bit like shooting a dead fox then", replied Tim,

"for all the time I have left on this world, it's hardly worth their while".

"Have you seen Charlotte?" asked Gabriel.

"No", replied Tim, "don't tell me you left her at the mercy of that villain Burnhouse".

"No, I dealt with Mr. Burnhouse and he won't be a threat to anyone for quite a while", said Gabriel, "but she followed me here and is now a volunteer nurse".

"A chip off the old block, my dear Charlotte, she won't stay idle for long", replied Tim.

"We both came here to find you", said Gabriel, "and so far I almost got myself killed.

"Don't be silly lad", replied Tim, "almost getting yourself killed is a far cry from actually getting yourself killed.

"Have you discovered anything since you have been here?" asked Gabriel.

"Couldn't find anything from those on the lower rungs of the ladder, so that's why I commandeered this uniform, to climb a little higher", replied Tim.

"In the name of God sir, don't get caught", said Gabriel in a pleading tone of voice.

"If God doesn't want me to get caught then I won't", replied Tim.

"Sir", said Gabriel as he struggled to find words.

"Why don't you just call me Tim, all my friends do, actually I don't have many friends", replied Tim.

"Tim sir, I forgot the letter", said Gabriel.

"What letter?" asked Tim.

"The letter Scrooge left for me to pass on to you", replied Gabriel.

"You have got to be joking?" asked Tim.

"I'm so sorry", replied Gabriel, "I was in such a hurry to catch the train".

"Is that old joker up to his tricks again?" asked Tim as he smiled broadly in the direction of Gabriel.

"I don't understand sir, I Mean Tim", replied Gabriel with a confused expression written across his face.

"You can't deliver any of his letters to me, their apparitions of time, they don't exist in our physical world", said Tim.

"But why did he give it to me?" asked Gabriel.

"He keeps sending me letters in the hope that someday I will either have joined him in the spirit world, or acquire the means to read them", replied Tiny Tim.

"He must love you a great deal", said Gabriel.

"That he does my young friend, a second father who I truly owe my life to", replied Tim as he bowed his head in thought.

"You said acquire the means to read them, so there must be a way to read his letters?" said Gabriel.

"The gloves of time", replied Tim as he continued to stare at his feet while in thought.

"The gloves of time?" asked Gabriel, "what are the gloves of time?"

"Gloves that if they are worn by those who are true of both heart and soul, can touch those things that are untouchable", said Tim as he lifted his head to look at Gabriel.

"Do you know where we can find them?" asked Gabriel.

"An old vagabond once told me when she had too much to drink from my limited supply of brandy, that she saw them somewhere in the Welsh mountains".

"Did she say where, or who's house or cottage they were in", asked Gabriel

"No", replied Tim, "she passed out while trying to open the second bottle".

"If only we knew exactly where", said Gabriel as he

rubbed his hand across his face.

"That can wait until another time", said Tim as he arose suddenly from his chair, "for now we have serious business to attend to, crucial my young friend in every considerable aspect of the word".

CHAPTER 8

"Reconnaissance", said the lieutenant, "you have to report to the Royal Flying Corps as soon as possible".

"Did they say what type of reconnaissance?" asked Gabriel as he finished packing his few clothes into his kitbag.

"You know the flying boys", said the lieutenant, "no doubt it will be something extremely dangerous, or exciting if you enjoy that sort of thing".

Gabriel had been taken unaware by the order that had just come through. He wanted to pay a visit to Charlotte and perhaps go for a stroll or cup of tea, but the order that arrived this morning had now removed any possibility. He knew little about the flying corps except for what he read in the papers, and what he read had little relevance to anyone who expected to live a long and prosperous life. Death notices which he tried in vain not to read sometimes appeared in front of his eyes and The Royal Flying Corps had been quite frequent.

"Good luck old chap", said the lieutenant as he shook Gabriel's hand, "I hope to see you back here sooner rather than later".

"Goodbye sir", replied Gabriel as he turned to depart through the door, "I hope so too".

Gabriel made his way out through the door and up the narrow gravel path that separated the buildings on either side. A motor vehicle was waiting as he turned out onto the opening, and as he opened the door to climb inside, the driver turned and spoke.

"I was told to give you this note", said the driver as he passed Gabriel a slip of folded paper.

"Thank you", replied Gabriel as the driver proceeded on their journey.

Gabriel wanted to put the note in his pocket and read it later but curiosity had every intention to kill him so he surrendered and opened it.

I HAVE DECIDED TO TAKE FLYING LESSONS.

TIM.

Gabriel put the piece of paper in his jacket pocket and sat silently beside the driver as they bumped and shook along the rugged road. He didn't know how to interpret the note he had just received from Tiny Tim, and furthermore he was unsure if Tim's actions were the acts of a courageous genius, or someone who should be a permanent resident of a secure facility. Tim never ceased to amaze him no matter what he did, but taking flying lessons was something he could not fully comprehend. Gabriel had tried very hard to conceal the hidden fear that was stirring inside him since his first encounter with the horrors of war. He knew that his life was in danger and only by the arrival of Tiny Tim, had he regained some strength to carry on. By knowing that Tim was never far away and would pop up in the most unusual places, Gabriel was able to look danger in the eye.

"Here you are", said the driver as they pulled up outside a cluster of tents and wooden buildings.

"Thank you", replied Gabriel as he departed from the vehicle and grabbed his kitbag from the back seat.

Gabriel stood and proceeded to take in the scenery around him, while spits of rain began to fall from the dark grey sky. Several biplanes stood lined up and facing him, while men worked at varies tasks of maintenance and cleaning. He began to pray into himself, and ask God to please allow him to remain firmly on the ground.

"Hello there", said a middle age officer with a thick handlebar moustache, "are you the new camera operator?"

"I'm not quite sure what I'm to do sir", replied Gabriel, "I was ordered here".

"Well if you're not quite sure what you are", said the officer, "I will remind you, you are a camera operator and that's all there is about it".

"I have never used a camera in my life sir, is there no one else who is better qualified?" asked Gabriel.

"We are losing camera operators around here as fast as they can send them", replied the officer, "so now you need to run along to that building over there and Captain George will brief you"

"Thank you sir", said Gabriel as he made his way to a wooden building next to a tent and knocked the door before entering.

"I take it you are the new camera operator", said a young officer lying back on an old worn leather armchair.

"I was told to report to Captain George sir", replied Gabriel.

"You have found the great man, come in and sit

down and tell me what you know", said Captain George.

Gabriel closed the door behind him and after leaving his kitbag against the wall by the door, he sat down on a wooden chair next to the Captain.

"I'm not a camera operator", said Gabriel, "I don't know why I was sent here".

"I will tell you why you were sent here", said Captain George, "but first you need to introduce yourself".

"I'm sorry sir", replied Gabriel, "my name is Gabriel Shivers and I came over from The War Office".

"Well Mr. Shivers", said Captain George, "you were sent here for the same reason the last camera operator was sent, and the one before that. To take photos of German positions on the ground and if you are lucky you might live for a full week".

"But sir", replied Gabriel, "what is the point in sending people up in the air to take photos, if they know they are going to get killed".

"I will tell you why Mr. Gabriel Shivers Esquire", said Captain George, "if we lose an airplane with a couple of men in it, well that is a risk worth taking, if we can find at least one German machinegun position, a hundred lives could be saved".

"It sounds like a good balance on the scales of rationality sir", replied Gabriel, "but from where I'm sitting, I can't agree".

"Indeed, and where would we be without disagreement?" said Captain George.

"Not at war", replied Gabriel.

"Precisely old boy", said Captain George, "and without a war none of us would ever get to endanger our lives and we wouldn't want that".

"No sir we wouldn't", replied Gabriel sarcastically.

"Now get along that's a good chap, Sergeant Doe will give you a quick lesson on the mounted camera and you'll be good to go tomorrow morning", said Captain George.

"Thank you sir", replied Gabriel as he departed the room and made his way towards a hanger situated to his left.

Gabriel did not like Captain George for the very plain and simple reason, he didn't seem to care whether people lived or died. To him it all seemed a game, some boy's club sport and all the foxes had human heads. He wondered if Tiny Tim was close by, or perhaps he had gone off further afield in search of more clues. He thought of Charlotte and wondered if he would ever see her again, if he would ever get to say the things he had been so cowardly to say.

"Hello mate", said a short plumb sergeant with short black greasy hair, "are you the new suicide jockey?"

"If you mean camera operator, no, but I do believe you may be about to give me a crash course on the very same", replied Gabriel.

"Ok old son", said the sergeant as he walked over to a camera mounted on the rear passenger's side of an airplane.

"Your job is simple, you pull your lever when the pilot puts his thumb up to inform you that you are over the target area", said the sergeant.

"That simple", replied Gabriel as he put his hand on the lever.

"Simple yes, but you then have to remove the plate and do it over and over again until the pilot signals for you to stop", said the sergeant.

"So how do I develop them?" asked Gabriel.

"That's a job for someone else", replied the sergeant,

just get them back here and we will do the rest".

"You seem to be quite knowledgeable on the working of cameras", said Gabriel.

"The best there is", replied the sergeant as he smiled at Gabriel.

"Then why didn't they pick you for reconnaissance?" asked Gabriel.

"I wanted to go but the airplane couldn't get off the ground", replied the sergeant, "besides if I was to get shot down who would train the next sheep who came along".

"Who indeed", replied Gabriel as he looked over the airplane from back to front and from side to side.

The airplane that Gabriel was to be a passenger in was the most beautiful piece of machinery that he had ever seen. The two sets of wings stretched out on either side like some great mythological bird of prey. He knew that this great flying machine could be the making of his death bed, but he couldn't help paying homage to its magnificence.

"Who will be flying it?" asked Gabriel.

"Any one of four pilots", Replied the sergeant, "they are all away to town so if you don't see them tonight, you'll get a rude awakening early in the morning".

"So, what you are telling me", said Gabriel "is that the pilot who will be taking me up in the morning will still be intoxicated from the night before".

"Very much so, but don't let that worry you there is not much traffic up there to bump into", replied the sergeant as he flashed Gabriel a wide grin.

As the sergeant guided him to his quarters, Gabriel reflected on the mess he found himself in and pointed the finger directly at his own stupidity. He had rushed off chivalrous and dashing from England to defend innocence, and now as the days drew him closer to his objective, the rising fear began to dare him to question his commitment. Had Tiny Tim discovered that their efforts were in vain and along with Charlotte, made their way back to London? Did Jimbo confess to all his black deeds and the children were now safely back in England and being cared for by loving families? And last but most certainly not the least, was the war about to end soon and he was risking his life for nothing? All these things and more pounded Gabriel's state of mind and as he sat down on the edge of the bed inside the tent the sergeant had taken him to, Gabriel allowed his conscience to come to his aid and accept the fact that the needs of the young, outweighed the needs of the older.

"In London town where I was born, and where I got my learning, sweet William Green took to his bed, for love of Barbara Allen."

Gabriel was awakened by a familiar voice singing outside his tent, and when he gathered his senses together he realized that dawn had already arrived.

"Get up you young rascal", said Tiny Tim as he put his head through the opening of the tent.

Although Gabriel was fully awake by this time, he tried hard to picture the scene before him with any form of common logic. Tiny Tim was dressed like a pilot, looked like a pilot but from what Gabriel had learnt about his new found friend, he was not a pilot.

"What, ash, please tell me no, in God's name man say it isn't true", said Gabriel as he crawled out from under the bed covers.

"My young friend", replied Tim as he made his way inside the tent, "you need to put a little more faith in the abilities of your elders, I am several years older than you and therefore my mind is much superior".

"You can't fly an airplane", said Gabriel as he got dressed quickly to combat the cold.

"I'll have you know young man that my trainer informed me just last night that I am one of the best pilots he has ever seen", replied Tim as he sat on the bed next to Gabriel.

"Was that before or after he drank the bottle of brandy?" asked Gabriel in a tone of sarcasm.

"Come to think of it, I believe he may have finished the second bottle", replied Tim, "but all things being equal, we have a number of important photographs to obtain before the rest of the chaps rise from their intoxicated slumber".

Gabriel knew from the note he had received that Tim was not far away, but as for him taking flying lessons, the thought in itself was put firmly at the back of his mind for fear of it becoming a terrifying truth. For the short time he had known him, Gabriel should have accepted the fact that the word surprise no longer attached itself to Tiny Tim. From around some corner, Gabriel knew that Tim would emerge clothed in some fantastical costume of amazement and each time would be more colorful than the last.

"I took the liberty of loading the airplane with camera plates", said Tim, "with some luck thrown in for good measure, we may get the photos we need".

"How is this going to benefit us?" asked Gabriel, "have you forgotten why we ended up in this mess in the first place?"

"Indeed my dear friend, a very natural response to shock, but as soon as we're up in the clouds, you'll feel right as rain again", replied Tim as he proceeded to observe a small insect crawling up the wall.

"What do you mean, what has shock got to do with why we're here?" replied Gabriel, "you're applying words that have no practical meaning to the topic".

"Shock my young friend arrives after many different scenarios and can confuse the victim into believing he is someone he is not", said Tim as he continued to follow the path of the insect.

"You mean like a pilot?" asked Gabriel as he tried to catch Tim's attention.

"A pilot or camera operator", replied Tim as he turned to look at Gabriel, "and those two imposters need to be on their jolly way".

The thick engine smoke of the airplane as it fired into life smothered the light mist that had greeted the cold dark December morning. Gabriel had taken Tim's advice and decided to wrap up warm, including heavy leather gloves and hat. The thought of what lay ahead bore heavy on Gabriel's mind and as much as he wished it would end, he knew that the road to conclusion was a long way off.

Tiny Tim turned the airplane towards the grass runway before them and began to accelerate, building the speed up as they watched the buildings get smaller and smaller behind them. Gabriel had seen an airplane taking off once from a field in Yorkshire and very much to his annoyance he realized that Tim should have been in the air by now. He could see the line of trees getting larger before them and with as much voice as he could muster, he shouted to Tim to do something quick. Just before they crashed headlong into the large solid looking trees, Tim managed to turn the airplane and head back in the direction they first came. The buildings that once disappeared behind them were now getting larger before them and as Tiny Tim continued full acceleration in a straight line, Gabriel had come to a very swift conclusion that the intoxicated instructor's assessment of Tim's flying skills, had been very much exaggerated.

"FOR THE LOVE OF GOD TIM STOP THE AIRPLANE", shouted Gabriel as loud as his voice could carry.

"WHAT DID YOU SAY?" shouted Tim in response, "DID YOU SAY YOU LOVED GOD?"

"I SAID STOP THE AIRPLANE WE ARE GOING TO CRASH", roared Gabriel.

"YES I KNOW THE AIRPLANE NEEDS A WASH, BUT THAT CAN BE DONE LATER", replied Tim.

Gabriel could see the cluster of buildings getting larger before them, and could do nothing but wait until the airplane came to a thunderous end as they introduced it to something solid. But once again and just before the crashed into the unsuspecting buildings, Tim turned the airplane around and journeyed back in the direction they had just came from.

"WHY DON'T YOU ACCEPT THE FACT THAT YOU ARE NOT A PILOT", shouted Gabriel.

"WHAT DID YOU SAY?" replied Tim.

Before Gabriel could call out one last plea for mercy, the airplane began to float and slowly climb up into the sky. Gabriel could see everything on the ground get smaller and suddenly disappear behind the mist. The terrifying fear that had taken hold of the pit of his stomach began to subside, paving the way for a mixture of pure excitement and raw euphoria. Never in his wildest dreams would he have believed he would be flying above the green fields of France or would he have strolled so far from his boring existence. His unfair assessment of Tim's ability to ever get the airplane off the ground had been quickly put to the side and replaced by the fair realization that he may not get back down again in a safe and respectable manner.

"LOOK DOWN THERE", shouted Tiny Tim as he pointed with his thumb down below them.

Gabriel looked through a clearing in the mist and could see clusters of soldiers around what looked like a machinegun position.

"TAKE A PHOTOGRAPH", shouted Tim as he proceeded to keep the airplane as straight and steady as possible.

Gabriel leaned over the side of the airplane and pulled the lever of the camera like sergeant Doe had instructed. He then removed the plate and after replacing it, he continued taking photographs of the positions below.

"WE WILL SCOUT AROUND FOR MORE POSITIONS", shouted Tim as he showed his thumb in an upward motion.

Whenever Gabriel could get a glimpse of anything through the mist, Tim would nod his head from side to side to inform him that it was of little use. Visibility was bad and all Gabriel could do was to stare hard into the mist below in the hope that something of interest would catch his eye. Suddenly he noticed a long line of heavy guns pointing towards the allied trenches.

"LOOK DOWN THERE", roared Gabriel as he pointed with his finger.

Tiny Tim followed his direction and quickly informed Gabriel that he had noticed.

"I'M GOING TO FLY AS CLOSE TO THEM AS POSSIBLE, MAKE SURE YOU HAVE THE

CAMERA READY", shouted Tim.

Gabriel leaned over the side of the airplane once again and placed another plate into the camera. As Tim began to descend to a lower altitude he grabbed the handle and began taking a photograph. He could see the German soldiers bending their necks to stare in their direction and wondered what might be going through their heads.

"KEEP AT IT", shouted Tim, "AS SOON AS THEY DISCOVER THAT WE ARE ONE OF THE ENEMY THEY'LL GET RATHER ANGRY".

Gabriel pulled the lever again and again, each time working quickly to load the camera before they were recognized as British. Suddenly the morning sky began to crackle with sparks and puffs of thick smoke, shaking the airplane back and forth. Gabriel continued taking photos as Tim wrestled with the controls in order to keep the airplane on a balanced course.

"WE NEED TO GET OUT OF HERE", roared Gabriel as he allowed that enough photographs had been taken.

"I CAN'T HEAR A WORD YOU ARE SAYING", Shouted Tim, "SOMEONE NEEDS TO TELL THEM TO KEEP THE NOISE DOWN I'M TRYING TO THINK".

"I SAID WE NEED TO GET OUT OF HERE", Shouted Gabriel at the top of his voice.

"ONE MORE PHOTOGRAPH", roared Tim.

Gabriel took hold of another glass plate and pushed it into the camera. While he was doing so, he realized that the camera had slide further down the bracket, which left him having to stretch further down the side of the airplane to take a photograph. Just as Gabriel was about to pull the handle, a large piece of shrapnel caught the right wing and threw it off balance. Gabriel slipped down the side and managed to catch hold of the wheel axle as his legs hung loosely towards the ground. He was unsure if Tiny Tim saw what happened, and knew if he didn't he would have to think fast.

"TIM, TIM, I'M DOWN BELOW", shouted Gabriel with all his might.

There was no reply from Tim and Gabriel began to realize as the fear quickly took hold, that he was going to die. He had discarded his gloves earlier to allow his fingers more movement to work with the camera, now his bare hands were blue with cold and Gabriel could not rely on them much longer. He could now hear the loud bangs from the German guns and came to the very speedy conclusion that he was getting closer to the ground. The mist began to clear as he looked down and to his utter surprise he could feel his feet being dragged through water. Gabriel felt his hands slipping as they surrendered to the inevitable and down he fell into the cold murky water and the reluctant acceptance of his fate.

CHAPTER 9

"Halt", said the German soldier, "Hinde hoch".
Gabriel crawled out of the water and stood before the two German soldiers who were shouting something he could not understand. It was only when one of them took hold of his hands and signaled to put them up in the air, that Gabriel discovered it meant put your hands up.

"Sprecher Sie Deutsch?" asked one of the soldiers.

"Don't understand", said Gabriel as he held his hands above his head.

"Englisch?" asked the soldier as his colleague began to search Gabriel for weapons.

"Yes English", replied Gabriel.

"komm mit mir", said the soldier after they had finished searching him.

Gabriel followed the first soldier as the second one tagged along behind, pointing the rifle menacingly towards his back. The position he now found himself in was not in the least expected, and a hundred things began to flow through his mind. He had not heard Tim's airplane crash so for the moment at least, he could accept that Tiny Tim had made it back to base.

He began to blame his own idiocy for falling out of the airplane and wondered what the Germans had in store for him. He heard of Prisoner of War camps being employed by both sides and rumors of prisoners being shot for trying to escape or antagonizing the guards, and as Gabriel followed the soldier into a large tent, he became quickly aware that he was now in a very dangerous place.

"So we have an Englishman", said the German officer as he stood in front of Gabriel, "or have I been too hasty in using the word man, looks more like a schoolboy, is this all the British have to fight us with?"

"I assure you sir", replied Gabriel, "there are many larger and older than me".

"Older?" said the German officer as he smirked at Gabriel, "my grandfather is older".

"Give him my best wishes the next time you see him", replied Gabriel as he tried not to react to the officer's insults.

"What are you doing in our sector?" asked the officer.

"We were testing a new armored plated airplane", Gabriel lied.

"You don't surely expect me to believe that", said the officer.

"I don't expect you to believe anything", replied Gabriel as he kept up the pretense, "all I am doing is trying to answer your questions clearly and correctly".

"It is not possible, such an idea is laughable", said the officer.

"I am sure when the idea was first presented, a lot of people laughed but I assure you it is very much real", replied Gabriel.

Gabriel looked into the German officer's eyes and

studied the changing expression on his face. He quickly realized that the lie he had told was beginning to have some effect.

"Such an idea would not even get off the ground", said the officer as he sat down on a chair next to a table.

"Such an idea did get off the ground", replied Gabriel, "otherwise how else would I find myself here".

"How did you find yourself here?" asked the officer.

"We miscalculated how much fuel we would need", Gabriel lied, "and when we realized we were running low I had to jump out to allow the airplane to make it back without falling into enemy hands".

"Would you like a drink or is it tea you English prefer?" asked the officer as his attitude towards Gabriel began to soften.

"Thank you sir", replied Gabriel, "a cup of tea would be greatly appreciated.

Gabriel took a chair by the table and listened to the officer give orders in German to a young soldier standing by the door. He began to regret the lie he had told about armored aircraft, as the officer in question might not have a sense of humor when he discovers the truth. For now, he knew there was no other alternative but to carry on with the perjury and at the very least it would give the German command a headache.

"So, these airplanes", said the officer as he began to pour Gabriel's tea, "do you have many of them?"

"No not many", replied Gabriel as he took the tea from the officer, "just a few hundred at the moment, but I shouldn't really be telling you this".

"Yes, yes I know you shouldn't", said the officer in a friendly tone of voice, "but I promise you as a gentleman, anything you tell me will go no further".

"You won't tell your superiors?" asked Gabriel as he tried to keep a serious pitch to his voice.

"Absolutely not", replied the officer as he managed a smile in Gabriel's direction, "between you and me I have a boyish fascination with airplanes".

"I understand", said Gabriel as he took a sip of his tea, "I used to have a boyish fascination too".

"You were saying just a few hundred at the moment", said the German officer.

"Yes, maybe three or four hundred, but the top brass were so impressed, they have ordered another ten thousand".

As soon as Gabriel had announced the last figure to the officer, a sudden coughing sound erupted from the German as he almost chocked on his tea.

"Are you alright sir?" asked Gabriel as he rushed to pat the officer on the back.

"Ahh hum must have gone down the wrong way", replied the officer.

"That happens a lot with me", said Gabriel, "the first time I saw an airplane I was drinking a cup of milk and out it went through the nostrils".

"I'm fine now", said the officer as he swept the palm of his hand over his brow.

"You speak very good English", said Gabriel as he tried to change the subject, "you could almost pass for an Englishman".

"I lived and worked in London before the war", replied the officer.

"What did you work at if I may be so bold?" asked Gabriel.

"I am sorry young man, we will have to part company", said the officer as he stood up from the chair, "you will be taken to a holding cell until we can make arrangements to transfer you to a prison camp". The officer signaled for the young soldier to call the guards and as Gabriel stood to wish the officer farewell, he knew that his deception had now reached a point of no return.

Gabriel sat down on the chair inside the cell and watched the soldier slam the door hard before locking it. Inside the cell it smelled of new paint and the grey mattress looked like it had never been slept in before. In this now hostile and lonely place of confinement, Gabriel thought of Charlotte and hoped she was safe and well. He wondered if Tiny Tim had made it back to base and thought of how his boring and lonely rooms in London would be easily exchanged for what he had now. Gabriel's thoughts were interrupted by approaching footsteps and the door to his cell being unlocked.

"comma mit mir", said the German soldier.
Gabriel followed the soldier up the short corridor and turned left into a small room with a desk and some chairs.

"setz dich", said the soldier and he indicated for Gabriel to take a chair.
Gabriel looked around the room and observed that the table top was littered with an assortment of various papers. He spied a bundle of small maps and without thinking he reached over and slipped one from the desk. Stealing a hurried look he noticed a lot of halfpenny sized red dots and before he was discovered, he secreted the map inside his underpants.

"Good evening sir", said a brown haired German officer in perfect English.

"Good evening to you sir", replied Gabriel as he

noticed he was of a much higher rank than the last one.

"My name is Colonel Dettmer, I hope the guards have been treating you well".

"I have no complaints as of yet sir", replied Gabriel.

"That is good", said the colonel, "I hope the as of yet never arrives".

"I hope so too sir", replied Gabriel.

"However, I must inform you that there is a problem with your story", said the colonel as he took a chair across the table facing Gabriel.

"A problem sir?" asked Gabriel.

"Yes a problem which could be very serious for you indeed", replied the colonel.

"I already told you sir I fell from an airplane", said Gabriel.

"Yes indeed", replied the colonel, "but if I was to tell you I was a survivor of a sunk battleship, you wouldn't believe me".

"And why would I not believe you?" asked Gabriel as he tried to figure out what the colonel was insinuating.

"It's as plain as the nose on your head, yes, and the uniform", answered the colonel.

Gabriel quickly realized that he was up in an airplane with an infantry uniform.

"You mean the army uniform and not one from the Royal Flying Corps?" asked Gabriel.

"The very thing young sir, please explain", replied the colonel.

"I was sent over from the army to go on a test flight sir and as it was only temporary I kept the uniform", said Gabriel in his defense.

"You see, someone else might not believe you and take you for a spy", replied the colonel, "but I myself have every trust in what you say".

"Thank you, sir,", replied Gabriel.

"However you may have to give me something to give to my superiors", said the colonel.

"Give you something sir? I don't understand", replied Gabriel.

"To prove you are with the Air Corps, you must have some experience with airplanes", said the colonel as he produced some note paper and laid it down before him on the desk.

Gabriel realized that he now found himself within a game and the colonel was closing in on Gabriel's half of the field.

"I have some knowledge of aircraft sir, especially the T24d", Gabriel lied.

"Before you tell me about the T24d, perhaps a spot of tea as you English say", said the colonel as he smiled at Gabriel.

As the colonel arose to order the tea, Gabriel began to think faster than he had ever thought before. He had little knowledge of airplanes, only that they flew and made lots of noise taking off. The colonel will be expecting a detailed description of the figment of his imagination and he prayed inwardly for a blueprint to appear before his eyes.

"Do you take sugar?" asked the colonel as he set the tea things on a table before them.

"Two lumps please", replied Gabriel.

"You will have to make do with honey I'm afraid", said the colonel as he stirred two spoonful's of honey into Gabriel's tea.

"Honey will be fine", replied Gabriel.

"Now, where were we, a yes the T24p let's hear about it", said the colonel as he sipped his tea.

"Well actually it's the T24d sir and it's an armored airplane", answered Gabriel.

"So tell me how this armored airplane manages to get into the air with such a heavy weight?" asked the colonel.

"It has four engines sir", answered Gabriel as he looked the colonel in the eye.

"Impossible, four engines would tear the airplane to pieces", said the colonel.

"No sir, the whole airplane is built entirely of steel so the engines have a solid base", replied Gabriel.
Gabriel stared at the German colonel and searched for any sign of disbelief. He watched him slowly reach for the pencil before him and begin to write something on the paper laid out before him.

"How many of these machines do you have?" asked the colonel.

"At least a few hundred, but I heard someone mention that another ten thousand were awaiting the order to commence production", Gabriel lied.
Gabriel could see that the colonel was worried and prided himself in keeping the charade up for so long.

"So who are you going to get to fly these airplanes?" asked the colonel.

"Trained pilots sir, I heard that there are thousands already trained and on standby awaiting orders", Gabriel lied.

"So tell me young man, if you have so many men available to fly these airplanes then why do you send children to fight in the trenches?" asked the colonel.

"I don't understand sir", replied Gabriel, "we don't accept children into the British army".

"You don't say, well I am sure I can convince you otherwise", said the colonel as he arose from his chair, "follow me".

Gabriel followed the colonel back down the short corridor and past the cell he had just been taken from. At the very end they turned to the right and down a short flight of stone steps. The colonel stopped beside a cell with a yellow door, turned the key to unlock it and flung the door wide open.

"Is this all the British have left to fight with?" asked the colonel.

Gabriel stared at the two children huddled up together on a bed in the cell. They both wore army uniforms which give the appearance that they were designed for someone older and their expressions of fear were clearly visible.

"The one on the left we call Ignorance, for various reasons", said the colonel, "and the one on the right we named him Want, as he always wants something to eat or drink".

"Can I speak to them please sir?" asked Gabriel.

"I will give you thirty minutes", replied the colonel, "perhaps you can get them to say something intelligent".

Gabriel walked into the cell and sat down on the bed next to the boys as the colonel slammed the door behind him.

"Hello young men", said Gabriel, "my name is Gabriel, could you tell me how you managed to end up as prisoners to the Germans?"

"I want some chocolate", said Want in a soft childish voice.

"I'm sorry", replied Gabriel, "I don't have any chocolate to give you".

"I want some milk then", said Want.

"No milk either I'm afraid", replied Gabriel.

"When are we going to play games again?" asked Ignorance.

"What games do you play?" asked Gabriel as he directed a smile towards Ignorance.

"We play soldiers and lots of people pretend to be dead", replied Ignorance.

"Who taught you to play these games?" asked Gabriel.

"Our teacher sent us away with a little man", replied Ignorance.

"And what did your teacher call this little man?" asked Gabriel.

"Toffee", said Want, "I want toffee".

"No toffee either", answered Gabriel as he waited for a reply from Ignorance.

"He called him sir", replied Ignorance.

"And what was your teacher called?" asked Gabriel.

"He was called sir", answered Ignorance.

Gabriel soon realized that those who had perpetrated these crimes had their tracks well covered. The children never got to hear any names and were easily tricked, owing to their inferior intellect and age. As orphans, no one would report them missing, allowing those who had illegal interests to walk away from their black deeds unpunished. As footsteps once again echoed in the corridor, Gabriel tried one last time to dig for even the tiniest scrap of information.

"Were there any names mentioned throughout your time of leaving England until you arrived here?" asked Gabriel.

"I want strawberries", said Want.

"Everyone called sir", replied Ignorance.

"Time is up", said the colonel as he flung open the door of the cell.

Gabriel left the cell and followed the colonel up the stone steps and back up the corridor. As they returned into the room Gabriel noticed that two guards were waiting.

"You are being moved to Berlin", said the colonel, "someone there has developed a keen interest in your T24".

"Why don't you release those children", said Gabriel, "there has been a huge mistake".

"They are British soldiers in uniform", replied the colonel, "however, we are not monsters and they will be looked after at least until the end of the war".

"Thank you, colonel,", said Gabriel.

As Gabriel was led from the building by the two soldiers he was confident that the colonel would keep his word. He also knew that since he had led them up a merry path, the highest authorities in airplane manufacturing would be grilling him in Berlin and would soon discover his practical joke was by no means amusing. So far, the only proof he had of child soldiers were locked up behind enemy lines and he knew if the Germans decide that he is a spy, that small morsel of information could soon be digested before a firing squad. He thought hard about escape but quickly realized as he was put between two guards in an open car, that that possibility got closer to impossibility.

The German car commenced its journey along the bumpy road and Gabriel looked across the beautiful green countryside, wondering if he would ever see such beauty again. He began to notice that the engine of the car suddenly started to rev up as it got louder, but still the car carried on in its steady pace. He looked at the soldier to his right and then to the one on his left, but both took no heed of the changing roar from the engine. He looked down at his feet and then upwards and to Gabriel's blood rushing surprise, there were two wheels of an airplane floating gracefully above his head. He did not have time to decide whether it was a good idea or not, nor had he time to figure out who it was flying the airplane. In one split second, Gabriel reached for the axle bar and in one swift motion of the pilot, he found himself being carried away to the freedom of the sky above.

As the airplane glided across the sky to freedom Gabriel could feel his bare hands beginning the process of losing sensation. He knew he must hang on with every living muscle of his body, as to fall from this height would mean certain death. He was surprised that someone had even contemplated risking an airplane and pilot to rescue him and was even more astonished as to how they knew he would be on the road at that particular time.

"TAKE THE AIRPLANE DOWN", shouted Gabriel, "I'M LOSING MY GRIP".

"WHAT DID YOU SAY?" shouted the pilot in reply.

"I SAID I'M LOSING MY GRIP", roared Gabriel.

"WHAT'S THAT YOU SAID, YOU WANT ME TO DO A FLIP", shouted the pilot in reply.
Gabriel felt his grip slipping and he tried with all his might to deliver something miraculous into his frozen hands. He prayed inwardly for some form of divine assistance in his hour of need before he shouted out one last time for the pilot to heed his call.

"TAKE THE AIRPLANE DOWN", shouted Gabriel as loud as his voice would carry.

"WHO ARE YOU CALLING A CLOWN?" roared the pilot in reply.

At that very moment Gabriel recognized the voice of Tiny Tim and knew yet again that a dangerous path lay below him. He couldn't fault Tim for his hard of hearing, nor could he fault him for trying to rescue him. He only wished he could see Charlotte again and share in the warm glow of her presence as she hooked onto his arm. He wanted so much to live, to grow old with someone he loved and breathe the sweet clean air of peacefulness. But Gabriel knew that all these things were only wishes and if destiny were to grant these wishes, they must be written first.

"GOODBYE TIM", shouted Gabriel as his hands slipped off the axel bar and he began falling to the mercy of what lay beneath.

CHAPTER 10

Gabriel looked down from the top of the tree and breathed a gasp of pure undiluted relief. The clouds that had suddenly appeared, somehow allowed the distance to the ground to be poorly judged and now Gabriel was once again snatched from the jaws of death. After recovering from the sudden shock of finding himself alive, Gabriel began to make his way slowly and very carefully down the tree to the grass below.

"So you have decided to rejoin us", said Captain George as he greeted Gabriel walking in the direction of the tents.

"Yes sir", replied Gabriel, "I hope my absence did not cause too much of an inconvenience".

"Not in the slightest, the pilot however was a real ace getting those photos back to base", said Captain George.

"Hurrah for the pilot", replied Gabriel as he continued on his way to his tent.

"Get your gear packed", Captain George shouted after Gabriel, "you have a two week pass; the car will be leaving in half an hour".

Gabriel entered the tent and sat down on the bed wishing he could go to sleep. A two week pass had come as a surprise and the only thing that excited him about it was an opportunity to see Charlotte again. Once again he found himself packing his belongings into his kitbag and walking out of the tent in another direction. He climbed in beside the driver and as the car sped off down the bumpy road, Gabriel decided to enquire about their destination.

"We are off back to London", said Tim as he raced down the road while paying little heed to the very large potholes.

Gabriel was not surprised to see Tim at the steering wheel and had now accepted the many talents of Tiny Tim.

"Will Charlotte be coming with us?" asked Gabriel as he tried to close his eyes to catch a nap.

"Charlotte is already on the train", replied Tim as he barely missed crashing into an oncoming horse and cart.

"Now there is a woman who loves her country", said Gabriel, "she even managed to be the first one on the train to make sure she gets back".

"As for loving her country", replied Tim, "the jury is still out until at least she gets the vote, but she is not the first one on the train".

"Don't tell me someone else has beat her to her pride of place", said Gabriel as he give up on the impossibility of having a nap.

"They certainly have, our good friend Jimbo is responsible for her presence on the train in the first place".

Gabriel could not believe what he was hearing from Tiny Tim and for a small moment of time he thought

Tim had said something else.

"How, what did you say, Jimbo has Charlotte?" asked Gabriel as he tried to come to terms with the terrible news.

"He has and is taking her back to London using fair means or foul", replied Tim.

"But how did he get out of prison?" asked Gabriel as he now sat upright and fully conscience.

"What worries me is not how he got out of prison", answered Tim, "but how did he convince Charlotte to accompany him back home".

"Do you think some kind of blackmail was employed?" asked Gabriel.

"Indeed", replied Tim as he forced someone on their bicycle to take evasive action, "I know Charlotte and she would not be easy to coerce".

As Tim and Gabriel pulled in at the railway station, the last carriage of the train was disappearing off into the distance. Tiny Tim turned the steering wheel towards the direction of the tracks and they sped up the railway track behind the train.

"As soon as we get close enough", said Tim, "climb onto the bonnet and use it to jump onto the train".

"And where will you be?" asked Gabriel as he watched the rear carriage getting closer and closer.

"I'll be right behind you", said Tim as he pushed the throttle as far as it would go.

Gabriel prepared himself for the task ahead and wondered for a brief moment, if Tiny Tim was really trying to get him killed. He knew Charlotte was on the train and with Jimbo by her side; one more act of chivalry was justly called for.

"Ok, get ready", said Tim excitedly.

Gabriel climbed over the windscreen and on to the

bonnet of the car, hunkering down to wait for his leap of death.

"Now", said Tim.

Gabriel sprang like a wild hare towards the back of the train and grabbed onto the safety rail with both hands. He managed to climb over the rail and waited for Tim to follow behind. Before Gabriel jumped, he was worried about Tim and how his lack of youthfulness would greatly impair his ability to perform the dangerous task. This concern was quickly thrown to the side when Tim leapt from the car and with one swift moment of nimbleness found himself standing next to Gabriel.

"I'm beginning to feel my twenty odd years", said Tim as they made their way inside the train.

Gabriel and Tim walked up the middle of the train and scanned each row of seats for Charlotte. As they moved further up the aisle they arrived at the first class carriage and discovered Charlotte in one of the private cabins.

"Hello there my dear", said Tim as he opened the door and walked inside, "I do hope these gentlemen are not keeping you from your appointment".

"Mr. Cratchit I presume", said Jimbo as he smiled in Tim's direction.

"Your presumption is right", said Tim, "Now my dear it's time you were coming along".

Gabriel looked at Jimbo and noticed his accomplice stare at him in a menacing way.

"Did any of these men harm you Charlotte?" asked Gabriel as he moved into the cabin beside Tiny Tim.

Charlotte never spoke but just smiled at Tim and Gabriel as if they were two strangers.

"Do you know these men dear?" asked Jimbo.

"No sir", replied Charlotte as she turned to stare out the window.

"Do you know my name?" asked Jimbo.

"Yes, your name is sir", replied Charlotte in a subdued voice.

"I think you may have got this young lady mixed up with someone else", said Jimbo as he directed a triumphant smile in Tim and Gabriel's direction.

Gabriel remembered the two boys in the German cell and knew that somehow, Charlotte had fallen into some kind of spell.

"I think we may be mistaken", said Gabriel as he turned to look at Tim.

"Mistaken, yes", replied Tim, "We'll have a look elsewhere".

"Good day gentlemen", said Jimbo as Gabriel and Tim departed from the cabin.

Gabriel and Tim took a seat by the window in the second class carriage and Gabriel told him what he had discovered behind enemy lines.

"He has either drugged her or hypnotized her", said Tim.

"Either way we need to devise a plan to get her back before it's too late", replied Gabriel.

"I am genuinely surprised", said Tim, "I never thought Charlotte would have allowed anyone to catch her napping".

"Strong willed and stubborn as she may be", replied Gabriel, "she is still human".

"We need to stay close until we reach home soil", said Tim, "we'll make our move on the train from Dover".

"Have you a plan?" asked Gabriel.

"Yes, but before we cross the channel, I need to send

a telegram", replied Tim.

As Gabriel and Tim continued their journey to Calais, Gabriel noticed a change in Tim's expression when he discovered Charlotte in her present state of mind. An air of emotional anger was ebbing from Tim's voice and Gabriel could not fault him for this flicker of grandfatherly love. Gabriel knew that to rescue Charlotte would take a fair amount of skill and resolution, and whatever Tiny Tim had stuffed up his oil stained sleeve.

"Excuse me sir", said the detective, "my name is detective Inspector Whitely and this is my colleague Sergeant Blackly, I wonder if you could accompany me to answer a few questions".

"Any questions you wish to ask, you are quite free to ask them here", replied Jimbo.

"Sorry sir, please accompany me to the next carriage", said the inspector.

"All of us?" asked Jimbo.

"Just you and your friend", said the detective, "the young lady may remain in her seat".

"May I enquire why?" asked Jimbo as he turned to look at his very frightened friend.

"Just a few words in relation to a robbery on the train, we are questioning everyone, it will only take a few minutes", replied the detective.

"The young lady is feeling poorly, surely we can talk here", pleaded Jimbo.

"My sergeant will remain with the lady to make sure no harm may befall her", replied the inspector.

Jimbo and his accomplice followed the inspector out of the cabin and into the next carriage. No sooner had they left when Tiny Tim and Gabriel entered the cabin and proceeded to escort Charlotte out and down to the far end of the train.

"Where are we going sir?" asked Charlotte as they made their way through the rows of seats.

"Don't worry my dear", said Tim, "we are taking you home".

With the long journey from Dover behind them, Tim, Gabriel and Charlotte were now back home in Gabriel's rooms in London. Charlotte was tucked up in bed safely in Gabriel's bedroom leaving Tim and Gabriel to figure out how to break the spell. Gabriel was worried that Charlotte may be lost forever in her confused state of mind, and could not think of any logical way to return her back to reality.

"I don't know, I just don't know", said Tim as he paced back and forwards across the room floor.

"Do you know of anyone who could either cure her or at least explain what has happened to her?" asked Gabriel.

"No one of this world", replied Tim as he continued to pace back and forth.

"When you said no one of this world", said Gabriel, "does that mean you know someone not of this world?"

Tim continued to walk back and forth across the room as he rubbed the palm of his hand across his forehead. Suddenly Tim stopped and quickly turned to Gabriel.

"The letter", said Tim, "the one you forgot to bring with you".

"It's on the windowsill in the bedroom", said Gabriel as both he and Tim rushed to find it.

"I can't lift it", said Tim in frustration.

"What's in it?" asked Gabriel.

"I'm not really sure", replied Tim, "but old Scrooge does get his times mixed up and he may have meant for us to read it now".

"Where is the glove of time?" asked Gabriel.

"Somewhere in Snowdonia", replied Tim.

"Where in Snowdonia?" asked Gabriel, "for God's sake Tim think".

"A black stone cottage, there is an old woman who owns a grey cat thought to be a hundred years old", replied Tiny Tim.

"Ok, we must be on our way", said Gabriel as he arose quickly from his chair.

"I need to stay here with Charlotte", replied Tim, "you have to go alone".

Gabriel had already accepted the fact that he would face hell and high water for Charlotte and that Tim would be the best person to protect her from the evil Jimbo.

"As soon as I find it I will return as fast as I can", said Gabriel as he buttoned up his coat and opened the door to depart.

"Take care, my young friend", said Tim as he bid his goodbye to Gabriel.

"You too", replied Gabriel as he took his leave from Tim and the sleeping Charlotte.

As Gabriel made his way up the rugged mountain road, he smiled to himself as he recalled Tim's description of the cat and how it was a hundred years old. Cats do not live to a hundred he thought and the oldest cat he had ever seen was a black one who lived to the ripe old age of twenty. He could feel his breath labor as he quickened his steps up the incline and looked around for Tim's black stone cottage. As he turned a sharp bend Gabriel could see an old man sitting on a stone smoking his pipe.

"Good day sir", said Gabriel, "I am looking for an old woman who lives in a black stone cottage, I would be grateful for any help".

"A black stone cottage, now let me see, if it was a white stone cottage you were looking for then that would be a bit of a problem boyo", said the old man as he puffed on his clay pipe.

"Why would that be a problem?" asked Gabriel.

"Why indeed", replied the old man, "because there are no cottages around here built from white stone, they are all black".

"Is there one with an old woman living in it?" asked Gabriel as he shielded his face from the clouds of tobacco smoke aimed in his direction.

"If there was a young woman living in it", said the old man, "that too would be a problem",

"Lucky for me", replied Gabriel in mild sarcasm, "all I have to do now is take my pick".

"Indeed", said the old man, "but that will be a problem or a blessing whichever way you want to take it".

"Could you please explain", replied Gabriel.

"Well boyo, the problem is, there is only one to choose from and the blessing might be that you find the right one".

"Thank you sir, could you please direct me to the solitary black stone cottage so that I might take my pick", replied Gabriel in mock humor.

"Just follow your feet for half a mile up the road and at the first bend you will see it tucked away on the right", said the old man.

Gabriel thanked the old man and continued up the

rugged road in search of the only black stone cottage. The thought of Charlotte lying in bed lost to the world forced him to overcome the blisters forming on his feet and move forward in a quick and even pace. When he reached the bend the old man described, he turned right and walked up to the grey painted door and knocked.

"Hello", said Gabriel as an old woman dressed in black clothes and sporting a grey shawl, opened the door.

"How may I help you dear?" replied the old woman.

"I wonder if you would be so kind and allow me to see your cat", said Gabriel politely, "a friend of mine told me about it and I have come a long way".

"My cat?" asked the old woman.

"Yes, your cat", replied Gabriel.

"But I don't have a cat dear", said the old woman.

"I'm so sorry", replied Gabriel, "I must have the wrong place".

"What's so important about this cat dear?" asked the old woman.

"It supposed to be a hundred years old", replied Gabriel as he turned to leave.

"Someone's pulling your leg dear", said the old woman.

"Indeed, they have", replied Gabriel, "good day to you and once again I apologize for disturbing you".

"What's your friend's name dear?" asked the old woman as Gabriel turned to leave.

"Tim Cratchit", replied Gabriel as he made his way from the cottage door.

"Would you like a cup of tea dear?" asked the old woman as she slightly raised her voice.

"No thank you", replied Gabriel.

"Well at least let me see to those blisters on your feet dear, they will be a lot worse by the time you get back to London", said the old woman.

Gabriel thought about what she said and agreed that his feet might not allow him a pain free journey.

"Ok, thank you kindly", replied Gabriel as he turned and entered the old woman's cottage.

As the old woman beckoned him to sit down on an armchair beside the fire, Gabriel surveyed his internal surroundings of four whitewashed walls, with various pictures taking their pride of place. Above the fireplace sat a small grey China cat between to candlesticks and a clay figurine and as Gabriel turned to look at the old woman making tea, he suddenly realized she mentioned London.

"How did you know I was from London?" asked Gabriel.

"I used to know someone from London once dear", replied the old woman as she sat a cup of tea before Gabriel, "and you sound just like him".

Gabriel knew that her story was wrong, as he had a Yorkshire accent and as he had not been in London long enough, that accent was in no way rearranged.

"Please madam", said Gabriel as he pleaded with the old woman, "a friend of mine and the niece of Tim Cratchit is very seriously ill and we need the glove of time".

Gabriel watched the old lady quietly put her cup on the small table beside them and turn to look Gabriel in the face.

"What is his niece's name dear?" asked the old woman as she searched Gabriel's eyes for a flicker of deceit.

"Her name is Charlotte", replied Gabriel in a

desperate tone, "please help us".

"Why do you need the glove of time?" asked the old woman as she continued to search Gabriel for some sign of trickery.

"Because Tim got a letter from Ebenezer Scrooge and he believes it will be able to cure her", replied Gabriel.

"You love Charlotte?" asked the old woman.

"Ah hum, well I do like her", answered Gabriel as he was taken aback by her prodding of his heart.

"You love her dear, I can see it written all over your face", said the old woman as she arose and walked over to a pine dresser and opened the door.

Gabriel watched as she removed a black cloth bag from the drawer and walk back to her chair.

"Now my dear", said the old woman as she removed a pair of gleaming white gloves from the bag, "I want you to promise me you will bring them back as soon as you have saved your sweetheart".

"I promise you madam with all my heart", replied Gabriel as he continued to stare at the heavenly glow of the gloves.

"You need to go quickly my dear", said the old woman as she handed Gabriel the cloth bag containing the gloves.

"I hope my blisters carry me back to London", said Gabriel as he arose from the chair.

"Don't worry dear, you won't feel a thing", replied the old woman.

Gabriel suddenly noticed the China cat come to life and proceed to chase a scurrying mouse into another room.

"My God", said Gabriel in disbelief, "the caaat, and fireplace?"

"He's very good at disguising himself my dear", replied the old woman as she threw a smile in Gabriel's direction.

"Is he a hundred years old?" asked Gabriel in amazement.

"A hundred and four my dear and now you must hurry", replied the old woman.

As Gabriel proceeded to leave through the door he had entered, the old woman stopped him and pointed to another door.

"No, my dear that's the front door."

"Are you sure madam?" asked Gabriel, "I am certain I entered through this door.

"I am sure dear, I should hope I know my own house", replied the old woman.

Gabriel walked to the door at the corner of the room and turned to thank the old woman before he parted.

"Thank you for everything", said Gabriel as he lifted the latch to open the door.

"Remember your promise dear", said the old woman as Gabriel walked through the door.

"I will and thank you once again", replied Gabriel as he walked through the door and out onto the streets of London.

CHAPTER 11

Tiny Tim opened the door and greeted Gabriel as he walked through clutching the cloth bag.

"Did you find the gloves my good man? "Asked Tim, as he closed the door quickly behind Gabriel.

"I have them" replied Gabriel, "Is she still sleeping?"

"Like a newborn baby", said Tim.

Gabriel handed Tim the cloth bag containing the gloves and followed him into the bedroom. Tim put the gloves on and to Gabriel's astonishment, Tim's hands disappeared.

"My God", said Gabriel, "I can't see your hands".

"Don't worry my good man", replied Tim as he proceeded to lift the letter from the window sill, "they are still here at the end of my wrists".

Tim opened the letter with his unseen hands, walked over to the sleeping Charlotte and began to read out loud.

THE LOCK INSIDE YOUR HEAD I SEE
I REACH MY HAND TO TURN THE KEY
THE LIGHT WILL STAY, THE DARK WILL GO
AND FROM YOUR HEART LIFE WILL FLOW.

Gabriel watched as Charlotte's eyes begin to flicker and

slowly open wide to receive the patient looks of both Tim and Gabriel.

"Ahh hum", muttered Charlotte as she stared around the room and back to Tim and Gabriel, "what happened, how did I get back here?"

"All in good time my dear", replied Tiny Tim, "but first we need to get you up on your feet".
Gabriel helped Tim assist Charlotte out of the bed and position her on the chair next to the stove.

"There my dear", said Tim as Charlotte sat down on the chair, "I'm sure you could use a cup of tea.

"Thank you, grandfather,", replied Charlotte, "I would love one".

"I need to return the gloves", said Gabriel.

"Yes you must", replied Tim as he filled the kettle and placed it on the stove.
Tim handed the cloth bag containing the gloves to Gabriel and wished him a speedy trip.

"I'll put you a cup out on the table", said Tim.

"No need", replied Gabriel as he made for the door, "I have quite a journey ahead of me".

Gabriel opened the door and said his goodbyes to Charlotte and Tim, before departing and walking into the old woman's cottage room.

"Hello my dear, I see you have kept your promise", said the old woman.

"Thank you so much", replied Gabriel as he handed the old woman her bag containing the gloves.

"You are welcome to them anytime my dear", said the old woman as she nursed her aged cat.

"I appreciate your kindness", replied Gabriel, "I hope we can meet again".

"That would be nice", said the old woman, "don't forget your tea".

Gabriel said goodbye to the old woman and opened the door he had arrived through. He expected to walk into his own room at home and be greeted by Charlotte and Tim and welcomed with a hot cup of tea. But to his surprise he found only the Welsh hillside and a torturous journey back to London.

"My good man", said Tim as Gabriel walked through the door tired, hungry and sporting two blistered feet.

"You look shattered", said Charlotte as she arose to offer Gabriel her chair by the stove.

"Thank you", replied Gabriel as he threw himself down on the chair, "I hope you didn't wait up all night for me".

"What do you mean wait up all night, you were only gone half an hour", said charlotte as she poured Gabriel a cup of tea.

Gabriel thanked Charlotte for the tea and inwardly blamed time for once again playing tricks with his mind and body.

"Grandfather was filling me in on the events in France and leading up till now", said Charlotte as she sat down on a chair next to Gabriel, "You certainly look as if you have been through the wars".

"Whether I have been through the wars, or just look as if I have been, is the least of my worries right now", replied Gabriel as he sipped at his tea, "right now my feet ache, my limbs may never work again and to add to the misery, Jimbo has a secret weapon in which we have little defense against".

"That is no longer the case my young friend", said Tim, "We have the words Scrooge sent us".

"I don't think I have the will or strength to walk back to the Welsh mountains", replied Gabriel.

"You won't have to my fine friend", said Tim, "I never forget anything, even when it comes to a rhyme through time".

"I can't think how Jimbo managed to get out of prison", said Charlotte.

"I can", replied Tim, "and that means Jimbo has friends in high places, or very high places".

"He has got to be stopped", said Charlotte as she removed Gabriel's empty cup from his hand and placed it on the table.

"Stopped he must be indeed my dear", answered Tim, "how to achieve that will take a great deal of ingenuity".

"In the meantime", said Gabriel as he struggled to pull himself up from the chair, "I'm off to sleep for forty days and forty nights".

Gabriel slowly made his way into his bedroom and was fast asleep before his body hit the mattress.

"Wake up", said Charlotte as she reached down to shake Gabriel's shoulder, "grandfather has been arrested".

On hearing these alarming words Gabriel quickly returned from the land of sleep and sat upright on the bed.

"When did this happen?" asked Gabriel while rubbing his eyes.

"An hour ago,", answered Charlotte.

"What did they arrest him for?" asked Gabriel as he climbed out of bed and followed Charlotte into the next room.

"They didn't say", replied Charlotte now showing signs of alarm in her voice, "Oh Gabriel we need to do something".

"Calm down", said Gabriel, "put the kettle on and let's get our heads around this over a brew".

"It must be something serious as a chief inspector made the arrest", said Charlotte as she prepared the tea things.

"That means nothing", replied Gabriel as he proceeded to analyze the present predicament, "all that tells us that someone at the top wants him silenced".

"We need to get him out", said Charlotte as she waited on the kettle to boil, "he's an old man".

"Try telling him that", replied Gabriel, "by now he has probably blown the bars of his cell with dynamite".

"God only knows what he has been up to in France", said Charlotte as she finished pouring the tea.

"Believe me, God is not the only one who knows what he has been up to in France", replied Gabriel before thanking Charlotte for the tea.

"Think of something please", said Charlotte in desperation.

"I am going to try and impersonate his solicitor", replied Gabriel, "I will try and get him released by hook or by crook".

"You might end up inside with him", said Charlotte.

"Then you will have to employ the act of foul play and blast a whole in the wall", replied Gabriel as he tried to remove some of the stress from the air.

"Let's go", said Charlotte as she reached to put her coat on, "before they lock him up in Brixton".

"I wish to see Mr. Timothy Cratchit if you please", said Gabriel as he stared at the policeman behind the desk.

"And who might you be?" asked the policemen.

"My name is John Hughes, I am Mr. Cratchit's

solicitor", answered Gabriel.

"I am sorry sir but you will have to come back in the morning, the sergeant will not be back until 9.00am", said the policeman.

"What is your name?" asked Gabriel as he removed a notebook and pencil from his coat pocket.

"Constable Manning sir", replied the policeman.

"I have a right by law to see my client anytime whether it be night or day", said Gabriel as he proceeded to write the policeman's name in his notebook.

"I will have to get authorization sir", replied the worried looking policeman.

"Well you would better get to it", said Gabriel as he returned the notebook to his pocket, "before you find yourself out of a job".

The policeman left the front desk and dialed a number on the telephone attached the wall.

"Yes sir", said the policeman into the telephone, "Mr. Cratchit's solicitor".

Gabriel watched as he continued to talk to someone on the other end and noticed the policeman's voice getting lower as he turned to look Gabriel up and down.

"Ok sir", said the policeman as he placed the phone back on the hook, "come this way".

"Thank you", replied Gabriel as he followed the policeman down the narrow corridor to the holding cells, "I'm glad that someone has decided to see some sense".

The policeman opened the door to a dimly lit cell and Gabriel walked inside.

"I will have to lock you in sir", said the policeman, "I'll call back in half an hour".

As the policeman closed the door firmly behind him,

Gabriel waited until the footsteps could be heard disappearing before he spoke.

"How did you manage to get yourself in here?" asked Gabriel as he sat beside Tim on the bed.

"On a trumped up charge, no doubt the work of our good friend Jimbo", replied Tim as he flashed a smile at Gabriel.

"What have you to smile about?" asked Gabriel, "look where you are".

"Well at least I have a good friend to keep me company", replied Tim.

"Only for a short while I'm afraid", said Gabriel, "in the meantime we must hatch a plan very fast to get you out of here".

"Oh don't be afraid my young man, and the word you meant to use was plural, not just one person", replied Tim as he flashed Gabriel another smile.

"No just you, they think I'm your solicitor", said Gabriel.

"Don't be ridiculous", replied Tiny Tim, "you didn't think they would fall for that old trick".

"I believe they did or how else would I be here", said Gabriel.

"The interview room is three doors up my good man", replied Tim, "if they had have fell for it, that is where we would be now".

Gabriel could only hope that Tim was not wrong, but somehow the realization that he had been uncovered was now quickly becoming all too true.

"I'm sorry Tim", said Gabriel as he stood up to walk around the cell, "I feel so stupid".

"Don't worry my fine fellow", replied Tim, "I appreciate your act of bravery on my behalf".

"You mean an act of idiocy", said Gabriel.

"Sometime an act of folly can resurrect itself as a breath of great courage", replied Tim as he tried to reassure Gabriel.

"Noble words sir, but useless against stone walls and iron bars", said Gabriel as he sat down on the bed next to Tiny Tim.

"Where is my granddaughter?" asked Tim.

"I told her if I wasn't out in an hour to go back home", replied Gabriel.

"Wise thing to do, wouldn't want her to get hurt", said Tim.

"Why do you keep looking at your watch?" asked Gabriel, "have you anything special planned for tonight?"

"Just a habit my good man", replied Tim as he continued to glance at his watch every few minutes.

"Your granddaughter is worried about you", said Gabriel.

"Now she has two to worry about", replied Tim before stealing another glance at his watch.

"In all the time I have known you", said Gabriel as he stood to look up at the night sky through the barred window, "I have never once noticed you looking at your watch and now when we cannot move an inch beyond this cell, you have looked at it about twenty times in twenty minutes".

"You may not have noticed me", replied Tim, "but that does not prove that I didn't do it".

"What time is it?" asked Gabriel.

"Almost five minutes to midnight", replied Tim as he looked at his watch.

"Your watch is slow", said Gabriel as he removed his watch from his waistcoat to check the time, "I have it at one minute to".

Suddenly Tim sprang from the bed with the speed and agility of a teenager and flung Gabriel onto the floor. He grabbed the mattress with one swift grip of his hand and had just covered Gabriel and himself when a loud bang shattered the night air and left Gabriel's eardrums ringing in utter surprise.

"Quick my young friend", said Tim as he threw the rubble covered mattress off and jumped to his feet,

"Time to say goodbye".

Gabriel staggered to his feet and followed Tim over the rubble, through the gaping hole in the wall and out onto the street. A motorcar screeched to a halt and Tim beckoned Gabriel into the back seat before taking off at speed into the night and away from the extremely confused policeman.

"This is my safe house", said Tim as he guided Gabriel down an alleyway and through a large oak door.

"My God", said Charlotte as she witnessed Gabriel and Tim close the door behind them and walk into the room still covered in dust, "you might have at least changed your clothes".

"Hello, my dear", replied Tim, "I do hope you reminded the tea".

"A woman never forgets anything", said Charlotte as she ushered them over to the chairs by the table, "I even managed the bread and Jam".

As Gabriel sat down at the table beside Tim, he noticed Charlotte looked happy as she poured the tea and cut the loaf of bread. Gabriel knew by the way she glanced occasionally in his direction with her vibrant sparkling smiling eyes, that she was also pleased to see him.

"How did you manage to pull that one off?" asked Gabriel as he thanked Charlotte for the tea and proceeded to help himself to some bread and jam.

"A friendly policeman who went off duty before you arrived and delivered a note to someone I knew", replied Tim.

"And that someone you knew was commissioned to blow a hole big enough for yours truly to return once again to the land of the free", said Gabriel.

"If Jimbo gets his way our freedom will be short lived", said Tim as he too helped himself to some bread and jam.

"He has got to be stopped", said Charlotte as she sat down between her grandfather and Gabriel, "I know I keep saying it but this thing is getting bigger than we thought".

"Bigger indeed my dear", replied Tim, "and it's going to get a whole lot bigger".

"What we need is someone we can trust to infiltrate the boys at the top club", said Gabriel.

"Indeed, my young friend", replied Tim, "someone who can tell us why the army are employing children to fight at the front".

"We need to keep Charlotte out of this", said Gabriel, "it's getting too dangerous".

"I can look after myself", replied a defiant Charlotte.

"Not if Jimbo catches you with his hypnosis again", said Gabriel.

"His magic can no longer work on Charlotte", replied Tiny Tim, "since Scrooge left us the rhyme and we were able to read it, none of Jimbo's tricks will work on any of us".

"He can still use the police and whatever dirty means he chooses to employ", said Gabriel.

"Indeed, that is why for the time being we must not return home", replied Tim, "and you my young friend must not let Charlotte out of your sight".

"Have you anything in mind?" asked Charlotte.

"Yes my dear", replied Tim as he arose from his chair and proceeded towards the door, "I have someone to see".

Gabriel wished Tim good luck and watched him depart into the night air in search of something known only to Tim. He watched Charlotte wash the few dishes and shut the stove down for the night, and wondered if he would be strong and wise enough to protect her from the evil circling around them. He put his hand over his mouth to muffle a yawn and realized he was still tired.

"I think we need to get some sleep", said Gabriel as he turned to look at Charlotte.

"I agree", replied Charlotte, "I hope you don't snore".

"I don't really know as I never stay awake long enough to find out", said Gabriel.

"Well if you do I will wake you up", replied Charlotte as she ushered Gabriel into the bedroom.

"Where will you sleep?" asked Gabriel at the realization that there was only one double bed.

"Right here beside you", replied Charlotte as she flashed Gabriel a smile.

"Oh no", said Gabriel as he began to blush, "we can't do that; I'll sleep on the armchair".

"Don't be ridiculous", replied Charlotte as she removed her shoes, "I haven't packed any night clothes so we will have to sleep fully dressed".

Gabriel removed his shoes and climbed into bed beside Charlotte before pulling the covers over both of them.

"If your grandfather caught us in bed together he would string me up", said Gabriel trying to hide his nervousness.

"Tell me a bedtime story", said Charlotte as she turned to face Gabriel.

Before Gabriel could reply, Charlotte's light snores could be plainly heard and Gabriel was left staring at her childlike features slumbering peacefully beside him. He closed his eyes and remembered how his life was without Charlotte and Tim and came to the swift conclusion that no matter how dangerous his existence had become, he would not change it for the world. He was glad of this time to reflect on his life with Charlotte and Tiny Tim, and more so when the three choir boys began singing softly from the bottom of the bed.

BAD IS GOOD AND GOOD IS BAD
SAD IS HAPPY AND HAPPY IS SAD
ANGELS WEEP WHEN FOOLS DRAW NEAR
THE CLOTH THAT HIDES THE FROZEN TEAR
UP IS DOWN AND DOWN IS UP
INNOCENCE DRINKS FROM A POISONED CUP
A FACE FOR YOU AND A FACE FOR ME
APPLES ROT ON THE SWEETEST TREE
WIDE IS NARROW AND NARROW IS WIDE
BEHIND THE CROSS THIS MAN WILL HIDE
KNOW THEM ONE AND KNOW THEM ALL
FOR HE WEARS A HAT THAT MAKES HIM TALL

CHAPTER 12

"I don't know what has come over you", said Charlotte as she hurried along the street beside Gabriel.

"Just trust me", replied Gabriel.

"But you haven't told me where we are going", Said Charlotte as she came to a stop outside a cathedral.

"In here", replied Gabriel as he guided Charlotte through the double doors of the church.

Gabriel and Charlotte walked up between the rows of seats and found a space beside two very old ladies. He wasn't sure if the vision of the singers the night before had any significance to where he was now, but the mention of cloth and tall hat had more than pronged his imagination.

"What are we doing here?" whispered Charlotte before joining the congregation in standing up at the entrance of the bishop and several other clergy.

"Trying to find the truth", replied Gabriel in a whisper.

Gabriel studied the bishop from the moment he entered and listened to every word that flowed from his mouth with all the sincerity of a midnight fox.

"LET US ALL PRAY FOR THOSE WHO ARE FIGHTING TYRANNY AMONG THE BATTLEFIELDS OF EUROPE AND ASK GOD FOR A SPEEDY AND VICTORIOUS END TO THE DEATH AND CARNAGE".

"Words slipping from the mouth with as much grease as a snake", said Gabriel in a low voice.

Before Charlotte had time to reply one of the old ladies reached behind Charlotte's head and clipped Gabriel behind the ear. On seeing how Gabriel had been humiliated by the elder female citizen, Charlotte could not hold back the laugh that flew out of her mouth. To Gabriel's amusement Charlotte received a similar dose of ear clipping that in the meantime put an end to the chattering couple.

At the closing of proceedings, Gabriel and Charlotte followed the throngs of church goers and stepped out into the morning air.

"That will teach you to behave yourself", said Gabriel humorously.

But once again before Charlotte had time to reply, Gabriel was subjected to a kick on the skin by one of the elderly ladies' hard leather boots.

"My God", said Charlotte as she tried to hide her amusement, "I don't believe you will be going back there again".

"Never again", replied Gabriel while he feinted a limp as they walked away, "I could end up getting a damn good thrashing the next time".

"My ear is still hurting", said Charlotte as they crossed the road.

"My ear's ringing louder than those church bells", replied Gabriel.

"I don't hear any bells", said Charlotte.

"You too", replied Gabriel as he stopped beside a row of houses.

"We'll wait here awhile", said Gabriel as he stared towards the front doors of the cathedral.

"Will you please tell me what we are looking for?" asked Charlotte.

"That bishop has got something to hide", replied Gabriel.

"How do you know this?" asked Charlotte.

"It came to me in a dream, or something", replied Gabriel as he continued to watch the front doors of the cathedral.

"I dreamt I was a princess", said Charlotte, "but I'm not standing outside Buckingham Palace".

"I rest my case dear lady", replied Gabriel as he pointed Charlotte in the direction of the cathedral.

"My God", said Charlotte as she looked towards the cathedral, "It's Jimbo and the bishop together".

"I've said it before and I'll say it again", said Gabriel, "this is getting bigger than us".

"What will we do?" asked Charlotte as she grabbed Gabriel's arm.

"First I'm going to get you back to the safe house", replied Gabriel as he ushered Charlotte in the direction of home.

"We need to tell grandfather", said Charlotte.

"That's if we can find him", replied Gabriel.

Gabriel turned left onto a narrow street and occasionally turned to look back to make sure they were not being followed. The revelation that Jimbo was in league with the bishop was scaring him and he could only wonder who next would join Jimbo's list of influential associates. He was worried about Charlotte and he first thought of leaving her at the safe house, but now changed his mind as he remembered his promise to Tiny Tim. He also knew that it would take more than Tim, Charlotte and himself to fight against the evil that was sprouting up in every direction. He hoped that whatever magic or whatever mystical force past and present that had arrived in his life, that they too would outnumber the forces of darkness.

"Don't be getting settled my good friend", said Tim as Gabriel and Charlotte walked through the door,

"there's a train leaving for Kent in an hour".

"Why are we going to Kent?" asked Gabriel.

"We are not going to Kent old son", replied Tim, "you are going and Charlotte and my good self will remain here until you return".

"What's so important about Kent?" asked Gabriel.

"Kettlewell Convalescent Home my young friend", replied Tim as he hurried to prepare Gabriel a cup of tea.

"What will he be looking for there?" asked Charlotte.

"A Royal Inniskillen Fusilier soldier by the name of David Conway", replied Tim as he offered Gabriel a cup of tea, "he was wounded in a shell blast and I was informed by a very reliable source that he may have information that will be useful to us".

"Are you trying to tell me that I have to travel all the way to Kent to speak with a shell shocked soldier", said Gabriel, "he might be away with the fairies for all we know".

"I said wounded by a shell, not shocked by one", replied Tim.

"Does he need to leave today?" asked Charlotte as she looked sympathetically at Gabriel.

"If he leaves now", replied Tim as he removed the half full cup of tea from Gabriel's hand, "he will be back in time for supper".

Gabriel wasted no time in making his way to the train station and quickly boarded the train to Kent. He wondered where Tim got his information about the soldier from and could only speculate on why he believed he could help them. The past few weeks had left him exhausted and his change of accommodation had allowed little sleep. As he listened to the shouts of all aboard and the movement of the train as it set off, Gabriel could not keep himself from falling asleep.

"Excuse me sir", said a tall thin man with a bald head, "we have arrived at Swanley".

Gabriel quickly awoke and thanked the man for his assistance. He made his way on foot from the train station and after asking directions, he soon found his way to the hospital.

"Good afternoon", said Gabriel to the nurse behind the desk, "I was hoping that I might get to see my cousin David Conway".

"What's your name?" asked the nurse.

"Gabriel Shivers", replied Gabriel.

"Go out through those doors", said the nurse as she pointed, "and you will find him sitting under the apple tree".

Gabriel thanked the nurse and made his way through the doors and out onto a freshly mowed garden. To Gabriel's annoyance there were several apple trees and a patient sitting under each and every one of them.

"Excuse me sir", said Gabriel politely, "are you David Conway?"

"No", came the reply from the patient.

"Are you David Conway?" asked Gabriel as he

moved to the second one.

"Certainly not", replied the patient with a bandage covering up the remainder of his arm.

"David Conway?" asked Gabriel.

"Go away", replied the third patient.

"Have I the pleasure of addressing Mr. David Conway?" asked Gabriel yet again.

"Why don't you push off and join a convent", replied a trembling patient.

"David Conway, I presume?" asked Gabriel.

"That is correct", replied the last patient.

"May I sit down?" asked Gabriel.

"You may", replied David.

"My name is Gabriel Shivers and I have travelled down from London in the hope that you may be able to help me", said Gabriel as he took a seat next to the wounded soldier.

"And what makes you think I can help you?" asked David.

"A friend of mine said that you may have information that could help us solve a mystery", replied Gabriel.

"And what mystery might that be?" asked David.

"We believe that there are rouge elements within the military who may be committing crimes", replied Gabriel.

"There are more people than you who believe that crimes are being committed by the military", said David, "crimes against humanity".

"Did you see anything unusual?" asked Gabriel, "anything that was out of the ordinary even in times of war".

"I saw many things that were unusual", replied David, "but one thing did shine out from all the rest".

"And what was that?" asked Gabriel.

"One night a few weeks ago we were on night patrol near the enemy trenches, when all of a sudden out of the blue a German machine gun opened up. As we were pinned down with one wounded I decided to attempt to take out the post by first throwing a grenade and then charging before they got a chance to recover. After throwing the grenade I leapt forward and when I arrived after the explosion, everyone was dead except a British officer", said David.

"What do you mean a British officer?" asked Gabriel, "surely you mean a German one".

"No, he was British", replied David, "he was badly wounded and before he died he said to tell Bishop I'm sorry".

"Are you sure that's what he said?" asked Gabriel.

"His voice was low but I'm sure he said tell Bishop I'm sorry", replied David.

Gabriel thanked David for his assistance and returned back to the train station to return to London. On the journey back he thought about what David told him and had come to the very swift and calculated conclusion that the Bishop Charlotte and he had seen earlier in the day, and the Bishop from the mouth of the dying officer were indeed the same person.

"Could you spare a penny for a poor old lady kind sir", said an old woman dressed in rags.
Gabriel reached into his pocket, removed two shillings and handed it to the old lady.

"Oh, thank you dear sir, here's a rose for time's sake", replied the old, ragged lady.

"Thank you", replied Gabriel as he left the train station to make his way back to Charlotte and Tiny

Tim.

As Gabriel neared the house he once again looked around him to make sure no one was following. On discovering all was clear he grasped the rose in his hand and made his way to the door of the safe house and knocked gently on the door.

"Good evening may I help you?" asked the tall thin man.

"Excuse me who are you?" asked Gabriel in surprise.

"Uriah Heep at your service", replied Uriah.

"Is Tim or Charlotte at home?" asked Gabriel as he eyed the very old man before him with suspicion.

"There is no one by that name living here", replied Uriah as he rubbed his two hands together.

"I'm afraid you're wrong", said Gabriel as his suspicions began to boil over, "If you please move aside I will see for myself".

"If you must", replied Uriah as he stepped aside for Gabriel, "but I'm only a humble clerk who lives a humble existence".

Gabriel walked past Uriah and made his way into the living room where along with Tim and Charlotte, they had sat down together. The site that lay before him was troubling to say the least, for the house resembled more of a pigsty than the pigsty itself. He walked into the room where Charlotte and he had stayed the night and all he could see before him was a single bed with unrecognizable bed covers.

"Are you satisfied?" asked Heep as he slid up behind him as quiet as a thief.

"I don't understand", replied Gabriel as he looked around in confusion, "this is the house where I slept last night".

"To beg your good pardon sir", said Heep, "but I

have lived here these last thirty years or more and I'm sure you didn't stay here".

Gabriel said nothing and walked back out through the door and embraced the cool breeze blowing down the alleyway. He made off in the direction of his rooms, while his mind was spinning with the unreal situation, he was now finding himself in.

"Good evening sir", said Gabriel as he walked through the main door of Tiny Tim's house.

"Good evening to you too sir, may I help you?" replied the ashen face man.

"Is Tiny Tim at home?" asked Gabriel.

"Who?" replied the man.

"I mean Tim Cratchit", said Gabriel.

"I'm afraid he is not at home, but his granddaughter is here", replied the man.

"If you please sir, can I speak to her it's rather urgent", said Gabriel.

"Just a moment", replied the man.

Gabriel was glad that Charlotte was here and perhaps she could throw some light on the dark predicament before him. He couldn't understand why someone else had taken over the house he had just left, and in such a short span of time, turned it into a dump.

"Good evening sir, can I help you?" asked Charlotte as she approached Gabriel.

"I do wish you would stop playing your games", replied Gabriel, "and tell me what's going on".

"I don't believe we have met", said Charlotte, "perhaps you have mistaken me for someone else".

"Listen Charlotte", replied Gabriel, "if this is some game you are playing I am not impressed".

"I am sure we have never met sir", said Charlotte as she looked at Gabriel as if he was a stranger.

"Please Charlotte", said Gabriel as he leaned against the wall for support, "I'm tired and I have got some information so please stop this nonsense".

"If you don't leave this house I'm sending for the police", replied Charlotte as she began to move backwards away from Gabriel.

"So it has come to this then", said Gabriel as the anger now began to flow through his veins, "you and Tim have been running me around like some idiot to satisfy your own disturbed pleasure".

"Go now sir please", replied Charlotte, now showing an expression of fear.

"Where will I go", said Gabriel as he straightened himself up, "I live here".

"You don't live here sir I have never seen you before, please get out", replied Charlotte.

Gabriel turned from Charlotte and walked back out through the doors. His heart began to beat to the rhythm of sadness and despair and as he made his way down the street, all he could think of was his own stupidity. He began to believe that everything he had went through these last few weeks had all been a grand illusion brought on by his own boredom. The time in France, the fight against evil and his time with Charlotte were pictures created by his mind and no longer existed. He turned left onto the main street and before he could take another step forward, something very strange caught his eyes and ears.

"READ ALL ABOUT IT, READ ALL ABOUT IT, TITANIC SINKS IN NORTH ATLANTIC, READ ALL ABOUT IT", shouted the newspaper boy at the corner.

Gabriel slowly walked towards him, unable to fathom what he was hearing and frightened of what lay before him.

"What going on?" asked Gabriel.

"RMS Titanic has sunk, it hit an iceberg and it's feared that many have drowned", replied the newspaper boy as he continued to call out the news.

"But that happened over four years ago", said Gabriel.

"No, only recently sir", replied the newspaper boy. Gabriel purchased a newspaper and looked at the headlines on the front page,

TITANIC HIT BY ICEBERG MANY LIVES LOST. Gabriel looked at the date on the newspaper and could not believe what he was seeing. 18th April 1912. He rolled the newspaper up and walked away, still trying to come to terms with his situation and accept the fact that something was terribly wrong.

"Excuse me sir", said Gabriel as he stopped an old man walking past, "Could you please tell me the day's date please?"

"Eighteenth of April sir", replied the old man.

"What year is it?" asked Gabriel.

"Why it's 1912 sir", replied the old man as he looked at Gabriel in astonishment.

"Thank you, sir,", said Gabriel.

"Are you ok sir?" asked the old man.

"Thank you", replied Gabriel as he continued on his journey to the park.

When Gabriel reached the park he sat down on the same bench that Charlotte and he sat on before, and gripped the newspaper he had in his hand extremely tight. He did not know what happened or indeed how he managed to find himself in the very place four years too early. The past weeks had revealed to him many strange and wonderful happenings, but this was one he did not want. He was now lost, a stranger to those he had met and gradually learned to love and no stranger to the years that lay before him. He looked at the water expecting to find ducks floating about in search of breadcrumbs, but the sun was beginning to slowly disappear and night would soon arrive to add darkness to Gabriel's black state of mind. Church bells began to ring in the distance, calling out for some holy event or just reminding everyone that bells speak louder than words. He heard the occasional laugh as ladies passed by; gently strolling with those they love, oblivious of the future war and perhaps the loss of those memories forever. Gabriel began to come to terms with his situation and was quietly greeted with a great emptiness as it embraced his desperate loneliness. He wanted so much to return to the danger and excitement of his own time and place, to be back beside the youthful old man and the strong willed Charlotte. The same Charlotte who banished him from the door of her home, the same Charlotte who feared him and the same Charlotte who would never receive the two-shilling red rose. Gabriel put the tortured newspaper in his pocket and before he left to wander the streets in limbo, he threw the rose into the water.

CHAPTER 13

"Where on earth have you been?" asked Charlotte as she rushed up to Gabriel on the street, "the train arrived almost four hours ago".

Gabriel stared into Charlotte's eyes for some form of deceit or falsehood, but he could find none. Her body language, the way she touched his arm and the tone of her voice convinced Gabriel he was back.

"Where have you been?" asked Charlotte as she hooked onto Gabriel's arm and guided him in the direction of the safe house.

"I don't know", replied Gabriel.

"What do you mean you don't know?" asked Charlotte, "don't tell you are taking leave of your senses".

Gabriel was telling the truth, he didn't know where he had been and he didn't care. He was so overjoyed to be back again that he wanted to throw his arms around Charlotte and never let go. He could not even begin to comprehend how life would be without her and the small dose he had just been administered was enough to bring tears to his eyes. He followed her through the door of their safe house and his heart glowed to see the smiling face of Tim greeting him with a teapot in his hand.

"I say old man", said Tim, "we were beginning to believe you had fallen down a pot hole".

Gabriel sat on the chair next to the table and accepted the steaming cup of Tiny Tim's brew.

"Are you going to tell us why you were late?" asked Charlotte.

"You wouldn't believe me if I told you", replied Gabriel, "I can't even believe it myself".

"Try us", said Charlotte as she stood over Gabriel with her arms folded in a manner that Gabriel witnessed many times before.

"I got lost in time", replied Gabriel.

"You certainly did get lost in time", said Charlotte, "we were worried half to death about you".

"I really mean I got lost in time", replied Gabriel, "over four years ago".

"Explain yourself", said Charlotte as she took a seat by the fire, "I'm waiting to hear you present your very tall male tale of why you were four hours late".

"I can't explain", replied Gabriel, "I left the train when it arrived at the station and low and behold I had stepped back in time".

"Did anything strange or unusual happen to you on the train?" asked Tim.

"No, I left the train and proceeded to make my way back here, except I stopped to give an old beggar woman two shillings", replied Gabriel.

"And you were rewarded with a red rose for your trouble?" asked Tim as he turned to smile at Charlotte.

"Yes", replied Gabriel as he returned his empty cup

to the table, "how did you know?"

"Ask me how I knew my fine fellow", returned Tim, "I too fell for the same trick many years ago".

"My God", said Gabriel "is she a witch?"

"Not in the spooky sense of the word but she does have very powerful magic", replied Tim.

"Then how did I return?" asked Gabriel.

"I do believe the answer to that is best kept a secret within our own emotions", replied Tim.

"It was you", said Charlotte as she looked hard at Gabriel, "I remember you coming to the door looking for grandfather and you give me the impression that you knew me, I thought you were some lunatic who had just escaped from the asylum".

"Believe me my dear", replied Gabriel, "I almost thought I was".

"And when you returned here", asked Tim, "Did you find that it was a Mr. Heep who answered the door".

"Yes, who was he?" asked Gabriel.

"Oh just someone who worked as a clerk and was sent off to Australia for twenty years for his fraudulent sins", answered Tim.

"How did I get back sir", said Gabriel, "I don't remember doing anything magical".

"I told you Gabriel old son, please call me Tim", replied Tim.

"That doesn't answer how he got back", said Charlotte as she looked into her grandfather's eyes.

"Now we don't really want to discuss that now", replied Tim, "we have other priorities to attend to".

"If there is something I should know Tim", said Gabriel, "I would be very grateful if you would share the information with us".

"No I don't believe you would like me to share it,

these things are best left until us young men are on our own", replied Tim.

"Us men is it", said Charlotte as she lifted her voice in protest, "I will not move another inch from this room until you men decide I am not a second class citizen who has no God given right to know what is going on in a so called man's world".

"I'm sorry Tim", said Gabriel, "maybe its best left for another time".

"I think if you get to know my granddaughter as long as I have", replied Tim, "you will discover that she is true to her word and will most certainly carry out her threat of not moving an inch from this very room".

"Then if it pleases you", said Gabriel, "and for the sake of good relations among us, I don't mind if we all know how I managed to return".

"When you returned here and found a stranger living here", said Tim, "you panicked and went back home believing that something strange was unfolding before your very eyes. I was not at home and my granddaughter whom you were acquainted with suddenly disowned you, you made your way to the only place your heart could guide you, because my young friend, your mind could no longer function. After some time you threw the rose the old lady give you into the water and left the park. Shortly after that my dear granddaughter found you wandering around like a lost puppy".

"That doesn't explain how he got back", protested Charlotte.

"The rose the old lady give you", asked Tim, "do you know who you were going to give it to?"

"I hadn't, well I was, maybe, I don't really know", muttered Gabriel as he tried to hide the true destination of the rose.

"I do believe we both know who the receiver was going to be", said Tim.

"If you both know then maybe you could enlighten me", replied Charlotte, "or is it just a man's little secret".

"Shall we let her in on our little secret?" said Tim.

"I'm, well you know, I'm not quite sure what you mean", stuttered Gabriel as he continued to cloak the true destination of the flower.

"You were bringing it back to my granddaughter", replied Tim in an almost apologetic tone of voice.

"Oh how nice of you", said Charlotte, "but please remember for the next time, I prefer pink roses".

On hearing the revelation from Tim's mouth, Gabriel's face shone as red as the very rose that boiled the conversation with embarrassment. He knew he could not hide from the facts before him and now realized too late, that Tim was trying to spare him from the object of Charlotte's amusement.

"And just by throwing the rose in the water", said Charlotte as she sensed Gabriel's discomfort, "Gabriel was suddenly transformed forward in time".

"No my dear", replied Tim, "by throwing the rose into the water he sent ripples of despair across the surface of time, allowing that very sorrow to send a signal to the one who's absence he grieved for most".

"And who did he grieve for?" asked Charlotte.

"The very person who found him wandering the streets", replied Tim.

"Are you sure he mentioned the Bishop?" asked Tim.

"Yes Bishop", replied Gabriel, "I can't understand what a British officer was doing in a German trench".

"My granddaughter filled me in on what you saw at the cathedral", said Tim as he proceeded to pace up and down in his own familiar way, "I guess we could put the two together and come up with a match".

"Meaning that the Bishop is fraternizing with the enemy", replied Gabriel.

"Indeed my partner in youth", said Tim, "what we need now is proof beyond any reasonable doubt and then we can bag this thing once and for all".

"This thing is getting much too big for the three of us", said Gabriel.

"That has become apparently clear my good man", replied Tim, "but the question we need to ask ourselves, who can we trust?"

"Apart from ourselves, we can trust no one", said Charlotte as she finished clearing the table of the tea things.

"Exactly my dear", replied Tim, "well almost".

"Almost?" asked Charlotte.

"Yes, almost my dear", replied Tim, "trust can be bought but loyalty has no price".

"So, you are saying we should pay for help?" asked Charlotte as she took a chair beside Gabriel.

"Precisely my dear, we must bribe someone in The War Office and pay another to keep a close eye on the Bishop", replied Tim as he continued to pace in rhythm to his words.

"Are we supposed to trust these people?" asked Charlotte.

"Certainly not my dear", answered Tim, "we receive their trust temporarily in exchange for gold, we do not give it, and loyalty remains within our own circle and never outside it".

"Do you know anyone who can be bought?" asked

Gabriel.

"Leave that to me my loyal friend", replied Tiny Tim, "tomorrow I want you to take my granddaughter to see an old Gipsy woman".

"And to what do I owe the pleasure of meeting someone so distinguished?" asked Charlotte dryly.

"After you see her tomorrow my dear", replied Tim as he stopped pacing up and down, "your sarcasm will be discarded by the wayside".

"We do need to infiltrate the bishop's circle", said Gabriel.

"As of this moment I'm off to instigate that very task", replied Tim as he donned his coat to leave, "I will see you two sometime later".

After seeing Tim to the door, Gabriel returned to take a seat beside Charlotte and contemplate on the day's events. The uncomfortable revelation that spilled his feelings for Charlotte out in the open had left him now feeling awkward in her presence. Although Charlotte shrugged it off as nothing more than charming, Gabriel caught her eye on more than one occasion and knew that Charlotte had been touched by the destination of his affections.

"Would you like another cup of tea?" asked Charlotte.

"No thank you", replied Gabriel.

"I wonder who grandfather has in mind", said Charlotte.

"I shouldn't wonder", replied Gabriel, "but there is no doubt he knows what he's doing".

"Gabriel", said Charlotte as her voice grew softer, "About today, I'm sorry I pushed grandfather".

"It's ok", replied Gabriel, unable to meet Charlotte's eyes, "I tend to get a little carried away".

"A little can sometimes grow much larger with patience and care", said Charlotte as she tried to meet Gabriel's eyes.

"I'm sorry the rose didn't make it", replied Gabriel.

"You are wrong, the rose did make it, the flower remained behind", said Charlotte.

Gabriel began to feel the blood rushing to his face once again as he tried to brave the situation before him. Charlotte now stood facing him and stared into his eyes as she began to make her way closer to Gabriel.

"Gabriel", said Charlotte as she stood beside him, "do you, do you love, do you love telling bedtime stories?"

Before Gabriel knew what had happened, Charlotte suddenly made her way to the bedroom.

"It's time we were in bed", she said, "We may or may not have a long day ahead of us tomorrow".

Gabriel followed her into the bedroom and watched her climb under the bedclothes and except for her shoes, she was fully clothed. He removed his shoes and lay down beside her. He knew one of two things about what happened a few moments ago. Either Charlotte felt the same way about him, as he did about her, or she was well versed in the art of playing with his mind.

"Tell me a bedtime story please", said Charlotte as she lay motionless on the bed.

"Once upon a time", began Gabriel.

And once upon a time again Charlotte's snores could be heard vibrating around the room. He wanted her to stay awake and listen to his stories, he wanted her to lay her head on his chest and he wanted to feel her breath close to his heart. But he knew what he wanted wasn't going to happen, and as Gabriel closed his eyes to sleep, his thoughts would not stray from the path of destiny that lay before him in the coming days.

"Across from the iron monger's he said", muttered Charlotte as she led Gabriel down a long narrow street.

"That must be it", replied Gabriel as he pointed to a strange looking single story building in urgent need of repair.

"Shall we say hello?" asked Charlotte as they stood outside the door.

"I know you have your doubts", replied Gabriel, "but Tim did say she was genuine.

"Let us get it over with", said Gabriel as he knocked on the door and pushed the door in response to the voice from inside.

"Good morning", said Gabriel, "we have been encouraged here by a friend who has faith in your gifted abilities to read the chapters of tomorrow".

"Get out", replied the gipsy as she snarled through the long grey tresses of hair.

"Pardon?" asked Gabriel as he was taken aback by the gipsy's choice of words.

"Get out of here and don't ever cross my door again", said the gipsy, "and how may I help you too?"

"Excuse me but I thought you just told us to leave", replied Gabriel as he eyed the old gipsy up.

"I wasn't talking about you", said the gipsy as she commenced to put some tobacco into a clay pipe.

"Then who may I ask were you referring to?" replied Gabriel, "there was no one else here".

"Did that rascal of a Tim Cratchit send you?" asked the gipsy as she continued to fill her pipe.

"Yes indeed", answered Gabriel, "he sends his greetings".

"No he does not young man", said the gipsy, "did your mother not teach you the consequences of telling lies?"

"Well I'm sure he meant to send them but knowing Tim it must have slipped out of his mind", replied Gabriel as he tried to worm his way out of the lie that had just been exposed.

"Tell me young man", said the gipsy as she applied a burning ember to her pipe, "what does Tim want?"

"He thought that you might be able to help us by reading our fortune", replied Gabriel.

"Follow me", said the gipsy as she led Charlotte and Gabriel into a room lit by several candles.

Gabriel and Charlotte stepped inside the room and complied with the gipsy's request to sit down at the other side of a small square table. She reached across and with a small knife she first cut a small snippet of Gabriel's hair and then repeated the same process with Charlotte. She then put the fragments of hair into a bowl and added an egg and a pinch of salt. Gabriel sat and said nothing, all the time studying the old gipsy's movements as she shook her hands over the bowl and muttered unrecognizable words.

"Slooooo naaaa gee joo ar terre mushan traaa", muttered the gipsy as she moved her hands over the bowl. She suddenly stopped what she was doing and looked into Charlotte's eyes and then turned slowly to Gabriel.

"Young man", said the gipsy, "you will return to the road that leads you across water and at the edge of that return, you will look your destiny in the eyes".

"You mean I must return to France?" asked Gabriel.

"You must return to where the truth is", replied the gipsy, "I am sure the truth is what you are looking for".

"Indeed, as long as that truth sets a great many free", said Gabriel.

"The needs of the many will most certainly outweigh the unexpected needs of the few", replied the gipsy.

"Then tell me", asked Gabriel, "are we on the right path?"

"The right or wrong path is not at issue here young man", replied the gipsy, "but the only path is the one you will take".

Gabriel thought about what the gipsy said and was still unable to see a clear picture through the frosted pane of her words. He did not want to push her for anything else save he might be subjected to the same barrage of riddles.

"Now young man", said the gipsy, "if you would please wait outside I have something to discuss with the young lady".

Charlotte looked at Gabriel in surprise but did not protest as Gabriel arose from his chair and reached into his pocket to pay the gipsy.

"Put your money back", scolded the gipsy, "I don't accept payment of any kind and beware those who do".

"Thank you", said Gabriel before he turned to leave.

Gabriel stepped out onto the street and waited for Charlotte to finish her woman's small or large talk, whichever it may be. The street was bare except for a young messenger boy on his hurried way to deliver a message. From what the gipsy woman told him, Gabriel was sure he would return to France. No doubt Tim would be finding himself alongside him, but Gabriel was unsure about bringing Charlotte back to such a troubled and dangerous place. The soldier he had talked to in Kent had convinced him that the Bishop was a prime suspect, and if all went well with

Tim's plans, the curtain would soon be drawn to reveal the whole truth and nothing but the truth.

As the door opened behind him to allow Charlotte to exit from the gipsy's house, Gabriel felt her hand grip his arm as she ushered him back in the direction they had come.

"Well my dear", said Gabriel in mild amusement, "did she say you are going to marry a royal prince and live happily ever after?"

"No", replied Charlotte as they turned left and onto the main street.

"I couldn't understand much of what she was saying", said Gabriel, "other than the fact that France is just over the horizon again".

For a brief moment Gabriel felt Charlotte's hand grip his arm tighter as they walked past the corner shop and straight across the cobbled street. He turned to look at Charlotte, trying to catch her eye, but noticed every time he attempted to do so her face would turn the other way. Gabriel tried several times to catch her attention and extract from her a reply of more than one word. He walked past the old blacksmith's shop and just before he reached the baker's shop he stopped.

"Charlotte dear", said Gabriel, "what's wrong?"

Charlotte turned and looked at Gabriel and before he could ask her again, she flung her arms around him and soaked Gabriel's face with the flood of tears that had been dripping from her eyes since they left the gipsy. He did not know why she was crying nor could he understand why she had chosen this moment in time to break the seal on her deeply hidden emotions. Gabriel wanted to hold her for eternity and tell her that everything would be fine. He wanted to reassure her that despite the dark shadow that had cast itself across her heart, his light would forever shine. He longed to whisper in her ear and tell her that the cause of her unhappiness might never happen, if only he knew what it was that might never be allowed to happen.

CHAPTER 14

The next day it was arranged to meet Tiny Tim at the park and Gabriel knew that something was about to happen, as Tim never returned home the night before. Charlotte was still wearing the scars from their visit with the gipsy and no matter how much he tried; Gabriel could not get her to reveal the contents of her troubled state of mind. They arrived at the park as planned and Gabriel could see no sign of Tiny Tim.

"I wonder where he has got to", Said Gabriel as he scanned the area for Tim.

"Right behind you", replied Charlotte as she turned around to see a well-dressed lady sitting on the summer seat.

"Where?" asked Gabriel.

"Right there", replied Charlotte as she pointed a finger at the lady smiling in their direction.

"Have you stepped over the threshold of insanity", said Gabriel, "that's not your grandfather, it's a woman.

"Let's ask her then", said Charlotte as she steered Gabriel in the direction of the lady.

"Good morning dear", said Charlotte, "I was wondering if you saw my grandfather anywhere?"

"Sorry my dear", said the lady in a high pitched voice, "but I did see your grandmother".

"That's wonderful", replied Charlotte, "may we sit

down and you can tell me where to find my grandmother".

"Certainly, my dear", replied the lady.

Gabriel took a seat next to Charlotte and began to study the lady now sitting beside them. The thick layer of makeup and the long tresses of dark curls could do nothing to hide the familiarity of the face that smiled back at him in mocking humor.

"My God", said Gabriel, "I have seen many strange and uncanny things these last few weeks, but this certainly has to get first prize".

"Grandfather", said Charlotte as she tried to keep the amusement from her voice, "I really like that dress".

"You have such a good sense of fashion my dear", replied Tim.

"Why in God's name are you dressed like that", asked Gabriel.

"Oh didn't I tell you?" said Charlotte before Tim could reply, "grandfather does get some strange ideas every once in a while".

"My good man", replied Tim, "I'm waiting here to catch the attention of a certain gentleman who regularly takes a morning stroll in this very park".

"Don't tell me", said Gabriel as he looked at Tim in surprise, "the bishop?"

"Indeed", replied Tim, "let's hope the dress catches his eye".

"Oh don't worry grandfather", said Charlotte, "no one will miss a bright colored flowered summer dress in the middle of winter".

"It's all I could find", replied Tim, "and besides, it may have the affect I'm looking for".

"Is there any other way?" asked Gabriel as he looked around him for any sign of the bishop.

"Certainly not", replied Tim, "Unless we sacrifice my lovely granddaughter and I am not about to do that".

"Don't be so over protective", said Charlotte, "I could have sat here dressed in my nightgown".

"This has got to be one of the most upside down and back to front ideas I have ever came across", said Gabriel, "and there's me thinking all along I was the only one losing my mind".

"It's time you two old people were off", said Tim, "I will meet up with you later at base camp".

"Are you sure you are ok?" asked Gabriel, "I mean seriously, this has gone well beyond the boundaries of reason".

"My dear chap", replied Tim, "I have lived my whole life dancing across the boundaries of reason".

"Is there anything we can do?" asked Charlotte, "like getting you a blanket or some hot soup".

"To the contrary my dear", replied Tim, "Get yourselves some hot soup at the corner tearooms, someone will give you an envelope and I would like you to bring it back to the safe house, preferable unopened".

"Goodbye Grandmother", said Charlotte as she stood up and ushered Gabriel in the direction of the tearooms.

"Good luck", said Gabriel as he made his way out of the park at Charlotte's side.

As Charlotte and Gabriel left the park, Gabriel began to contemplate the sight he had just witnessed and pondered on the idea that perhaps Tiny Tim no longer possessed the ability to flirt with reality. Finding him dressed like a woman had caught Gabriel off guard, and he only hoped that Tim would soon return to his former self.

"What are you having?" asked Gabriel as he took a chair across the small table from Charlotte.

"I think I will have what the master ordered", replied Charlotte, "a bowl of hot soup and some rolls".

"You mean the mistress", said Gabriel before he ordered two bowls of soup and rolls.

"Whatever takes your fancy", replied Charlotte as she forced a smile in Gabriel's direction.

"You don't think Tim has got lost a little and strolled onto the path of insanity?" asked Gabriel.

"I have known my grandfather for a long time and I can firmly say without any reservations, that nothing surprises me", replied Charlotte.

"Well he certainly knows how to surprise me", said Gabriel.

"Let me reassure you of one thing", replied Charlotte as she leaned over the table to allow her words to stray no further than Gabriel's ears only, "my grandfather will take any risk, perform any act, go to any length to right any wrong, and he is one of the most courageous and loyal human beings you will ever have the pleasure to meet. Whether he is dressed like a woman or a chicken, he does so out of necessity only and not to fodder the minds of other men's assumptions. Tiny Tim is a legend to those who know him and an eccentric to those who wish not to know him. Tiny Tim is as mad as a hatter and as gentle as a new born lamb and above all he is my grandfather. He is your friend and probably the only sincere friend you will ever truly know, so write these words down on the parchment of your mind Gabriel Shivers and nothing will ever surprise you about Tim again".

As the waitress arrived with the soup and rolls, Gabriel took a moment to gather together the words that Charlotte had just spoken. The love of a granddaughter towards her grandfather was truly bonded and witnessed by every word that flowed from Charlotte's soul. He knew only too well how much Charlotte loved Tim, but the gates of that love had been thrown wide open, to reveal a breath of whispering beauty.

"Miss Charlotte, I presume?" asked a short and stocky well-dressed gentleman who stopped beside their table.

"Your talent for presumption is truly amazing", replied Charlotte as she continued to eat her soup and roll.

"I have a note here for your grandfather and I can see he has no doubt passed some of his circus skills onto you my dear", replied the stranger.

"I take it that's where you are off to now?" asked Charlotte as she still refused to be put off her soup.

"Good day", replied the gentleman as he disappeared out through the door.

"Whatever is ruffling your feathers there is no need to take it out on an innocent party", said Gabriel as he looked at Charlotte from across the table.

"No to both your assumptions", replied Charlotte as she finished her soup.

"What do you mean no to both?" asked Gabriel.

"No, I haven't had my feathers ruffled, and no he is not an innocent party", replied Charlotte as she now stared at Gabriel.

"How do you know if he's innocent or not?" asked Gabriel as they both paid the bill and left to go, "you don't even know the man".

"He may not know me", replied Charlotte as they stepped out onto the street, "but I surely do know him".

"Where have you met him before?" asked Gabriel as they made their way back to the safe house.

"He left a tack on my chair at school", replied Charlotte, "I don't forget anyone who tried to hurt me".

"My God", said Gabriel, "children do get up to mischief; it's a fact of life".

"He targeted me because I was a female", replied Charlotte.

"That indeed is surely an assumption if ever I heard one", said Gabriel as he waited for a motorcar to pass before crossing the street.

"He didn't target any of the boys in the same way, only I bet he wished he had have after I finished with him", replied Charlotte as they stopped outside the safe house door.

Gabriel didn't push Charlotte for an explanation on 'after I had finished with him', for the tone in her voice had left little to the imagination. As they entered the room, Tiny Tim was already back and dressed as his old self.

"Ahh my old friends", said Tim as Charlotte and Gabriel entered the room and sat down, "did you get the note I was expecting?"

"Yes", replied Charlotte as she handed the note to her grandfather.

As Tim read the note Charlotte arose and began to prepare the kettle and tea things.

"How did you get on at the park?" asked Gabriel just as Tim finished reading the note.

"Splendid my good fellow", replied Tim, "the bishop adored my beautiful attire and has arranged that we meet for tea at his house tomorrow night".

"You are going?" asked Gabriel, unsure whether Tim was going to reply yes or no.

"Most definitely, I wouldn't miss it for the world", answered Tim as he put the note into his jacket pocket.

"Be careful grandfather", said Charlotte as she sat down at the table to wait on the kettle to boil.

"Don't worry my dear", replied Tim, "the bishop is always nice to ladies".

"Until he finds out you're not a lady", said Gabriel.

"I have no intention of letting him find out my good man", replied Tim.

As the three sat down together to have a cup of tea, Gabriel thought about what Tim was doing to try and obtain information for the greater good. What Charlotte had told him at the tearooms had left him viewing Tim's assignment through a clearer lens and he too truly wished that Tim would come to no harm. He was still waiting for Tim to enlighten them about the contents of the note, but decided that if it was important, he would tell them in his own good time.

"We can't have a cup of tea", said Charlotte as she looked at Tim frustrated.

"What's wrong?" asked Gabriel, "can I help?"

"There is nothing you can do my fine fellow", replied Tim, "it's just one of those things that happens every now and again".

"I wish I knew who was playing these tricks", said Charlotte as she set the empty kettle at the bottom of the stove in defeat, "I would give them a feast of my mind".

"If you tell me what is wrong, I may be able to help", replied Gabriel.

"It's no good", replied Charlotte, "we'll just have to wait until another time or day".

"Allow me", said Gabriel as he lifted the kettle off the floor and filled it with water.

"Trust me", said Charlotte as she looked at Gabriel with a grin on her face, "It's best to leave it".

Gabriel took no notice of Charlotte and as he waited for the kettle to boil, he poured some tealeaves into the teapot before setting it down on the table. When the kettle reached boiling point, Gabriel lifted it from the stove and walked over to the table to pour its contents into the teacup. He poured the water slowly, taking care not to spill any over the clean white tablecloth, but to Gabriel's astonishment the kettle emptied and there was not one drop of water in the teapot.

"In the name of God", said Gabriel as he looked at the teapot with his mouth wide open, "what is going on?"

"It's best not to interfere with the process of those we cannot see", replied Tim.

"But where has the water gone?" asked Gabriel.

"I guess someone somewhere is having a nice cup of tea", replied Charlotte as she struggled to prevent her laughter from escaping.

"But it has to go somewhere?" asked Gabriel as he struggled to believe what he had just seen.

"Listen my friend", said Tiny Tim, "you have seen ghosts, held a magic glove, travelled back in time and read a letter posted from a different dimension, so don't let something as trivial as the disappearance of a few kettles full of water upset you".

Gabriel put the empty kettle back where he had found it and decided that in the best interests of his mind, Tiny Tim was correct.

"When are you going to tell us what was in that note we just delivered?" asked Charlotte as she sat down on an armchair in front of the stove.

"Oh dear", replied Tim, "Forgive me for not disclosing the particulars of my forthcoming plan".

"And what is your forthcoming plan?" asked Charlotte.

"Our good friend Mr. Shivers will be spending tonight, compliments of the King", replied Tim, "and I don't mean on a royal bed".

"My goodness", said Charlotte as she looked straight at Tim, "what have you brewed up now?"

"When Jimbo somehow managed to get out of prison, he put the blame on one of his associates by the name of Joe Barnaby", replied Tim, "Mr. Barnaby has agreed to talk for a sum of money and you my friend will take his statement".

"Have you paid him yet?" asked Gabriel.
"His wife and children have received half and the other half will be delivered on receipt of useful information", replied Tim.

"How long am I to stay in prison?" asked Gabriel.

"Just for tonight my fine fellow", replied Tim, "my benevolent granddaughter will pay your fine early in the morning, and before you know it, you'll be sipping tea with us once again".

"Don't mention tea", said Gabriel, "I prefer to banish the word tea from my vocabulary forever".

"How will he get locked up?" asked Charlotte, "surely he can't just walk up to the prison gate and tell them he is wanted for nonpayment of a fine".

"You will rise from your chair and walk up the alleyway and out onto the main road", said Tim, "a policeman will ask if you are John Smith and on accepting the guise of your fraudulent name, you will be escorted to The Clink my fine fellow".

"Don't worry Gabriel", said Charlotte as she stood up to follow Gabriel to the door, "it's only for one night".

Gabriel walked up the alleyway and out onto the main road just as Tim had instructed. Before he could turn right or left, he felt a hand on his shoulder before a voice asked him.

"Are you John Smith?"

"I am", replied Gabriel as he turned around to confront a policeman with the biggest grin written across his face that he had ever seen.

"There is the grave matter of an unpaid fine", said the grinning policeman.

"I guess you are going to have to take me to prison", replied Gabriel, "for I have no intention whatsoever of paying it".

"Excellent", said the policeman still grinning, "Please accompany me to The Clink".

Gabriel walked alongside the policeman and within a few short minutes he found himself standing outside the large steel doors of the prison.

"A nonpayment of a fine", shouted the policeman, "Mr. John Smith for incarceration".

One of the heavy doors opened enough for a prison warder to take the required documents from the policeman, and before anyone could take another breath, Gabriel found himself following the warden into the prison.

"Now Mr. Smith", said a pimple faced warden, "you are here for nonpayment of a £25.00 fine, and you will stay here until such time as someone pays it, or you have served enough time in lieu, have you any questions?"

"No sir", replied Gabriel.

After Gabriel had removed all items of value from his pockets, he followed a warder down a dark corridor and out onto a wider corridor with long lines of doors stretching out on both sides. When they arrived at number twenty one, the door was opened and on entering, quickly closed behind him.

"Mr. Barnaby?" asked Gabriel as he stood facing the pitiful figure before him.

"Yes", replied the prisoner.

"My name is John Smith; I believe we have some talking to do", said Gabriel as he moved to sit down on the bed beside him.

"Did my wife get the money?" asked Mr. Barnaby.

"She got half and the remainder will be delivered tomorrow if the information you have is relevant to our cause", replied Gabriel.

"I wouldn't have asked for money", said Mr. Barnaby, "only I am in here and my wife and little ones are going hungry".

"I am truly sorry to hear that", replied Gabriel.

"I have been stitched up good and proper", said Mr. Barnaby, "and now Jimbo is free to do whatever he wants".

"What can you tell me about Jimbo?" asked Gabriel.

"First and foremost, a nasty piece of work", replied Mr. Barnaby, "he will stop at nothing to achieve his black aims and anyone who gets in his way will suffer the consequences".

"Is Jimbo involved in recruiting child soldiers?" asked Gabriel.

"Come to think of it he may be", replied Mr. Barnaby, "in all honesty sir I don't know".

"But you must have known what he was up to, you worked for him?" asked Gabriel.

"He certainly was involved heavily with the orphanages here in London, but I don't know nothing about child soldiers", answered Mr. Barnaby.

"Have you ever heard him mentioning the Bishop?" asked Gabriel.

"Indeed sir, more than once the word Bishop sprung up from his conversations", replied Mr. Barnaby.

"Anyone else?" asked Gabriel.

"He did mention a General Arkwright, but I am unsure where he fitted in with his plans", answered Mr. Barnaby.

"Why did Jimbo go to France?" asked Gabriel, "there must have been something that interested him other than fighting for his King and country".

"That he kept to himself, but knowing Jimbo's black soul, there was nothing good going to come out of it", replied Mr. Barnaby.

Gabriel lay down on his own bed and thought about what Mr. Barnaby had told him, and other than the mention of a General Arkwright, he was no further forward. Charlotte would call and pay his fine in the morning and he would leave, but he could not help the pity that had been welling up inside him for Mr. Barnaby. As he closed his eyes to invite sleep to hurry away the hours, Gabriel thought about Tim's upcoming meeting with the Bishop and only could pray that Tiny Tim knew what he was doing.

"Fleming", said Mr. Barnaby.

Gabriel was almost asleep when the name came rushing into his head like a heard of wild animals.

"What did you say?" said Gabriel as he opened his eyes wide.

"Lieutenant Fleming", replied Mr. Barnaby, "Jimbo mentioned a lieutenant Fleming".

CHAPTER 15

"I am almost certain that the Lieutenant Fleming I knew and the one Barnaby mentioned are the same people", said Gabriel as he sat down at the table between Charlotte and Tiny Tim.

"We know that David Conway mentioned a dead British officer and if they are the same people, then Lieutenant Fleming is no longer with us", said Charlotte.

"We know that both the bishop and Lieutenant Fleming were mentioned in connection with Jimbo", replied Tim, "but this General Arkwright is a whole new player".

"I think Barnaby was sincere when he said Jimbo kept him at arm's length", said Gabriel.

"Let's hope so my good man", replied Tim, "I'll try and mangle some more information from the Bishop tonight".

"What sort of a man was Lieutenant Fleming?" asked Charlotte as she moved from the chair at the table and acquired a more comfortable armchair by the stove.

"The kind of man I thought I could trust", replied Gabriel.

"Remember what I told you about trust", said Tim, "for now keep it within the circle of us three only".

"Is there any way we can help Barnaby's children?" asked Gabriel.

"You are so soft hearted", replied Charlotte as she threw Gabriel a mocking smile.

"Barnaby I'm afraid has made his bed my young friend", replied Tim, "the day he took up employment with Jimbo was the day he ceased caring for his family".

"But it's not his wife and children's fault", said Gabriel.

"That is a fair argument my good fellow, but what if his wife knew what he was at and turned a blind eye", replied Tim.

"I think the question he is really trying to ask grandfather is, will the innocent children go hungry?" said Charlotte.

"In the interests of humanity I will have a word in the ear of a few people I know", replied Tim, "perhaps they could find something for the wife and the eldest boy to do".

"Are you going to give them the rest of the money?" asked Gabriel reflecting concern in his voice.

"I believe Barnaby has earned it by revealing two very important names", replied Tim, "and if it makes you happy my dear fellow I will throw in a few extra five pound notes".

"There, I am sure Gabriel is forever thankful to you grandfather", said Charlotte, "I am waiting for him to throw himself at your feet and exalt you with glorious praises".

"I would prefer a cup of tea but I'm afraid to entertain the idea for fear of the floor opening up and swallowing us", replied Gabriel.

"Don't worry Gabriel old son, no time for tea", said Tim as he stood up from his chair at the table, "My beautiful and charming niece and your good self will be calling into the shop at the corner and collecting a package for me".

"Can it wait until later?" asked Charlotte as she showed signs of not wishing to be disturbed from the comfort of the armchair.

"It's very important and most of all", replied Tim,

"Why leave until later what can be done now".

"Will you still be here when we get back?" asked Gabriel as he stood up from his chair.

"I may or may not", replied Tim, "I have to get myself looking nice for our good friend the Bishop".

As Charlotte and Gabriel left the safe house to attend to Tim's errand, Gabriel tried to brush away the uneasy feeling that had been peppering his mind. Lieutenant Fleming was no doubt dead and the way things were happening around him, Gabriel could only wonder if he would be next. He worried about Charlotte and had come to the conclusion some time earlier that any bullet would have to pass through him first. He knew Tim was playing with fire but accepted the fact that answers to burning questions must be obtained by whatever means necessary.

"Good day Mrs. Turnstyle", said Charlotte as both she and Gabriel entered the shop, "I have come to collect a package for my grandfather Mr. Tim Cratchit".

As soon as Charlotte uttered the last words, Gabriel flung himself in front of her and tumbled to the ground. At the same time a gunshot rang out and shattered the glass on the door behind them. Without allowing time for thought he reached up with one hand and turned the door handle, allowing him to pull Charlotte through the open door and out onto the cobbled street. Another shot rang out and a split second before Charlotte and Gabriel stood up to run, the shop window fell out onto the street in a hundred different fragments of glass.

"Run Charlotte run", shouted Gabriel as he hurried Charlotte along the street as fast as both their legs could carry them.

Charlotte never spoke a word as she allowed Gabriel to hurry her away to safety, along the main street and quickly down the alleyway leading to their safe house. Gabriel occasionally looked back to reassure himself that no one was following them, before stopping at the front door and entering the house.

"Hello dears, back so soon", said Tim as he continued to apply makeup to his broad masculine face, "my dear niece what is wrong?"
Gabriel helped Charlotte to the armchair she had left moments earlier and on first reassuring himself that she was not hurt, he took a chair at the table and proceeded to catch his breath.

"What happened?" asked Tim, as he put his arms around his out of breath and visible shaken granddaughter.

"Someone, saw it fitting, to take a couple of shots, at us inside the corner shop", replied Gabriel as he tried to catch his breath.

"My good God", said Tim, "Oh my God I am so sorry".

"It wasn't your fault", replied Gabriel, "we all have to take the responsibility and share the risks equally".

"But it was my fault", said Tim apologetically, "I

forgot to tell you that the package was to be collected under a different name".

"My God I didn't even see it coming", muttered Charlotte, "what use am I to anyone?"

"Don't be so cruel to yourself", said Tim as he held Charlotte's hand, "it's difficult for anyone to expect the unexpected".

"But Gabriel saw it coming", replied Charlotte, "he put himself between me and the shooter and was on top of me on the floor in less than a heartbeat".

"Now I am not quite sure if I agree to the concept of a young man lying on top of my granddaughter", replied Tim as he tried to dampen the seriousness of the situation, "but I will make an exception in this case".

Charlotte first looked at her grandfather in annoyance at what he had just said and then very quickly burst into laughter. Gabriel wanted to laugh too; he wanted to treat the near death experience as a funny side of the face of life, he wanted to pull Charlotte up from the armchair and lift her high in excited joy. But as the fear and adrenalin rush began to subside, Gabriel could feel the jaws of anger begin to feast on his manhood and the realization that Charlotte could have been killed was becoming only too clear.

"A nasty business shooting at a young lady in that way", said Gabriel unable to hide the anger in his voice.

"Young man", said Tim as he took a seat at the table, "there are forces within and around us that could all too easily step on the quicksand of madness. The anger that I feel at this very moment, I have learned to suppress by the very realization that sometime soon these people will get their comeuppance. Someone could have killed my granddaughter and in doing so the very gates of hell would have been flung open to allow vengeance in all its fury to burn all before it. By the grace of God and thanks to your good self she has not come to any harm and by that grace alone we will find a way to end this and put those responsible, some place where they can never be allowed to harm another human being again".

"How did you know?" asked Charlotte as she lifted her head to look over at Gabriel.

"The shopkeeper's face", replied Gabriel.

"I didn't notice any difference in her face, she always looks as if the world was about to end", replied Charlotte.

"I could see it in her eyes", said Gabriel, "her eyes could not hide the fear that was being projected in our direction".

"A very wise observation for someone of your age", said Tim, "indeed, the eyes cannot cloak what the face can hide".

"You won't be keeping your appointment with the Bishop now?" asked Charlotte.

"Indeed, I will", replied Tim as he continued to apply makeup to his face, "even more so as a consequence of what has just happened".

"No grandfather please", pleaded Charlotte, "it's too dangerous".

"My dear girl", replied Tim as he reassured his granddaughter, "the comforts of my years on this earth have given to me the opportunity to absorb a wealth of experience on the art of survival. Do not have any concern for my welfare my dear but perhaps show a little concern for those who have the unfortunate task of challenging me".

"In any case", said Gabriel as the teapot before him

began to make a hissing noise, "do take care".

It took Gabriel a little while to come to terms with what he was seeing before his very eyes. The teapot which no one had attempted to use since yesterday had somehow come to life and steam began to float from the top of the lid.

"The teapot", said Gabriel, "It's warm, hot, something weird is happening".

"It's ok I'll pour the tea", said Charlotte as she stood up from the armchair and began to fill cups from the freshly filled teapot.

"At least you have your teapot back", said Tim as he set the lady's wig on his head.

"Well that is at least something to cheer us up", replied Charlotte as she set a cup of steaming tea down before Gabriel.

Gabriel did not wish to prod anymore into the mysteries of the stranger than fiction teapot before him, instead he gladly drank his tea and give thanks for small but strange mercies.

"I can't sleep", said Charlotte as she turned around on the bed to face Gabriel.

"Perhaps a bedtime story would do the trick", replied Gabriel as he tried to look into the sleepless eyes of Charlotte.

"You saw fear in Mrs. Turnstyle's eyes", said Charlotte, "tell me what you see in mine".

"I can't see anything", replied Gabriel, "the room is too dark".

"Then tell me what you would like to see", said Charlotte as she moved closer to Gabriel.

Gabriel could feel Charlotte's breathe on his face and the light scent of her perfume was now sending welcoming signals to his senses. The thought of them both lying close together in the stillness of darkness had laid bare the cloth of his inner most desires, and that very moment would be forever priceless in the vaults of his soul.

"I want you to hold me", said Charlotte as she lifted her head slightly to rest it between Gabriel arm and chest.

Gabriel allowed Charlotte to rest her head on his chest as he reached over with his other hand and held her tight. A motorcar passed by outside their window and from a distant alleyway, a dog could be heard having a confrontation with a cat.

"I want you Gabriel", said Charlotte as she pushed herself even closer to Gabriel, "I want you to protect me, please don't let them kill me".

Gabriel could feel his heart beginning to swell from the pounding passion that gushed forth from a rising dam of terrible beauty, and from those very words, he could not contain the blade of sorrow that lunged forth to bury itself deep into his heart. The thought of someone killing Charlotte had released the stonemasons from the dungeons of untainted chivalry, and around her, protected walls of knightly defiance were springing up to surround her desire to live. He would gladly accept the bullet meant for her, he would without question swallow a thousand bullets for Gabriel knew that Charlotte's death would be a far greater pain than he could ever bear.

"Don't worry my dear, sleep peacefully", said Gabriel as he heard the soft snores of Charlotte sleeping peacefully.

"Get up", shouted Tiny Tim, "take up your bed and

walk; we have a miracle to perform".

Gabriel jumped up from the bed and as soon as he came to his senses, he realized Charlotte had already left the comfort of the bed before him.

"What's going on?" asked Gabriel as he looked at his watch, "my God it's 5.00am".

"5.03am to be exact", replied Tim, "we need to conduct a council of war".

When Gabriel walked into the room he found Charlotte sitting at the table and Tim commandeering the armchair beside the dying stove. As he sat down at the table beside Charlotte he threw her a look as if to question the early morning rise, but Charlotte offered no unspoken answer.

"As you both know I had a delightful appointment with the Bishop last night and delightful it was in every sense of the word", said Tim.

"I really hope this is good", replied Charlotte as she let out a yawn.

"It's more than good, it's excellent, it's fabulous", said Tim.

"You mentioned a miracle?" asked Gabriel.

"A miracle indeed, well more treason I suppose", replied Tim.

"What madness have you conjured up this time?" asked Charlotte as she flung a worried glance in Gabriel's direction.

"We are going to spring someone from a prisoner of war camp my dear", said Tim, "and not only are we going to get him out, but we are also going to make sure he gets back to Germany safe and sound".

"Oh no you don't", shouted Charlotte as she stood up from her chair, "I'll be damned if I betray my country".

"Calm down granddaughter", said Tim, "you really need to hear what I have to say first".

"I don't need to hear anything grandfather", replied Charlotte as she added some edge to her reply.

"I really feel we need to hear Tim speak first Charlotte", protested Gabriel, "but I do stress that to betray one's country anytime is unforgiveable, but in time of war it is the blackest of all crimes".

"Ok grandfather", replied Charlotte, "let's hear why you believe we should betray of country".

"As you know I met with the Bishop last night", said Tim, "and the more claret he had, the looser his tongue became".

"Why don't you tell us the real reason why the Bishop's words flowed so freely", said Charlotte as she stared at her grandfather.

"Well I might have had a little help from by great aunt Bess", replied Tim.

"His great aunt Bess taught him how to mix a little recipe which in turn limited the person who consumed it to tell the whole truth and nothing else only the truth", said Charlotte as she looked at Gabriel.

"Indeed, ok my dear", replied Tim, "and after the Bishop consumed the recipe mixed with a little claret he emptied things out of his mouth so fast I had to take breaks in between in order to digest the large quantities of truth. Among the many things that are not relevant to our investigation, and are between him and his God, he mentioned that German agents and sympathizers had penetrated not only our chain of command, but the very heart of our security services.

"So why by assisting a German prisoner to escape are we helping our cause?" asked Charlotte.

"Because my dear", replied Tim, "two days from

now he is going to be shot as a spy".

"If he is a spy and I'm not saying I agree with killing, but I believe by helping him escape we are putting other British lives in danger", said Charlotte.

"Perhaps if he really was a full grown German spy, but it is highly likely that he is one of the conspirers and in exchange for his life, he will give us invaluable information", replied Tim.

"What if we risk so much to get him out and he refuses to cooperate?" asked Gabriel.

"Then great aunt Bess will have to be deployed", said Charlotte as she managed a smile in Gabriel's direction.

"All joke on the side my much older looking than me friends", said Tim, "If we manage a positive result from this daring escapade, we may at last get a look inside Pandora's box".

As Charlotte arose from her chair to light the stove, Gabriel digested carefully what Tim had said and knew they had no other choice. The slow progress they were making so far would take for eternity to uncover the reasons behind the employment of child soldiers. He wanted an end to the affair as soon as possible as the probability of another attempt on their lives was around some unexpected corner.

"Where is the POW camp?" asked Gabriel.

"Outside a village in Northamptonshire called Pattishall", replied Tim, "before I came back here, I called at a master forger I knew and have arranged papers for us, we can collect them before we board the train".

"I bet he was delighted to be awakened so early in the morning", said Charlotte.

"He works during the night and sleeps through the day so a bit like normal working hours for him", replied

Tim.

"Grandfather", said Charlotte as she sat the kettle on the stove to be boiled, "I believe we are going too far with this one".

"I must agree with you", replied Tim, "it is becoming dangerous to say the least and I would prefer if you would stay behind".

"No way", said Charlotte in defiance, "If it has to go ahead I want to be there to make sure you two don't make a mess of things".

"Quite right", replied Gabriel, "nothing like a spot of female company to oil the cogs of our scheming industry".

"On a lighter note", said Charlotte as she finished making the tea, boiled eggs and bread and butter, "you did mention that the Bishop had revealed information that was only relevant between his God and himself".

"No my dear", replied Tim as he sat around the table with Charlotte and Gabriel, "When I said between God and himself I meant it wholeheartedly".

"He must have spilled other things that might be of interest to those wanting to broaden their understanding of the male habits", said Charlotte as her eyes tried to search for Gabriel's.

"You don't see us boys trying to understand the female habits, we care to let sleeping dogs lie and I advise you to do the same", replied Tiny Tim.

"I believe what your grandfather is trying to politely say", said Gabriel as he smiled under his breath "is that there isn't any point in trying to understand the female mind, as most females cannot figure out their own mind".

"Gabriel Shivers", protested Charlotte, "I never took you for a chauvinist".

"Since when does forming an opinion constitute an act of chauvinism?" asked Gabriel.

"When your opinion in not mine", answered Charlotte.

"Indeed", said Gabriel still trying to keep a smile from appearing across his face, "I must remember to entitle myself to your opinions in the future".

"Do you see grandfather", replied Charlotte as she turned to smile at Tim, "if he continues to exercise my opinions I might even consent to be his wife".

CHAPTER 16

"I believe the man speaks fluent French", said Tim as they approached the entrance to the POW camp, "once we get him to France it shouldn't be too difficult for him to reach his own lines".

"I have a terrible feeling coming over me", replied Charlotte.

"I would appreciate it my dear", said Tim, "if you would keep your terrible feelings to yourself until this little part of our adventure is over".

"How do you know we are not walking into a trap?" asked Gabriel as the entrance to the prison camp grew larger before them.

"I don't know, but I will let you know in about five minutes", answered Tim.

As Charlotte, Tiny Tim and Gabriel approached the entrance to the POW camp, Gabriel could feel a storm brewing up within the pits of his stomach. Collecting the forged documents before boarding the train had been no problem, and even the train journey had been a pleasant one. But now that the severity of the task was looming before them, Gabriel found it difficult to conceal his fear.

"Good afternoon", said Tim as they stopped outside the two large gates, "we are with the International Red Cross and we have come to inspect the conditions of the German prisoners you are so kindly looking after".

"Can you just wait here a moment", said the elderly guard at the gate.

"Can I please go home now", said Charlotte as she stood almost motionless before the camp gates.

"Very sorry for keeping you but I'm told you are not on the list", said the soldier on his return.

"Not on the list, not on the list", replied Tim as he stood before the soldier, "I would surely hope not or someone's head would be rolling".

"I don't know what you mean sir", said the soldier.

"Isn't it obvious?" asked Tim, "we are they red cross and it wouldn't be any point doing unannounced visits if you were already expecting us".

"Excuse me", said the soldier as he went off to speak with someone else.

"You are pushing it grandfather and now I really want to go home", said Charlotte as she feigned a smile towards a second guard.

"Good afternoon", said a tall captain with one arm, "may I have your papers please?"

"Under the agreement of the Hague Convention we have the authority to inspect prison camps unannounced", said Tim in a tone of authority.

"I am quite aware of the agreement", said the captain, "but what puzzles me is we already had an inspection this morning".

"sir", said Tim as he looked the captain in the eye, "as you are fully aware of the Hague Convention, you may have noticed that the inspection this morning was carried out by those representing the first Hague

Convention".

"And then who may I enquire are you?" asked the captain.

"We represent the second Hague Convention", answered Tim, "and if you are still here this time next year you will get to meet the third".

The captain looked at Tim as if he was trying to digest what he had just heard.

"Are you trying to obstruct us from carrying out international law?" asked Gabriel.

"Perhaps you have something to hide?" asked Tim.

"Perhaps, I mean no, please forgive me", said the captain, "Will you kindly follow me".

Gabriel breathed an inward sigh of relief as the gate opened slightly and allowed the three bogus inspectors to pass through. Although he knew that only the first hurdle had been passed, Gabriel felt that by fooling the captain once, it could be done again.

"Please sign the log book", said the captain as they passed through a small office with a clerk behind the desk.

Gabriel signed the book first under his bogus name, and then followed by Charlotte whose hand began to visible shake.

"A bad case of the shakes there love", said the clerk behind the desk.

"Had a late night at the palace ball and one too many glasses of Champaign", replied Charlotte as she tried to keep her voice from faltering.

"Don't I know the feeling love, the morning after the night before", said the clerk.

As Charlotte finished filling in her name, Tiny Tim took his turn and Gabriel couldn't help noticing that he took more time than normal.

"Oh one more thing sir", said Charlotte as she turned to face the clerk.

"Yes love?" asked the clerk.

"Don't ever refer to me as your love again or I will have your bureaucratic backside nailed to the nearest lamppost", said Charlotte angrily.

"No, no love, sorry Miss", replied the clerk in surprise.

"Let me join you on your inspection", said the captain as he continued to follow the bogus inspectors as they passed through into the main camp.

"Certainly not", replied Tim, "our inspection cannot be signed off unless we have access to the prisoners on their own".

"Very well", said the captain reluctantly, "I will be in my office if you need me".

As the three bogus inspectors walked among the prisoners, they stopped occasionally to ask them questions about their stay and if they were being fairly treated.

"And how is the food?" asked Tiny Tim.

"The food is nothing to be writing home about", said one prisoner who spoke very good English.

"And where is home my good man?" asked Gabriel as Charlotte proceeded to take down notes.

"Bonn", replied the prisoner.

"Do you have any prisoners here by the name of Hans?" asked Tim.

Suddenly the prisoner began to laugh and began to shout out the name Hans. About twenty prisoners crowded around them before the prisoner replied,

"Take your pick".

"What about a Hans Aderman?" asked Tim as he viewed the ring of smiling prisoners.

"Sich entfernen", shouted the English-speaking prisoner.

The prisoner waited until the other prisoners had dispersed before he spoke.

"What do you want of me?"

"You are Hans Aderman?" asked Tim to make sure.

"Yes", replied Hans.

"It is of our opinion that you might like to be back home in Berlin sometime soon", Said Tim.

"There are a great many prisoners in here who would like to be back home", replied Hans, "why do you ask such a foolish question?"

"Depends on what you mean as foolish", replied Tim, "Foolish that it could not happen or foolish that I even suggested it?"

"You may look like a fool", said Hans," but looks in your case are very deceiving".

"We know who you are", said Tim, "and if you are willing to offer us information in exchange for a way out of here, then we may do business".

"I'm all ears", replied Hans.

"We are seeking information in relation to child soldiers", said Tim.

"I am willing to oblige", replied Hans as he surveyed the area around him to reassure himself that no one else was listening, "but how do I know that you will keep your word".

"You will have to trust us", said Tim.

"I'm not in the habit of trusting three complete strangers", replied Hans.

"Perhaps we could meet halfway", said Tim, "you give us half of the information now and we will get you to France, the other half can wait until we get you to a ship".

"I prefer if you get me to France first and then I will give you what you ask for", answered Hans.

"I'm afraid our business is concluded here", said Tim as he turned to look in the direction of Charlotte and Gabriel.

"I will call the guards and have you exposed", said Hans.

"And I could have you shot by those very same guards for trying to kill me", replied Tim as he stared at the German long and hard.

"Ok half it is", said Hans after realizing that Tiny Tim was not going to back down.

"The child soldiers?" asked Tim.

"The child soldiers were never meant to be a fighting force, more of a morale booster for German soldiers. A rumor was circulated within the ranks of the German army that Britain and France had not only lost the will to fight but had lost so many men they had to recruit boys. Most of the German soldiers dismissed it as rubbish, but when children began to be captured or killed, that rumor was becoming even more believable."

"In order for this to be carried out there must be agents working within the British system", asked Tim, "who are these agents?"

"Those names are part of the second half of our agreement", answered Hans, "but let me tell us this, while I have been in here I have thought a lot about my own two sons back home in Berlin and as a father I do not condone the use of children in this way".

"But you have participated in it", said Tim.

"I'm only a messenger", replied Hans.

"The only way we can stop this barbaric act is to find those responsible and hold them to account", said Tim as he began to walk around in a small circle.

"When you get me safely to a ship I will give you two names", said Hans, "that you have my word".

"We are now going to walk into your compound to inspect the conditions inside", said Tim as he began walking towards an open door.

Gabriel walked beside Charlotte as they followed Tim and Hans in through the compound door and away from the prying eyes of the guards. As soon as they reached the interior of the building, Tiny Tim began stripping off his clothes to reveal another similar suit underneath.

"Get dressed in those", said Tim as he handed Hans the garments, "and here are your papers".

As soon as Hans finished dressing, all four made their way to the clerk's office.

"I think we have seen everything we needed to", said Tim as he proceeded to sign out.

"I have enough loves in my life without another one", said Charlotte as she signed herself out.

"The security in this camp is very good", said Gabriel as he too signed his name on the register.

As the four imposters made their way to the front gate and freedom, a shout from behind them caused them to stop suddenly.

"Three of you", said the captain, "I distinctly saw only three of you walk into this camp".

As Gabriel's heart began to beat wildly, he noticed Charlotte pushing her hand tight against her leg in an attempt to suppress the shaking.

"I really do not have time for this nonsense", said Tiny Tim as his voice reached a higher pitch, "I have an appointment at The War Office at four and I care not to be delayed".

"Clerk!" shouted the captain, "get out here at once".

"Yes sir", said the clerk as he stood beside the captain.

"I saw only three people come into this camp", said the captain, "how many do I see before me?"

"Four sir", replied the clerk.

"How many did you see?" asked the captain.

"Well, Ahh there could have been four sir", replied the clerk.

"What do you mean there could have been four?" asked the captain angrily.

"I will check the register", replied the clerk.

"Bring it here I will check it", said the captain.

"You do realize that you are harassing international inspectors", said Tim, "make no mistake; I will make sure the prime minister hears about it".

As the clerk returned with the book, the captain looked at the list of names and then to the four imposters before him.

"Your papers please?" asked the captain.

The captain looked at each set of papers one at a time and upon returning them, he wished all four imposters good day and began walking back in the direction of the camp office.

"Take no heed of him", said the clerk before following the captain, "he's new here, only arrived this morning".

As the four imposters continued their way to the train station, Gabriel could feel a large weight being lifted off his shoulders and replaced with a lighter bag of relief. As he turned to Charlotte he could see the color returning to her cheeks right before his eyes and up ahead, Tiny Tim walked alongside Hans as if they were strolling in the park.

"How do you suppose to get me across the water?" asked Hans as he took a seat next to Tim.

"We have secured a passage for you on a ship crossing the channel", replied Tim, "when you get to the other side a man will meet you and ferry you in a motor car and drop you off as close to your lines as possible".

"How do I know that you do not have someone waiting to arrest me on the other side?" asked Hans as he looked suspiciously at Tim.

"sir", replied Tiny Tim, "we have just committed an act of treason to get you out of there; perhaps that on its own is sufficient proof of our sincerity".

Gabriel leaned his head against the window of the train carriage and closed his eyes. The revelation that children's lives were being sacrificed on the altar of propaganda had shocked him to say the least, and if what Hans had told them was true, then somewhere within the British establishment, cruel and narcissistic people were conducting traitorous acts against their own country. What started off as a list of names on a piece of paper and a note slipped under his door, had now become an extremely dangerous situation with life threatening consequences.

"General Arkwright", said Hans as they stood at the bottom of the steps that passengers used to board the ship, "he was one of the pawns used by others".

"What others?" asked Tim.

"I was only allowed names on a need to know basis", replied Hans, "what I do know is that the people calling the shots have some kind of club or organization".

"Have you ever heard of a Bishop being introduced during any conversation?" asked Tim.

"Now that I think of it yes", replied Hans, "he may be one of those calling the shots".

"Why do you think that?" asked Tim as he looked at his watch to check the time.

"I overheard a conversation in which someone said that Bishop or the Bishop, would not be happy", replied Hans.

"Can you think of anyone else or anything that will help us to get to the bottom of this madness?" asked Tim.

"There is a man who goes by the name of Jimbo", replied Hans, "he is a small potato but a nasty piece of work who will do anything for money".

"I'm afraid we are out of time", said Tim, your ship will be sailing soon".

"I am sorry I could not be more helpful", replied Hans.

"Not as much as we are", replied Tim.

"If you care to trust me with an address", said Hans, "I could keep my ears and eyes open and if anything related to your investigation turns up, I will forward you a note".

"Very kind of you but I don't believe that as soon as you find your way back to Germany, you will care much about us", replied Tim.

"I don't like what is happening as much as you, there are certain lines that we as humans should never cross and I truly believe that this is one of them", said Hans.

"Your ticket and papers are in the inside pocket of the jacket you are wearing", said Tim, "You are a Dutch engineer and are returning from visiting your sister in England".

Before he boarded, Hans reached out to shake Tim's hand. Gabriel noticed that Tim was reluctant at first, but eventually took the German's hand and wished him luck. They watched as Hans ascended the stairs to the deck of the ship and Gabriel smiled as he turned to give them one final wave of his hand before disappearing into the ship.

"As much as I hate to admit it", said Tim as they left to return to the train station, "I rather liked that chap".

As Charlotte, Tiny Tim and Gabriel entered through the door of their safe house, Charlotte breathed a sigh of relief as she quickly threw herself down on the armchair beside the unlit stove.

"I am never doing that again", said Charlotte.

"It certainly was a nerve rattling experience", replied Gabriel as he began working on lighting the stove.

"I wonder if Hans gets back to his wife and children, will he tell them how he escaped", said Charlotte.

"I am sure he will", replied Gabriel as he put a match to the stove, "it will be passed on to each generation and no doubt exaggerated as the years go by".

"Perhaps when the war is over he will write to us and thank us properly", said Charlotte.

"He might even send you a box of German chocolates", replied Gabriel jokingly.

"Or a bunch of flowers as real gentlemen do", said Charlotte before rising to fill the kettle.

"I knew a man once who used to grow flowers for one reason only", said Gabriel.

"What was the reason?" asked Charlotte as she prepared the table with cups and saucers.

"To give every lady in the village over the age of eighteen a flower on Valentine's Day", replied Gabriel.

"Now that is what I call romantic", said Charlotte.

"That's what I call dangerous", replied Gabriel,

"especially when the husbands and fiancés got jealous and forced him to seek alternative lodgings further afield.

"Anything exciting in the newspaper grandfather", asked Charlotte as she gazed over at Tim quietly reading beside the table.

Tim closed the pages of the newspaper and after folding it neatly he placed it on the table beside a vase of dried flowers.

"The bishop is dead", replied Tim.

CHAPTER 17

"What in the name of God are we doing here?" asked Charlotte as she continued to follow Gabriel to the entrance of the cathedral.

"God may certainly put his name to it if he wishes", replied Gabriel as they stopped outside the cathedral entrance, "but today we are here to pay our disrespects and at the same time scan the mourners for any dodgy looking characters".

"Grandfather should have come here himself instead of sending us to stand out in the freezing cold", said Charlotte as she moved closer to Gabriel.

"Your grandfather has other important business to attend to", replied Gabriel.

Almost twenty minutes had past when the doors of the cathedral opened wide and the bishop's coffin was carried out and placed inside a horse drawn hearse. Gabriel studied carefully the many mourners, who began to walk behind the hearse as it moved off to take the bishop to his final resting place. The news of the bishop's murder had stunned him and Gabriel knew that if those very people could kill a man of God, then Charlotte, Tim and he were in very serious danger. He studied the faces of the men, both young and old and waited patiently to see if anyone would jog his memory.

"I don't see anyone crying", said Charlotte.

"The majority of those who attend the funerals of important people are not there to cry", replied Gabriel as he continued to carefully watch the faces of the long line of mourners, "they are there to be seen only".

The long slippery line of black clad mourners seem to go on forever as Gabriel looked for someone or some clue that would sit out from the crowd like a swollen thumb. He studied the faces, the color of the hair, those with hats and those without; he watched their expressions, the way they walked and how long they could hold their somber expressions of simulated grief.

"Do you see her?" asked Charlotte as she pulled Gabriel's mind away from the fixation.

"See who, what?" answered Gabriel.

"Her", said Charlotte as she pointed to a lady walking along slowly and applying a handkerchief to her eyes.

"Have you seen her before?" asked Gabriel as his eyes now focused on the only person who seemed to be crying.

"Yes, I have", replied Charlotte, "and not only did I see her before, but I also know her name".

"I don't believe there is anything else we can do here", said Gabriel as he nudged Charlotte in the opposite direction of the never ending crowd, "let's have some breakfast and you can tell me all about her".

"Mary Green", said Charlotte as they waited on the waitress bringing them their order of scrambled eggs and toast.

"Where did you see her before?" asked Gabriel as he lowered his voice.

"She was a volunteer nurse in France", replied Charlotte, "very well-mannered but kept very much to herself".

"That is interesting", said Gabriel, "Maybe she had other motives for being in France".

"I caught her crying over a dying soldier", replied Charlotte, "it was one of the few times she spoke, other than to give or receive instructions".

"An interesting reaction of a could be assassin", said Gabriel as he continued to lower his voice.

"Oh my God", said Charlotte as she suddenly put her hand up to her mouth.

"Keep your voice down", replied Gabriel.

"I suddenly remembered something", said Charlotte as she leaned across the table, "that night I caught her crying; she spoke of her home here in London and of her family. She said she was an only child and lived in a house along with her parents facing the park. But what stands out the most is she said she had an uncle who was a clergyman".

Gabriel thanked the waitress for their order and proceeded to pour both Charlotte and himself a cup of tea. He thought about what Charlotte had just told him and began to believe that it may be more than a coincidence that the lady in question had an uncle a clergyman, and she was the only one they could see crying at the funeral.

"Did she mention which park she could see from her window?" asked Gabriel.

"No", replied Charlotte, "but she did mention that this particular park had ducks who enjoyed the attention from visitors, especially those carrying bags of delicious bread".

"Wonderful my dear Charlotte", said Gabriel

mockingly, "ducks that like to be fed in a park in London, do you know how many parks there are in London with ducks who are all partial to free handouts of bread?"

"No, please tell me my dear Gabriel", replied Charlotte as she threw Gabriel an artificial smile.

"Too many to remember and this is no time for games", said Gabriel, "We need to talk to Miss Green".

"And what are we going to say", replied Charlotte, "hello Miss Green, do excuse us but is your uncle the bishop who has just been murdered?"

"You could say, hello Mary, nice to see you and I am so sorry about the tragic loss of your uncle", said Gabriel.

"I'm sorry", said Charlotte as she reached out to pat Gabriel on the arm, "I know we need to talk to her".

"We need to finish up here and try and find out where she lives", said Gabriel as he drank the last dregs of his tea and placed two shillings on the table.

"Should we talk to grandfather first?" asked Charlotte as she arose from the table to leave.

"Tim has other things on his mind", replied Gabriel as they made their way out through the door, "and besides, we might not see him for another week".

As Charlotte and Gabriel made their way to the first park they could think of, Gabriel hoped that Mary Green would be easy to find. If the Bishop was indeed her uncle, Gabriel knew that within the momentary sphere of her grief, now was the time she would be most vulnerable.

"Let's sit down", said Charlotte as they entered the park.

"We should be looking for the house of Mary Green, replied Gabriel as he looked down at Charlotte sitting on the summer seat.

"She lives just over there", said Charlotte as she pointed to a red brick two story house overlooking the park.

"How do you know that?" asked Gabriel as he looked towards the direction Charlotte was pointing.

"Because she said she could see ducks swimming in a pond outside her window", replied Charlotte.

"And to strengthen your argument my dear Charlotte", said Gabriel, "All the other ponds in London do not have ducks floating about".

"I am sure they do", replied Charlotte as she smiled up at the bewildered Gabriel, "but they don't have a solitary swan befriending the ducks like this one".

Charlotte and Gabriel walked up to the front door of the red brick house and applied the brass door knocker. A few moments later a maid answered the door.

"Good afternoon", said Charlotte, "could I speak with Mary Green please, I worked with her in France".

"Please wait here, I will see if she's available", replied the maid.

As they waited outside the door Gabriel wondered why someone would stoop so low as to traffic in children. He had a gut feeling that Mary Green was involved some way and only hoped that their meeting would uncover some clue to lead them to the ring leaders.

"Please come in", said the maid on her return, "go straight into the drawing room please, she will be down in a minute".

As Charlotte and Gabriel were led into the drawing room, Gabriel could sense a strong air of religious values ebbing from every wall. A picture of Jesus and the twelve apostles hovered angelically above the fireplace, while on the wall above a dark leather sofa, a large crucifix reminded all that death was only the beginning.

"Charlotte my dear, how nice it is to see you", said Mary as she walked into the room.

"The pleasure is all mine Mary", replied Charlotte as she arose to take Mary by the hand, "I heard about your uncle and both Gabriel and myself have come to offer you our sincerest sympathy".

"Thank you so much, it has been a trying time indeed", replied Mary as she sat down next to Charlotte on the sofa.

"Indeed it must be", said Charlotte as she looked at Mary sympathetically, "if there is anything we can do please don't hesitate to ask".

"Would you like some tea?" asked Mary.

"If it is not too much trouble", answered Charlotte.

"No trouble my dear", said Mary as she arose to give orders to the maid, "I just got back and was about to have a cup myself".

"I feel so sorry for her", said Charlotte as Mary temporary left the room.

"A wolf in sheep's clothing perhaps", replied Gabriel.

"That is very hard to accept", said Charlotte, "why would she volunteer to help our injured soldiers in France?"

"I don't know, but I hope you can extract that information from her", replied Gabriel.

"Tea won't be long", said Mary as she returned to the room.

"Have the police found out who was responsible?" asked Charlotte.

"Nothing yet and I won't be holding my breath",

replied Mary.

"So you have no faith in the police then?" asked Charlotte.

"My uncle may have stepped on a few toes too many", said Mary as the maid arrived with their tea, "I'm afraid his death may be a blessing to those who wish to keep their disguises".

"Did your uncle ever mention a General Arkwright?" asked Charlotte.

Mary's tea cup came to a sudden stop and hovered between her mouth and her chest. She sat quiet for what felt like minutes before she turned and glared into Charlotte's eyes.

"My God, who are you?" asked Mary.

"Please Mary, please trust us, we mean you no harm", replied Charlotte.

"I would like you both to leave now", said Mary as she returned her teacup to the table.

"Please listen to what we have to say first", replied Charlotte as she reached out to touch Mary's arm, "we believe your uncle was involved in illegal activities".

"My uncle was a good man", said Mary, "a great humanitarian and a firm believer of practicing what he preached".

"General Arkwright is not a good man", said Gabriel as he joined in on the conversation, "you were taken aback when his name was mentioned, why?"

"You are correct when you said General Arkwright was not a good man", replied Mary, "when you mention his name, I remembered something my uncle told me about him".

"Could you please share it with us Mary", asked Gabriel.

"He told me a few months ago after General

Arkwright left our house, there goes a walking cloud of blackness".

"We believe that your uncle may have been involved with ungodly activities alongside General Arkwright and a man called Jimbo", said Charlotte.

"My uncle was no friend of General Arkwright or this man Jimbo", replied Mary, "this piece of trash called Jimbo paid my uncle a visit and in the very house of God, threatened his life".

At the closing of these words Mary burst into tears and was quickly comforted by Charlotte.

"There, there my dear", said Charlotte as she put her arm around Mary, "I know this is not a good time to be pouring over your uncle's grievances, but we are only trying to help".

"Hundreds of children as young as twelve are being sent to die in the trenches", said Gabriel as he took a chair closer to Charlotte and Mary, "these children are orphans and therefore have no one to ask questions about their disappearance".

"Oh God", replied Mary as she applied a handkerchief to her eyes, "You know, oh please God help someone to stop this".

"Did your uncle mention this to you?" asked Charlotte,

"Yes", replied Mary, "he was trying to get to the bottom of it before he was murdered".

Gabriel thought about what Mary had said and remembering back to when he saw Jimbo in conversation with the Bishop, he could only assume that it was when Jimbo was sent to threaten him. The word Bishop had been flung at him from all directions, and now he began to wonder if he was being cheerfully led down the garden path all along.

"You uncle was a very prominent man of the cloth", said Gabriel, "why did he not try to stop it?"

"There are very powerful and dangerous people behind this", replied Mary, "my uncle threatened to declare it from the pulpit in the cathedral and now he is dead".

"If what you are saying is true", said Charlotte, "then we too are on the same side, is there anything else you can help us with?"

"Only what you already know", replied Mary, "but if I find anything among my uncle's belongings I will let you know".

"I will leave you an address where to deliver it or send it", said Charlotte as she began to write an address on a piece of paper.

"My uncle did mention that there was someone directing General Arkwright, and he was the one to stop", replied Mary.

"Once again you have our deepest sympathy my dear", said Charlotte as they arose to go, "please don't hesitate to call on us any time".

Charlotte and Gabriel made their way through the park and back to the safe house to consult with Tiny Tim. As they walked down the narrow alleyway that would lead them to the front door, Gabriel was becoming worried that Mary had convinced Charlotte of her uncle's innocence. He had saw a visibly upset niece pouring praises on her Godly uncle and what Gabriel feared most, was Mary's acting abilities could be well and truly honed.

"I feel so sorry for poor Mary", said Charlotte as they made their way through the front door and into the main room.

"Don't be smothering her in sympathy yet", replied

Gabriel as he took a chair at his usual place by the table, "your poor Mary may be much richer in deceit than we could possibly imagine".

"You men are all the same", said Charlotte as she sat next to the stove, "as soon as a woman shows any sign of genuine heartache, you brand her an imposter".

"Well my dear", said Tiny Tim who had arrived back home some thirty minutes earlier, "Gabriel does have a point".

"Don't you start grandfather", replied Charlotte, "A barrage from one male today is quite enough".

"But Charlotte my dear", said Tim, "it's a woman's natural instinct to open the floodgates whenever she wants something from a man".

"And if she wants something from a woman, don't forget I was there too", replied Charlotte.

"Did you find out anything interesting on your trip to the bishop's funeral?" asked Tim.

"Indeed my dear grandfather", replied Charlotte as she threw a sideward glance towards Gabriel, "we have found out that the bishop was indeed innocent of all charges and in fact was murdered because he was on the trail of the same criminals as us".

"Charlotte is convinced of the bishop's innocence by the very fact she knew his niece in France and she shed a few tears", said Gabriel.

"Indeed", replied Tim as he commenced cleaning an old blunderbuss he had laid out on the table, "if that is the truth then we are in more trouble than I thought".

"I thought we were in enough trouble already", said Charlotte.

"Trouble in the sense that we are back to the starting line and everything we have risked this far has been for nothing", replied Tim.

"Maybe not", said Gabriel, "what if the bishop's niece was lying and her true intentions were to reflect the guilt away from her deceased uncle".

"That would be the most desirable outcome my friend", replied Tim as he continued cleaning his antique pistol, "but one has to look at all possibilities and then ask the real question, why was he murdered?"

"Perhaps he threatened to expose them for more money or a higher position", said Gabriel.

"Or perhaps he threatened to reveal their activities because he was a righteous human being and a true man of God", replied Charlotte.

"Whatever story turns out to be true", said Tim, "We are stuck in a rut until we can discover which one it is".

"Why are you cleaning that old pistol grandfather?" asked Charlotte, "you know it's more dangerous to yourself than to those you are firing it at".

"It has served many generations faithfully before me and I have no doubt it will continue to serve a very many more after me", replied Tim.

"Now when we are on the subject of firearms", said Gabriel, "I was wondering if you know anywhere that I might acquire one".

"What do you want with a gun?" asked Charlotte, "have you not seen enough guns in France".

"In France guns were pointed and fired at the enemy when the threatened to advance", replied Gabriel, "When our enemy comes, what are we going to use to defend ourselves, your umbrella?"

"My God", said Charlotte "has it really come to this?"

"I'm afraid it has my dear granddaughter", answered Tim, "Gabriel is right, we need to prepare to return fire".

Before Gabriel could reassure Charlotte that a gun would be used more to preserve life, rather than take it, a knock suddenly came to the door. Gabriel walked slowly to the door and before releasing the safety chain they had devised earlier, he reassured himself first that no enemy was standing at the other side. After taking the telegram from the boy Gabriel thanked him with a shilling and locked the door securely behind him.

"It's for you", said Gabriel as he handed the telegram to Charlotte.

"Who on earth would be sending me a telegram at this time of the day?" replied Charlotte as she removed the sheet of paper from the envelope and began reading.

"Probably from a secret admirer", said Gabriel jokingly as he returned to his chair beside the table.

"It's a telegram from Mary", replied Charlotte as she continued reading.

"Has she written to tell you that owing to her fantastic performance earlier, she has been accepted to play the lead role in the new theatre performance beginning next month", said Gabriel at the same time throwing a smile in Tim's direction.

"She says that she was going through some things on her uncle's writing desk", replied Charlotte, and she would like to know if we have heard of a linen merchant mentioned in our investigations".

"Did she mention a name?" asked Tim as he attentively waited for what Charlotte had to say.

"His name is Will Crossman", answered Charlotte, "according to Mary they call him The Bishop due to the tall hat that he wears to compensate for his small stature".

Gabriel's head began echoing with the words again,

again and again.
WIDE IS NARROW AND NARROW IS WIDE
BEHIND THE CROSS THIS MAN WILL HIDE
KNOW THEM ONE AND KNOW THEM ALL
FOR HE WEARS A HAT THAT MAKES HIM
TALL

CHAPTER 18

"Take this", said Tim as he handed Gabriel a pistol, "I will continue to put my trust in the one I have".

"Where did you get this in such a hurry?" asked Gabriel as he slipped the luger inside his pocket.

"Hans give it to me as a souvenir, he said it would always remind me of the day I joined the German army", replied Tim as he threw a large grin in Gabriel's direction, "he said he was going to use it to try and escape".

Despite Tim's attempt at trying to cheer him up, Gabriel could not bring himself to return a smile or reply to Tim's mellowing of the act of treason. He knew he had a dangerous mission ahead and the weapon in his pocket bore witness to that very fact.

"Now remember", said Tiny Tim, "you are representing an inventor by the name of Jacob Solomon who has invented a machine that can produce cloth five times faster than current methods".

"And what if he gets so excited about the idea that he wants to meet Mr. Solomon in person", replied Gabriel.

"Then you must reassure him that if he is interested,

a meeting can be arranged at his premises", said Tim, "remember the purpose of your mission is to have a look around, study the character and form of Mr. Crossman and report back to us".

"And where can I find you?" asked Gabriel.

"As close to the building as possible without raising suspicion", answered Charlotte as she reached out to put a reassuring hand on Gabriel's arm, "in the unlikely event of trouble raising its ugly head, we want to help get you out of it as quickly as possible".

"Good luck my elderly friend", said Tim before Gabriel walked off in the direction of the factory, "I would go myself only someone at the factory might recognize me".

Gabriel walked off in the direction of the collection of large red brick buildings before him as the morning mist gathered around like smoke from a phantom fire. He had volunteered to take Tim's place at the request of Charlotte and now as he moved closer to the entrance, the pit of his stomach began to send run away signals to his legs. But Gabriel knew that despite his fears, he could not run or hide from whatever lay before him. He also was aware that Tim would have gladly took his place had the risk been equal or even greater, but in the hope that their plan might have a chance of succeeding, Tim would have to stay on the outside.

"Good morning", said Gabriel as he approached a security box outside the factory gate, "I am here to see a Mr. Will Crossman if you please".

"Is he expecting you?" asked the elderly guard at the gate.

"No, but I have very important information to relay to him", replied Gabriel.

"What is your name?" asked the guard.

Gabriel found himself unable to answer; he had discussed everything with Charlotte and Tim right down to the last detail except what he should call himself. He knew he had to engage the cogs of his slow starting early morning brain and he had to do it fast.

"John Smith", replied Gabriel.

The guard lifted a telephone inside the hut and for what Gabriel thought was forever, he returned and invited Gabriel in through the heavy Iron Gate.

"Ok sir", said the guard as he opened the gate enough to let Gabriel through, "through the door on the right and at the top of the stairs you will find a door with his name clearly written".

"Thank you sir", replied Gabriel as he made his way through the gate and into the lion's den.

At the top of the stairs Gabriel could see the name Will Crossman clearly stamped at the top of the door like the engraving of a headstone.

"Come in", said a voice after Gabriel knocked three times on the door.

As Gabriel walked in and stood facing the man before him sitting behind a dark oak desk, he could hear his heart knocking hard on the wall of his chest. Beside him on the desk perched a taller than average tall hat and next to that lay a thick ledger bearing the remnants of a thousand secrets.

"Good morning", said Gabriel as he looked down on the man before him, "Do I have the pleasure of addressing Mr. Will Crossman".

"Please have a chair", replied Mr. Crossman, "you told the guard at the gate you had important information you wished to share".

"Yes indeed", said Gabriel as he took a chair before the desk, "information I hope can be of mutual interest".

"Did they find Cratchit yet? Asked Crossman as he mistook Gabriel for someone else.

The word Cratchit was flung at Gabriel with such a blast that it nearly knocked him off the chair. By that question alone, Gabriel knew that danger was throbbing from every wall and how he conducted himself in relation to the question was tantamount to his safety.

"Excuse me", replied Gabriel as he looked Crossman firmly in the eye, "I'm here on business".

"Then state your business", said Crossman as he returned his stare to the ledger before him.

"I represent a client by the name of Mr. Jacob Solomon", replied Gabriel, "he wished me to convey his thanks to you for agreeing to see me and prays that a man in your standing of character and enterprise would appreciate the progress of industry".

"Get on with it I haven't got all day", muttered Crossman as he continued to go through the ledger.

"My client has invented a machine that will weave cloth five times faster than any other of its day", replied Gabriel as he studied Crossman for any form of excited response.

"And?" asked Crossman as he lifted his head to face Gabriel.

"Well sir, as you are a loyal and dedicated producer of uniforms in a time of our country's greatest need, he has decided that you should have the opportunity of purchasing what he calls a great leap forward in cloth production", replied Gabriel.

"So this Mr. Solomon of yours wants me to buy into

some puff and bang contraption of forged madness", said Crossman.

"I assure you sir it is no mad man's fancy", replied Gabriel, "I saw it with my very eyes and am soundly convinced that other gentlemen in your line of business would be more appreciative".

"Five times faster you say", said Crossman, "if it coughed out cloth at twice the current speed I should like to get my hands on it, but that what you are claiming is beyond reason".

"Beyond reason is a fair assessment to make from behind a desk", replied Gabriel as he arose from his chair, "but those who chose to get up and look reality in the eye, will find that beyond reason is standing right beside them".

"Ok", said Crossman as he realized Gabriel was rising to leave, "where can I see this miracle machine?" "I can arrange a demonstration and fix a date that is convenient to you sir", answered Gabriel.

Gabriel took little notice when the knock came to the door and a man entered, he waited on Crossman's reply and wished he would hurry, as a quick exit from this dismal office could not come too soon.

"You will find me here most week days and if not you can leave a message with my friend here", said Crossman as he nodded in the direction of the person who had just entered the room.

When Gabriel turned around to face Crossman's friend he felt a thousand sticks of dynamite explode within the pit of his stomach. His heart began to thud loud warning noises in the direction of his eardrums as the blood rushed through his veins with all the ferocity of a high waterfall.

"Ahh, and there's me thinking we would never meet

again", said Jimbo and he reached inside his jacket for a firearm.

Gabriel pulled the luger out of his pocket and quickly pointed it in the direction of Jimbo. He felt his hand shake as he pulled the trigger, but to Gabriel's horror nothing happened.

"Cratchit should have taught you how to use that thing before he give it to you", said Jimbo as he produced a revolver from his jacket and pointed in Gabriel's direction.

Gabriel did not wait in the slim hope that Jimbo's firearm would behave in the same manner as his. He flung himself at the large pane of glass to his right and found himself falling to a lesser of two deaths. When Gabriel hit the ground below he expected to feel a great amount of pain screaming through his body as his brain surveyed the damage. But to his surprise and utter relief he found himself on top of a large bundle of cloth. Hurriedly he picked himself up from his soft angelic bed and ran to the main gate and into the jaws of the elderly guard.

"Open the gates now", said Gabriel as he produced the luger for the guard to see.

"I don't believe you will use that", replied the guard defiantly as he refused to open the gate.

"But I will", said Tim as he pushed his arm through the bars in the gate and produced his antique pistol.

The guard suddenly began to laugh at the sight of Tim's threat but soon stopped when Tim fired off a warning shot in the direction of the factory.

"Ok I'll open it", said the guard.

Gabriel followed Tim as they ran across the road and down an alleyway in the direction of the waiting Charlotte. As Gabriel turned to see if they were being pursued he noticed flames coming from the direction of the factory. At the same time he could hear Charlotte scream from behind a high stone wall, a noise that injected new life into Gabriel's tired legs. He ran like he never ran before as Charlotte's screams grew close and then closer. He threw himself at the stone wall and on reaching the top; he dropped his body down between the highly distressed Charlotte and the threat now facing her.

"I hate them, I hate them, my God I hate them", shouted Charlotte as she stood holding her hands to her eyes.

"Now, now my dear", said Tim as he walked through the side door that Gabriel failed to notice, "they have gone away now, let's not get stressed".

"I hate them grandfather, I hate them so much I want to scream", replied Charlotte as she clung to Tim's coat.

"Now's not the time my dear", said Tim as he rushed Charlotte and Tim down the alleyway and back in the direction of the safe house.

"I thought she was being murdered", said Gabriel as he sat down beside Tim at the table, "I almost broke my neck jumping that wall".

"Your act of chivalry has been duly noted my good man", replied Tiny Tim, "but sometimes what you hear is not always what you see".

"But a rat, my God she probably scared the poor creature to death", said Gabriel, "and no doubt half the neighbors".

"Ever since she was little she hated rats, for reasons known only to herself", replied Tim.

"I am not overly fond of the creatures myself but to

behave in that manner would be unthinkable", said Gabriel as he tried to stem the flow of adrenalin still rushing around his body.

"Some time, somewhere you will encounter something that will drive you to the very edge of insanity, I hope you don't, but everyone has to face their terror sooner or later", replied Tim.

"I have already faced it today", said Gabriel as he arose to lift the kettle off the stove.

"I saw Jimbo going in through the gate so I left Charlotte where we found her and proceeded to take up a position close to the guard's hut", replied Tim.

"I'm glad that you did", said Gabriel as he began pouring the tea, "I had no idea how to fire that gun you give me".

"Unfortunately Hans had no bullets for the gun when he give it to me", replied Tim as he thanked Gabriel for the tea, "Otherwise he would have escaped without our assistance".

"What was the use of giving me an obsolete gun?" said Gabriel as he flashed a not too happy look in Tim's direction.

"Indeed", answered Tim as he returned a smile, "how braver would you have been without it?"

"At least we know that Jimbo is tied up with the large hatter and in addition the factory has probably been burnt to the ground", said Gabriel.

"I will have a nosey outside later and see what I can find out", replied Tim, "by some stroke of luck there will be nothing left but the ashes of both Bishop and Jimbo".

"I need you to find me some bullets for that luger and if not, another firearm", said Gabriel.

"Are you sure you are ready to take a life?" asked Tim

as he looked into Gabriel's eyes.

"If I save a life by taking one, then I have no qualms", replied Gabriel.

"You can still protect a life without taking one", said Tim, "I have lived my whole life without spilling one drop of blood and I have saved many lives".

"I have no doubt that Jimbo was aiming to remove me from existence when he pulled that gun today", replied Gabriel, "tell me how I could have escaped that without defending myself".

"But you did my dear friend", said Tim, "you were able to use alternative measures to preserve your wellbeing and no one got killed".

"But what if that window was not there or a consignment of cloth had not been so conveniently placed to break my fall? Asked Gabriel.

"Then something else would have turned up", answered Tim, "remember, these opportunities are only placed before those who are pure of heart and soul".

"Have I missed anything?" asked Charlotte as she returned from her nap in the bedroom.

"I was just telling Gabriel here if you had to face a rat or Jimbo, Jimbo would have the pleasure of your company", said Tim.

"Enough about rats please", replied Charlotte as she took her seat beside the stove.

"It certainly was not a clever idea to hide somewhere and then announce to everyone within a square mile of your whereabouts", said Gabriel as he looked Charlotte in the face.

"Almost as clever as that idiotic display of bravado by jumping over a wall, when it was quite plain to even a blind man that there was an open door right in front of you", replied Charlotte as she returned Gabriel's stare with equal fire power.

"Now, now my dear elderly children", said Tim as he tried to defuse the situation, "let's not resort to biting and pulling hair, we need all the unity we can muster to confront what lies ahead".

"How do we stop it, that indeed is the question", said Gabriel as he changed the subject.

"We have the general, Bishop and our good friend Jimbo", replied Tim as he arose from his chair and began pacing the floor, "we need proof, written proof that will convict them beyond a shadow of a doubt".

"I don't believe that kind of evidence will be lying about in Bishop's office", said Gabriel as he turned towards Charlotte to catch her attention.

"Nothing can ever be as solid as a rock", muttered Tim as he continued with his thinking march, "there is always a crack somewhere if you look close enough".

"While you two are busy dusting off the rock in search of a crack, I will keep my idea all to myself", muttered Charlotte from the comfort of her chair beside the stove.

"Please my dear Charlotte", replied Gabriel as he once more tried to catch her attention, "we would be only too happy to share your idea".

"How to trap the general", said Tim as he mumbled to himself, "a spot of blackmail, humm perhaps not".

"Why don't you offer Jimbo money to let the cat out of the bag", replied Charlotte.

"My dear", said Tim as he suddenly stopped pacing the floor, "you may have struck the nail precisely on the head".

"Offering Jimbo money would be like waving a red rag in front of a bull", replied Gabriel as he smiled in

Charlotte's direction.

"But one thing Jimbo has got to lose worth more than money", said Tim.

"What could be worth more than money to Jimbo?" asked Charlotte.

"His life my dear", answered Tim as he sat down next to Gabriel, "the crime he is guilty of is a hanging offence".

"Perhaps if we helped him to obtain immunity by saying he was working with us, instead of against us", said Charlotte.

"My dear granddaughter, Gabriel, we are beginning to stray from what we are trying to achieve here", replied Tiny Tim, "that is to stop what is happening and bring all those to justice. Jimbo is as guilty as the rest and if we are ever going to stop the spirits of those children from haunting us for eternity, then he too must pay the piper of retribution".

"I'm sorry grandfather", said Charlotte, "I just thought it would be an easy answer to a difficult problem".

"However, I have an idea and the sooner it is executed the better for all", replied Tim as he arose from his chair, "I just happen to know the best thief in all of London".

"Where are you going?" asked Charlotte as she jumped to her feet to follow Tim to the door.

"To set a thief to catch a thief", replied Tim as he shut the door securely behind him.

"My God", said Charlotte as she returned to her chair beside the stove, "Whatever is he up to now".

"I would go with him", replied Gabriel, "but I need to keep my ugly face off the streets for a day or two".

"You can say that again, you certainly scared those

rats away", said Charlotte jokingly, "or was it the sight of a madman flinging himself over the wall".

"Probably both", replied Gabriel agreeably, "Nothing like an ugly face and a touch of insanity to frighten the life out of anything living".

Gabriel thought about the hours before and his speedy escape from the clutches of death. Tim was right when he commented on how brave he would have been if he knew the gun was not loaded. He knew Charlotte had put them in great danger by screaming, but he was prepared to forget in the interests of good relations.

"Gabriel?" asked Charlotte as she interrupted his thoughts.

"Yes", replied Gabriel as he stared into Charlotte's eyes.

"I didn't mean it about you having an ugly face", said Charlotte.

"I know", replied Gabriel, "I just had a look in the mirror earlier and I look just as handsome as ever".

"And I do very much appreciate you diving over that wall, whether it was stupid or not", said Charlotte, "Sometimes by seeking to protect the things that mean most, we are blind to the obvious".

"What is this great and powerful light that blinds us to the obvious? Asked Gabriel as he continued to look into Charlotte's starry eyes.

"Let me show you", said Charlotte as she arose from her chair and walked towards Gabriel, "let me convey to you this great and terrible beauty that even the purest of admiration cannot touch".

As Charlotte's lips moved closer to his, Gabriel felt a thousand stars explode above his head as the windows came crashing in around them. The room flung into darkness and all Gabriel could think off at that very moment in time was carrying Charlotte to safety.

CHAPTER 19

"My God", said Charlotte as she tried to catch her breath, "what happened?"

"I don't know", replied Gabriel as he brushed the dust and fragments of rubble from his clothes, "but if this is Jimbo's idea of a joke then I will never laugh again".

"What will we do?" asked Charlotte as she grabbed Gabriel's arm.

"We need to find out first what happened", answered Gabriel, "then perhaps Tim will have returned.

The explosion some moments before had left both Charlotte and Gabriel not only dazed, but badly shaken. He was sure that somehow Jimbo and company had discovered their whereabouts and decided to remove their thorn in the side from the planet, once and for all.

"My dears", said Tiny Tim as he rushed towards Charlotte and Gabriel gasping for breath, "I heard the news and rushed back to see if you had been hit".

"We are ok grandfather", replied Charlotte as she leaned against the gable wall at the top of their street.

"You heard what news?" asked Gabriel.

"That a German Zeppelin had dropped bombs in this area", replied Tim as he applied a handkerchief to his brow.

"At least that is one consolation", said Charlotte, "now we know Jimbo wasn't responsible after all".

"I wouldn't like to bet that Jimbo had no hand in this", replied Gabriel as he turned to look down at the ruins of their safe house.

"Where will we go grandfather?" asked Charlotte.

"As a matter of fact, I had plans to change our temporary lodgings", replied Tim as he ushered Charlotte and Gabriel away from the scene.

As the three friends commenced their walk past the butcher's shop and around the next corner, Gabriel surveyed the damage around him. Apart from their safe house, a fire across from the cobblers and the plume of blue smoke rising from the local distillers, the German Zeppelin had done little damage. He had read about airships in the newspaper and the concept of changing how we travelled in the future, but now even this wonderful leap of progress had been turned into an object of death.

"Mind your head", said Tim as he opened the door of their new safe house and made his way into a small room equipped with a table and chairs, two armchairs and an open fire with a kettle hanging from a crook.

"Not what you would call the pleasures of home", said Charlotte as she lay claim to one of the empty armchairs.

"Safe and snug as three bugs in a jug", replied Tim as he captured the remaining armchair.

"It's a rug grandfather", said Charlotte.

"No rugs here my dear", replied Tim as he threw a smile in Gabriel's direction, who now had to content himself with the hardest chair in the house.

"I tested the bed and came to the swift conclusion that a better night's sleep would be acquired on the cobbles outside", said Tim.

"I don't care where I sleep", muttered Charlotte, "I am so tired".

"Please yourself my dear and make yourself at home", said Tim as he arose from the chair, "I will be spending the night with an old friend who has all the luxuries of comfortable living".

As Gabriel wished Tim good night and locked the door securely behind him, he could hear the soft cotton snores floating towards him from Charlotte's armchair. He knew that the best place to sleep would be the bed, however torturous it may be so proceeded to remind Charlotte that armchairs were for sitting on, not sleeping.

"Your efforts are futile", said a voice within the room.

"Who's there", replied Gabriel as he quickly scanned the room for the owner of the voice.

"She will not wake up until my presence is no longer needed", said the voice.

"Who are you, do I know you?" asked Gabriel as he placed a hand on his leg to try and stop the shaking.

"Mortals are such primitive creatures", said the voice, I almost despair of the whole human race".

"Where are you, I can't see you?" asked Gabriel as the initial fright began to slowly subside.

"Trapped in these damp walls, always trapped between a damp place and man's stupidity", replied the voice.

"What is it you want of me, can I help you?" asked Gabriel.

"No", replied the voice.

"Do you want to help me?" asked Gabriel.

"No", replied the voice again.

"Why did you come then?" asked Gabriel.

"To help", replied the voice.

"Help who?" asked Gabriel as he began to show signs of frustration in his voice.

"And now my lord, I rest my case", replied the voice, "beyond any hope, absent of even the most minute fragment of reason".

"I don't understand", said Gabriel as he tried to discover the direction of the voice.

"I blame these idiotic walls for man's refusal to evolve", replied the voice, "Oh how I long for a utopia without walls".

"And don't forget the damp", said Gabriel as he tried to reason with the unreasonable.

"Hope, hope at last, someone who has restored my faith in walls", replied the voice.

"Do the walls have ears?" asked Gabriel as he struggled to make sense from what he was hearing.

"Terrible ears, ears that bleed this very moment from the pitiless thorns of gentle sorrows", answered the voice.

"Please, I throw myself before the mercy of the wall", said Gabriel as he knelt down on the floor, "I humbly beg that I might share what he shares".

"Stop crying Tom", said a male child's voice, "Mr. Jimbo promised we will be out of this Mill by Friday morning and off to a life of plenty in France".

"I'm scared John", replied Tom, "I'm cold and hungry and I don't trust the short man with the big hat".

"Don't worry", said Tom, "this time next week we

will have mothers and fathers just like everybody else".

"Can I suck my thumb?" asked John, "it helps me to sleep".

"Ok but don't let Mr. Jimbo catch you, remember what he said about behaving like a grown up", replied Tom.

Gabriel didn't hear the voices stop or the voice of Charlotte calling him from across the room. He felt his body shake wildly and a deluge of tears flowing down his face. He felt the welcoming arms of Charlotte comfort him in his hour of need and glowed inwardly as she pressed her face to his, twin heartbeats together bathing in their river of grief.

"I don't know why or what or how", said Gabriel as he lay beside Charlotte on the bed of a thousand lumps.

"My God", replied Charlotte, "when I awoke and found you on your knees crying on the floor, I felt at that very moment what you were feeling, I can't describe it, almost as if I was connected to you in some way".

"There was times when I began to ask myself, what I was doing here?" said Gabriel as he grasped Charlotte's hand tightly in his, "I will never ask that question again".

"Grandfather will be back in the morning", replied Charlotte, "we need to get those children out of there before Friday".

"This time you are not coming", said Gabriel, "Absolutely not, never and I don't care if I have to tie you up".

"The only way you will stop me Mr. Shivers is shoot me with your useless gun", replied Charlotte as she pressed hard on Gabriel's hand.

Gabriel held Charlotte until the voices disappeared from the street outside and until her snores could be heard tip toeing around the room. Before he closed his eyes he prayed for innocence lost and courage found. He prayed for the cold and hungry, for a hidden generation and trapped voices within every dreary, damp wall.

"Don't question, don't consider and for God's sake grandfather just take it as fact", said Charlotte as she began to raise her voice.

"If we are going to break into the hatter's factory at night, I am sure I would like to know the source of the information", replied Tim as he commenced his walking back and forth.

"We have to go tonight, or Gabriel and I will go ourselves", said Charlotte as she paused from pouring tea.

"Why the secret my dears?" asked Tim, "I thought we were in this together".

"The walls", said Gabriel as he interrupted the argument between Charlotte and Tim, "the walls give me the information".

Tim suddenly stopped from his pacing and began to digest what Gabriel had just told him. Gabriel watched him slowly reach inside his pocket and remove a small brown paper bag.

"You are going to need these", said Tim as he handed Gabriel the bullets for the luger.

"Give me a gun", said Charlotte as she finished pouring the tea, "or get me one, if these people want to live dangerously then so be it".

"My dear", replied Tim as he sat down at the table.

"No dear grandfather I will not be convinced any

differently", said Charlotte, "I will shoot the first person who gets in my way".

"Why don't you get yourself painted up and keep the night watchman busy while Gabriel and my good self-have a look around inside", replied Tim as he smiled in Charlotte's direction.

"If we find any children, where will we hide them?" asked Charlotte, "Oh don't tell me, you have an old friend".

"I love a woman who understands me so well", replied Tim.

"So, we go tonight?" asked Gabriel.

"Indeed, my good friend, why leave what can be done tonight until tomorrow night".

"Hello there sir, what's a nice man like you doing all on their own", said Charlotte as she stopped beside the guard at the gate.

As Charlotte kept the guard talking, Tim and Gabriel cut the wire at the darkest side of the fence and scurried inside.

"I hope she keeps his eyes pointing away from the building, I have to use a lamp", said Tim as Gabriel and he made their way across the yard and up beside a small green door.

"Have you done this before?" asked Gabriel as he watched Tim proceed to pick the padlock securing it.

"No", whispered Tim, "but how difficult can it be?" Gabriel watched Tim attempt to pick the lock and at the same time mutter unintelligent words under his breath. He could hear Charlotte's voice breaking into false laughter across the yard while someone somewhere wished another someone goodnight.

"Excellent", said Tim in triumph as he removed the

lock and quietly opened the door.

Gabriel drew his pistol as they entered the inside of the mill and at the same time Tim applied a match to an old lamp that he carried with them.

"Be careful old son", said Tim as he guided them both through the factory, "We don't want to trip over something and have to call for a doctor".

The thought of having to call a doctor out in such circumstances almost made Gabriel laugh, but was suddenly discouraged from doing so by the revelation of the lamp. Sitting crouched down together were two sets of frightened eyes reflecting the light within the darkness.

"Hello", said Gabriel softly as he knelt down beside the two boys, "we are not going to hurt you".

"He's right my dear fellows", said Tim as he two sat down beside the two boys; "we have come to help you".

"How would you two boys like to sit down to a feast of cakes and sweets, followed by a soft warm bed", said Gabriel as he rubbed his hand over the top of the youngest looking boys head.

"Did Mr. Jimbo send you?" asked the eldest looking boy.

"Mr. Jimbo is an evil man who is trying to trick you", replied Tim.

"I knew he was, I told you so John", said Tom.

"We want you to be as silent as mice please", said Gabriel as he stood back up on his feet.

The two boys followed Tim and Gabriel as they made their way out of the factory and back into the night air. The climbed back through the hole in the fence and proceeded back in the direction they arrived.

"Where were you?" asked Gabriel as he noticed the

familiar figure of Charlotte approach them, "I thought you were keeping the guard off our back".

"The guard is temporary out of action, he decided to allow the liberty of the movement of his hands so I had to deploy a largatacka wallop", replied Charlotte as she took the boys hands in hers.

"What's a largatacka wallop?" asked Gabriel as they quickly made their way up the street.

"You do not really want to know", replied Tim.

Gabriel stared at Charlotte as she happily cut thick slices of chocolate cake and poured generous amounts of milk for the two boys. He was relieved that the operation to spirit the boys away from under Jimbo's nose had been successful, and for that one short moment in time, peace had set into their lives.

"You are going to have to question them", whispered Tim as he made his way towards the door,

"I need to arrange somewhere safe for them until this thing has ended".

"Will you be back tonight?" asked Gabriel as he reached to close the door behind Tim.

"If I can arrange something, if not don't expect me back until morning", replied Tim as he made his way quickly into the night.

"Did you like Mr. Jimbo?" asked Gabriel as he took a seat next to the smiling boys.

"No sir", replied Tom, "he slapped me across the face for asking questions".

"He told us we were going to France to be part of a real family", said John, "but something just wasn't right".

"Sooner or later we are going to need you boys to make a statement in relation to your treatment", said

Gabriel, "these are bad people and you are going to have to hide away until we have enough evidence to stop this".

"Will we be cold and hungry sir?" asked John as he paused from eating his cake.

"No, you will be cared for by good and kind people", replied Gabriel as he smiled at the children.

"I trust you sir and the Miss too", said Tom.
Gabriel's questions were interrupted by three loud knocks straining the timbers of the front door.

"It's grandfather returned", said Charlotte as she made her way to the door, "I'll get it".

"Take your time and eat your cake", said Gabriel, "when you are finished you both will be going to stay somewhere no one can harm you".

Gabriel stood up from his chair and listened for any signs of Charlotte and Tim's voices. He made his way to the door and the realization that something was wrong hit him like a right hook from a heavy weight boxer.

"Stay here", said Gabriel, "don't let anyone in unless the recite the password, tiger claws".

Gabriel slammed the door behind him and proceeded to run as fast as his shaking legs would carry him. He reached the top of the side street and after quickly looking around; he took off in the direction of the barber's shop. At the barber's shop he noticed a motor car pull up and from a side alley; two men were struggling with what looked like a lady with a hood covering her head.

He was glad he had loaded the gun and received simple instructions from Tiny Tim on how to use it. He ran to the car and pointed the gun in the direction of the driver.

"Get out now, I swear to God I will kill you", shouted Gabriel as he tried to camouflage his fear with bold words.

Suddenly a gun was pointed in Gabriel's direction and just as Gabriel swerved to the side, a bullet passed by where he had previously been. He knew there was no time for assumptions or words of reconciliation, he lunged at the two kidnappers with the full weight of his body behind him and all four scattered across the cobbled street like skittles. Gabriel grabbed Charlotte tightly with both arms as one of the men tried to pull her in the direction of the car. He raised his weapon and fired a shot that shattered a glass window of the car. He aimed in the direction of the second kidnapper and was relieved that all had decided to hand in their resignation and quickly make good their escape.

"The children, the children", shouted Charlotte as she flung the hood off her head and began running in the direction of the safe house.

Gabriel picked himself up off the street and was soon hot on Charlotte's heels. He began to consider the painful truth that Charlotte's abduction could have been a ploy to draw them away from the house, and prayed inwardly that the two children were safe.

As Charlotte and Gabriel approached the house they were confronted by two oncoming bloody characters whose retreat was evident by the fear written across their faces. On passing, Gabriel caught one of the men on the side of the head with his luger and followed his tumbling body as it hit the hard stone surface of the alleyway floor.

"Who sent you?" shouted Gabriel as he pointed the luger at the man's bruised and terrified face.

"Please sir; don't kill me I have a wife and four

children to support", replied the frightened man.

"Last time", shouted Gabriel, "who sent you?"

"A man, by the name, of Jimbo", replied the man as his breathing labored.

"Go back and tell Jimbo the gloves are off, the party is over and we are coming to destroy him and his cluster of vermin". Shouted Gabriel as his leg shook violently.

The man hurriedly lifted himself off the street and disappeared beyond the shadows of the gas lights that flickered in the night air.

"I give those chaps a jolly good thrashing", said Tim as Gabriel entered the room.

"I could see that by their expressions", replied Gabriel, "well done Tim".

"And you too my good friend for denying them the company of my treasured niece", said Tim as he patted Gabriel on the back.

"There will be time enough for awards of bravery later", said Charlotte as she took the boys hands, "I pray grandfather you have somewhere for us to hide".

"Indeed my dear, always expecting the unexpected", replied Tim as he led the way out through the door,

"but first we need to drop our young friends off were Jimbo will never think to look".

"And where is that?" asked Gabriel as he walked behind Charlotte and the two children.

"At the police commissioner's house", replied Tim.

CHAPTER 20

"At least it has a decent bed", said Charlotte as she walked out of the bedroom.

Gabriel looked around the room and save for having an extra armchair, the room looked no different than the one before. He wondered how many more rooms they would have to share until closure, or how many more bullets would search until one actually found them. He was glad that the children were now safe with the police commissioner's family and he only hoped that many more would find their peace.

"I knew him since I was a boy", said Tim as he sat down on one of the well-worn armchairs, "as a matter of fact I even boxed his ears a time or two".

"I said it before and I will say it again", replied Charlotte as she removed her coat, "you are full of so many surprises grandfather".

"Can the police commissioner be trusted?" asked Gabriel as he too gives into the comfort of an armchair beside Charlotte.

"Probably the most trusted public servant in good old London town", replied Tim.

"How did they know where we had the boys?" asked

Charlotte, "are you sure those trustworthy and honorable friends can be trusted".

"That is something I have yet to look into my dear", replied Tim, "in the meantime we must keep several steps ahead".

"Christmas is only a few weeks away", said Charlotte as she stared at the empty table as if imagining a feast,

"I could eat a whole turkey right now".

"You won't find a shop open at this hour", replied Gabriel as he too began to feel the hunger pangs, "I'll go out in the morning and get us some things".

"I once feasted on a turkey that was twice the size of me", said Tiny Tim as he closed his eyes as if to remember the festive moment.

"I don't believe you", replied Charlotte as she looked at Tim in disbelief.

"I certainly did, it was delivered one Christmas morning by an anonymous benefactor", said Tim.

"You mean to say you ate a turkey sent to you from someone you didn't know, talk about throwing caution to the wind", replied Charlotte.

"When I was a boy growing up, no one would ever look a gift horse in the mouth", said Tim.

"If someone knocked on that door this very moment with a gift of a Christmas hamper", Gabriel interrupted, "I certainly would not be sending it back".

"Such is the idiocy of men", said Charlotte as she began to nod her head from side to side, "while you both are lying chocking and coughing on the ground, I could always say I told you so".

"Tomorrow I would like you to call on an old rag and bone man by the name of Ned", said Tim, "the commissioner furnished me with an interesting story before we left".

"What's so interesting about a rag and bone man?" asked Charlotte "is he really the mastermind behind all this?"

"Not so my dear", replied Tim, "but it seems he acquired a number of army uniforms that were apparently rejects from the factory due to their rather small measurements".

"Now that is indeed an interesting piece of information", said Gabriel as he arose to go to bed.

As Charlotte and Gabriel made their way through the throngs of people on their way to work, Gabriel glanced at almost every face for signs of recognition. He knew that floating around London. was someone or some persons waiting for a chance to cross their paths with violence. The luger swung heavily in his pocket as they walked briskly and Gabriel had no qualms about using it at the slightest sign of danger.

"This is it", said Charlotte as she gently pushed Gabriel towards the door.

"Good morning", shouted Gabriel as they entered the musty air of the shop.

"If you want to buy something then it is indeed a good morning", said an old man dressed in a long grey overcoat and matching hair, as he stooped while walking towards them, "If you don't want to spend money then the morning is like any other at this time of year, dull and duller".

"I should like to part with some of my hard earned cash and make your morning as fair as summer", said Gabriel as he smiled in Ned's direction, "It depends if you have something that might take my fancy".

"I have everything under the son except ladies underwear", replied Ned, "come to think of it I might have some of those in an old box somewhere".

"We are not really after underwear right now", said Gabriel as he tried to keep the smile off his face, "but as it is my young brother's birthday tomorrow and he likes playing at soldiers, I was hoping you would have an old tin hat or something along those lines".

"Or even better still", said Charlotte as she joined in the conversation, "A soldier's uniform made for a boy".

"Follow me into the back, I was expecting Tim to call himself", replied Ned as he shuffled his stooped body towards the back of the shop.

"Where's my ten bob?" asked Ned as he stopped beside a bundle of khaki green uniforms.

"Tim sends his compliments", said Gabriel as he handed the ten shillings to Ned.

"I got these from a house keeper of a big house across from the infirmary", said Ned as he pocketed the money, "The boss wanted her to throw them away but as she always has a soft spot for my handsome self, she give them to me instead".

"Do you know who lives there?" asked Gabriel.

"A retired surgeon by the name of Parker I believe", replied Ned, "and anything else will cost you another ten bob".

"Do you have anything else to add?" asked Charlotte as she removed another ten shillings from her coat pocket.

"Cross my hand with silver and take your chance", replied Ned as he reached his hand out for the money.

"A great many arguments are going on in that house", said Ned as he deposited the second payment into his pocket, "a few months ago they were a loving couple and now the housekeeper is waiting for one to murder the other".

"Did she mention why they were at loggerheads?" asked Charlotte, "any mention of strangers calling at the house".

"Not as such, but she did comment on how much alcohol the surgeon was consuming", replied Ned.

When Charlotte and Gabriel left the old shop, Gabriel stopped a taxi and ordered it to take them to The Infirmary. As they rolled along the cobbled street, Gabriel was only too aware that the pound spent at the rag and bone shop was money well and truly spent.

"You are not going to confront that surgeon", said Charlotte, "we should talk to grandfather first".

"We need to strike while the iron's hot", replied Gabriel, "something is stirring inside that house and the once devoted wife is not happy about it".

"I hope your right", said Charlotte as they rattled on in the direction of The Infirmary, "I am getting so tired of petty leads".

As the taxi pulled up beside The Infirmary, Gabriel paid the driver and helped Charlotte out of the car. He stared at the big house glaring at them from across the street and glowed inwardly at the realization that a breakthrough was getting closer.

"Can I speak to Mr. Parker please?" asked Gabriel as both he and Charlotte stood at the front door of the surgeon's house.

"Mr. Parker is not seeing anyone today", replied the housemaid as she began to close the door.

"Tell him it's Jimbo with another consignment of uniforms", said Gabriel.

Charlotte and Gabriel waited on the housemaid to deliver the message to her boss, which turned out sooner than they thought when Mrs. Parker came angrily to the door herself.

"I told you before, ahh", said Mrs. Parker as she stood with her mouth half open.

"Not who you thought my dear", said Gabriel, "but I am sure we can come to some kind of agreement about your husband's relationship with the aforementioned".

"Please go away, I have no idea what you are talking about", replied Mrs. Parker.

"We have no relationship with the scallywag named Jimbo", said Charlotte as she smiled in Mrs. Parker's direction, "we can help your husband escape the hangman's noose, but only if you talk with us now".

"Follow me", said Mrs. Parker as she led Charlotte and Gabriel into the study, "please wait and I will fetch my husband".

Charlotte and Gabriel took a seat beside each other in the study and almost simultaneously stared in awe at the great collection of books that painted the four walls with literary expression.

"Good day to both of you", said a tired and worn out looking surgeon, "my wife seems to be under the illusion that you can help me, but I'm afraid I am beyond all forms of mortal help".

"Good day to you sir", replied Gabriel as he waited for the surgeon and his wife to sit down opposite them, "I trust you know what we have come to talk about".

"My wife has nothing to do with what happened between me and Mr. Bishop", said Mr. Parker as he held his wife's hand in his, "I am a weak man whose weakness has caused nothing but pain and disharmony in this very home".

"Sometimes our greatest weakness can be our

greatest strength", replied Charlotte, "by what you know of Bishop could help to save thousands of lives".

"Would you like to tell us how you came to be taken in by Bishop?" asked Gabriel.

"About eight months ago I was invited by a colleague to accompany him for a drink at a little club he and some of his friends had put together. I hesitated at first but was convinced by the realization that I could perhaps raise money among the members for various charitable projects. It was the second or third night visiting the club that my colleague introduced me to Mr. Bishop. At this meeting we only conversed for a few minutes, but when I made a joke to my colleague on his size, I was surprised to be met with an icy cold reaction and a stare that was as sharp as the very scalpel he uses", said Mr. Parker.

"So when did Bishop approach you again?" asked Gabriel.

"The very next night I was to meet my colleague, but he failed to turn up", continued Mr. Parker. "After waiting for about half an hour I then decided to leave but was stopped in my tracks by Bishop who begged that I join him for a night cap. I reluctantly agreed and after sitting down in a seat near the arch window, Mr. Bishop moved in for the kill. He asked me if I would like to be a permanent member of the club and when I informed him I would need to think about it, he then promised me lavish amounts of funding for my projects".

"May I ask what projects you were working on?" asked Charlotte.

"My husband was involved in raising money to help poor children receive expensive and complex treatment, treatment that would have otherwise been unavailable to them", answered Mrs. Parker.

"And did you receive any of this funding you were promised?" asked Gabriel.

"That night he told me to put him down for a hundred pounds, but thankfully I never received a penny from him", replied Mr. Parker.

"This club, did he mention what it was called?" asked Gabriel.

"He called it the Pillar of Blood Society, an ancient society that has been around for hundreds of years", replied Mr. Parker. "A few days later his friend Jimbo called with a load of soldiers' uniforms and said I was to keep them until I received further instructions. I told him to leave them in the shed behind the house and almost forgot about them until one night something strange happened. I was disturbed in the early hours of the morning by a noise in the shed; I immediately loaded my shot gun and went to investigate. What I found when I opened the door was a sight that will haunt me until the day I die. About twenty or thirty children were putting on the uniforms that Jimbo delivered a few days before. I asked Jimbo to explain himself and he informed me that as I was now part of the club, I should expect dire consequences if I broke the silence. I called at the club the following night and told Bishop that I refused to be any part of his society and would be informing the police. Mr. Bishop smiled and then threatened to kill my wife and then make sure I got the blame for it. For a number of months I hid the episode from my wife but at the same time I was dying inwardly. My work at the hospital suffered considerably as a result of my heavy drinking, and it was only when my wife caught me with a loaded gun to my head, that I decided to tell her the story".

"No matter what you think", said Mrs. Parker, "my husband is a man of honor".

"That I have no doubt", replied Gabriel, "your husband is also an innocent man who was tricked by snakes like Bishop".

"Would you be willing to testify before a judge?" asked Charlotte.

"I have no fear for my own life", replied Mr. Parker as he turned to look at his wife, "but I will not put by good wife in harm's way".

"If we could put you and your wife somewhere safe until we trap Bishop and his gang, would you be willing then?" asked Gabriel.

"If I had a guarantee of safety for even my wife alone, then I would gladly stand before a judge and make Bishop Pay", replied Mr. Parker.

"After we leave I want you to send the housemaid away and lock the doors", said Gabriel as he stood up from his seat, "pack only what you can carry and answer the door to no one and I mean no one unless they call out a codeword".

"What is to happen?" asked Mrs. Parker.

"Someone will call for you and call out the code word Silent Thunder", replied Gabriel as both charlotte and he made their way towards the door.

"Young man", asked Mr. Parker as he moved closer to Gabriel, "are you sure this is safe?"

"Trust me sir, both your wife and you will be in the safest hands in all of London", replied Gabriel as he wished them good day and returned to the cold wet December air.

"Indeed, yes indeed", said Tiny Tim as he proceeded

to march back and forth inside the small room of the safe house.

"Can you get them to the police commissioner's house?" asked Charlotte as she poured the boiling water into the teapot.

"Certainly my dear", replied Tim as he held his hand on his head, "three thousand Christmas candles".

"What do you mean by that?" asked Charlotte.

"Something one of the children heard Jimbo saying", replied Tim as he struggled to work out the next move.

"Sounds like a large congregation holding candles while singing Christmas carols", said Gabriel as he sat down at the table and thanked Charlotte for the tea.

"You will get them out of there tonight grandfather, Mrs. Parker is very worried about her husband and Mr. Parker is more worried about her", said Charlotte.

"Yes indeed, consider it done, the more the merrier", replied Tim as he continued to pace and rub his head in thought.

"I can't see why the children's stories and the Parkers statements are not enough to move against Bishop", said Charlotte.

"It may be enough to arrest him", replied Gabriel, "but a good lawyer would have him out again in a few hours, we need more".

"Three thousand Christmas candles, a grand flash in the dark", mumbled Tim.

"I do wish this was all over and I can get back to normal living again", said Charlotte.

"Of course, Christmas carols, Church services, to put at three thousand windows", Tim continued to mumble to himself as he marched up and down the small room.

"And there's me thinking all along you were enjoying

our great and noble adventure", replied Gabriel as he smiled in Charlotte's direction.

"Who lights large quantities of candles, Buddhist monks, Catholics with three thousand sins, three thousand homes without gas or electric?" Tim continued to mutter as he tried to figure out the problem that had sprung up to nag his inner self.

"I wonder what is eating grandfather", said Charlotte loudly as she tried to catch his attention, "someone's cup of tea is getting rather cold".

"Tim, sir", said Gabriel as he reached over to tap Tim on the shoulder, "Your tea".

"I'm afraid tea will have to wait", replied Tim as he stopped pacing and removed his hand from his head, "I need to pay a visit to the commissioner; to make sure tonight's flit will go as planned".

Before Charlotte or Gabriel could wish him goodnight, Tim was out through the door like a flash and pausing only to remind Gabriel to secure it behind him.

"Now that is what I call fast for a man of his age", said Gabriel as he returned from locking the door.

"Something is gnawing at his mind", replied Charlotte, "grandfather would never leave a cup of tea untouched for nothing".

"Do you trust the police commissioner?" asked Gabriel as he sat down on the armchair next to Charlotte.

"If grandfather trusts him then I too award him with that honor", replied Charlotte as she leaned back in the chair and closed her eyes.

"How did Jimbo's thugs know where we took the children?" asked Gabriel.

"Only an idiot could answer that question and you are suitably qualified", said a familiar voice.

Gabriel quickly jumped up from his chair and scanned the room for a physical presence. He reached over and began to shake Charlotte and like before, the chances of wakening her were impossible.

"Then tell me Mr. Ebenezer", said Gabriel as he once again tried to hide the obvious shaking in his voice, "how would an idiot answer the question?"

"Behind every window is a set of eyes and behind those eyes is a mind trying to figure out where the next loaf of bread will come from", answered Ebenezer.

"So it could have been anyone on the route here", replied Gabriel.

"Or everyone my fine fellow", returned Ebenezer.

"We have met before", said Gabriel as he continued to search the room.

"We have had that pleasure, but the time and place does elude me", replied   Ebenezer.

"What do I owe the honor of this visit?" asked Gabriel.

"Stupidity in your part and blindness from my dear boy Tiny Tim", replied Ebenezer.

"Stupidity and blindness?" asked Gabriel, "I myself admit to the crime of stupidity on occasion, but Tim has perfect eyesight".

"Then tell him to watch where he is going", replied Ebenezer, "he reminds me of a drunk man trying to negotiate his way up a dark alley".

"I don't understand", said Gabriel, "Tim has always found his way rather well".

"He is being blinded by three thousand tiny flickering flames leading him up a path in a wax covered garden", replied Ebenezer.

"Where should he be led?" asked Gabriel.

"He should be looking for three thousand beating

hearts, all pulsating to the same rhythm", replied Ebenezer as his voice began to fade away.

"Pulsating to what rhythm?" shouted Gabriel.

"Fear", replied Ebenezer as his voice disappeared.

"I am so, so tired", said Charlotte as she arose from the chair, "I'm off to bed".

CHAPTER 21

In the midst of the silence of the night, Gabriel's eyes opened wide. No motorcar passed by, no drunken songsters or dog's warning bark could claim responsibility for his sudden awakening. The voice drifted off on its return to where it sleeps and all Gabriel could remember were the words, Time to Go. Charlotte turned and heard his soft whispers and almost in unison they both left the warmth of the bed and departed out through the door while not one word passed between them.

The cold damp early morning air offered them no comforts as they made their way through the aroma of freshly baked breads and a factory whistle screaming from somewhere in the distance. Gabriel trusted the voice and Charlotte trusted Gabriel and behind them the hammering of gunshots could be heard echoing from the empty walls of the room they had just left.

"Where is grandfather when we need him most?" asked Charlotte as she broke the silence.

"Right here my dear", replied Tiny Tim as he stepped out of a dark patch in a doorway.

"Bishop is one finely tuned instrument of anger",

said Gabriel as all three continued walking in the direction of nowhere in particular.

"Indeed my fine fellow", replied Tim, "an instrument that will soon be playing its own requiem".

"Have you any other safe houses nearby?" said Charlotte as she shivered and hooked onto both Tim and Gabriel's arm.

"Not at this present moment in time", replied Tim as he reached into his inside pocket and produced a brown envelope, "but you two will not need one, you're off to Belgium".

"Where are you going grandfather?" asked Charlotte as she suddenly stopped outside a tobacconist.

"Everything you need including new identities and instructions are in this envelope, I will catch up with you both later", replied Tim.

"Are we getting close sir?" asked Gabriel as he placed the envelope in his coat pocket.

"My young friend", replied Tim as he proceeded to walk off in another direction, "we are standing on its toes".

When Charlotte and Gabriel walked into the camp, they expected little scrutiny being applied to their identities. Their papers informed those who challenged them that Gabriel was part of a war department team sent on a fact finding mission and Charlotte was his capable and trusty secretary. However, General Arkwright also believed them to be as black hearted as he and secret members of the Pillar of Blood Society. And now thanks to the never ending genius of Mr. Tim Cratchit Esquire, Charlotte and Gabriel were now entering the core of the vipers nest.

"Mr. Tom Drennen and Miss Elizabeth Barton to see

General Arkwright", said Gabriel as he boldly handed over their papers to the young soldier at the desk.

"Excuse me for a moment", replied the soldier as he left his desk and after knocking on a room door, entered and announced Gabriel and Charlotte's presence to someone inside.

"He will see you now", said the soldier as he returned to his desk.

With Charlotte close behind, Gabriel made his way through the open door and for the first time came face to face with what looked like Mr. Bishop's twin brother.

"Good day general", said Gabriel as he reached down to shake his hand, "I am sure you know as much about us as we know ourselves".

"Sit down", replied the general, "what can I do for you?"

"I am sure you have heard the words, to thread the needle of time".

The general arose from his chair and made his way towards the door; he opened it and told the young soldier to leave the building. On his way back to his desk he stopped beside Charlotte and stared with cold dark eyes into her face.

"To thread the needle of time indeed", said the general as he returned to his chair behind the desk.

"I trust you have been fully briefed by the Society on the task before us", said Gabriel as he tried to keep the anger from filtering through his voice.

"What has the Society planned for Christmas day?" asked the general as he now directed the cold dark stare towards Gabriel.

"I don't care much for your games sir", replied Gabriel as he returned the general's stare with one of his own.

"If you were truly sent from the Society, then you would know what we have planned for Christmas Day", shouted the general as he banged his fist on the table and caused Charlotte to jump up from her seat.

"Listen to me you little piece of vermin meat", shouted Gabriel as he stood up and looked down at the general, "Instead of three thousand candles, how about you being subjected to the same treatment".

On hearing these words the general's expression turned from one of anger to that of a small boy who had just been scolded by his parents.

"Please my dears, you can never be too careful", said the general as he arose from his chair, "let me offer you some refreshments".

"We didn't come here for refreshments" replied Gabriel, still not allowing the anger in his voice to retire.

"I am fully aware of your mission, please sir sit down", said the general.

Gabriel stared hard into the face of the general before taking his seat once again. The luger in his inside pocket seemed to be throbbing, breathing heavily and calling out for Gabriel to use it on the excuse for a human being before him. The resemblance to Bishop was strange to say the least, but Gabriel knew the general if not related, was every bit as rotten as Bishop and all his followers.

"Have you thought about how we are to carry it out?" asked Gabriel.

"Fire a few shells at the German trenches and let the little beggars feast on a festive swarm of German machinegun bullets", replied the general as he burst into a strange rattle of laughter.

Gabriel's blood began to boil, he wanted to end the general's life here and now, he yearned to see the scab of putrid thoughts disappear and make the world a better place. The general continued to laugh as Gabriel arose and reached inside his coat pocket to retrieve the luger. He felt Charlotte's hand gently press his arm and in that small moment of madness, Charlotte's touch allowed him to return to his senses.

"We will meet outside the gate at four o'clock", said Gabriel as he ushered Charlotte through the door they entered, "I need to inspect the candles".

The fresh December air flowed over Gabriel's face as he made his way outside and away from the inhuman character of General Arkwright. He leaned against the gable wall of an old ruined barn and before long Charlotte had wrapped her arms around his waist to take comfort from the only humane figure she could trust.

"We have got to hold onto our sanity", said Charlotte, "for God's sake do not fall apart or all our dangerous and grueling work will be for nothing".

"It is difficult to be saintly when you move among monsters", replied Gabriel.

"Good will always overcome evil, no matter what we see around us", said Charlotte as she moved away from her embrace.

"Let's have a look around", replied Gabriel as both he and Charlotte made their way out through the gate.

"Did grandfather mention in his note where we would meet up?" asked Charlotte as she hooked onto Gabriel's arm.

"No, but you know Tim, whenever he's needed he always shows up", replied Gabriel.

Charlotte and Gabriel stopped and looked across at the town of Ypres. Smoke was still billowing from the ruins of some buildings and Gabriel wondered how many lives were wasted in its defense. He could see trenches reaching out across the landscape and to his right, more trenches were being dug. A few weeks ago he had heard a newspaper boy call out the news of a large and bloody battle that took place in this very place, and now Gabriel was standing right before its aftermath.

"Do you see anything that could house a large number of soldiers or children?" asked Gabriel.

"Certainly not with a roof on it", replied Charlotte.

"Where did they hide them?" said Gabriel as he strained to see through the mist.

"We will soon find out", replied Charlotte as she pulled Gabriel's arm, "It's almost four o'clock".

As Charlotte and Gabriel came up to the gate, a motorcar was waiting and General Arkwright had already taken his place in the back seat. Gabriel helped Charlotte inside first and then climbed in beside her.

"I trust you had a pleasant walk", said the general as the car made its way down the bumpy road.

"If what you call destruction pleasant, then I would prefer an alternative", replied Gabriel.

"Nothing like the sight of shell damaged buildings and the smell of battle to fire up the old appetite, what", said the general.

Gabriel never responded to the general's black sense of humor and decided to refrain from any conversation until it was necessary. The evening sky began to cloud over, giving way to the trickle of rain and within the silence of his own thoughts; all Gabriel could think about was the terrible anger that was now raging up inside him. He only knew when the general spoke of something horrid, by the pressure of Charlotte's finger prodding his side to warn him of any reaction. He blocked the words out by bringing up memories of childhood and the joy of the long summer holidays spent in laughter and the smell of freshly mowed hay. The car coming to a sudden stop beside an old church brought Gabriel back from his memories and the dire realization that he would have to say something to the general.

"So this is where we keep the candles", said Gabriel as he stepped out of the car before helping Charlotte.

"The ironic part of all this is, they used to light three thousand candles in this church on Christmas day", replied the general.

"How will we get them to the trenches?" asked Gabriel as he walked towards the church door, "three thousand children in uniforms will not go unnoticed".

"It's all taken care of; a few of our chaps will take over from the guards at the opening and on Christmas Eve night we will march them in and over the top", replied the general.

Gabriel opened the church door and was followed close behind by Charlotte, they made their way across the floor to what was once upon a time the alter. He could smell the dampness seeping from its walls and somewhere within the walls a faint smell of roses began to grow stronger.

"Oh I'm so sorry", said Gabriel as he looked at the young nun before him, "I thought this building was derelict".

"I am sure you could be right", replied the nun, "but being right and wrong at the same time does not justify one or the other".

Gabriel stared at the young nun and quickly realized she had only one eye. The skin on her face carried on and over where her eye should have been, almost as if her lack of an eye socket had been natural.

"Have you come to pray my children?" asked the nun.

"Perhaps", replied Charlotte, "I wonder if I could have a word with you in private".

"Would you please leave us Gabriel", said the nun. Gabriel bid the nun good evening and made his way across the empty church and back out through the doors.

"You didn't tell me it was occupied", said Gabriel as he walked over to the general who was now leaning against the car smoking a large cigar.

"It's empty, has been for many years", replied the general as he blew a puff of cigar smoke in Gabriel's direction.

"I have just spoke to a nun in there", said Gabriel.

"Humm, probably just called to pay the place a visit", replied the general, "she won't stay about for long".

"Will Bishop be here on Christmas Eve?" asked Gabriel.

"Why didn't you ask him?" replied the general as he removed the cigar from his mouth and stared Gabriel in the face.

"You know Bishop, one minute he's here and the next he's over there", said Gabriel as he met the general's gaze, "he was to brief us thoroughly before we left but he got called away on urgent business".

"He better be here on Christmas Eve, I don't like starting the festivities without him", replied the general as he continued to puff his cigar.

"Is everything ok?" asked Gabriel as Charlotte

approached the car.

"Just women's talk", answered Charlotte.

"I'll take you back and show you to your billet", said the general, "we have that gold assignment to deliver tomorrow".

As Charlotte and Gabriel climbed back into the car, Gabriel looked back at the old church and for one brief second, he thought he saw a great beam of light reflecting from the stain glass windows.

"What is the name of that church?" asked Gabriel as they moved off.

"They call it Saint Dita's after a one eyed nun who was supposed to have worked miracles over two hundred years ago", replied the general.

For a short while Gabriel stared straight ahead, not daring to question any facts about the two hundred year old legend. As they turned a corner he could feel Charlotte's hand close over his and from the side of his eye, he saw the tears running abundantly down her face.

"I wonder where grandfather is?" asked Charlotte as they sat outside the stone barn and makeshift accommodation.

"As I said before he will turn up when we either need him most or we are least expecting him", replied Gabriel as he placed the oil lamp on the ground before them.

Gabriel looked out below the level of the night sky and watched the flashes of shellfire somewhere in some distant place. The billet the general had dropped them off at was simple to say the least; the complete furniture consisted of two single beds with rock hard mattresses and two chairs that had seen much better days. The mention of a gold drop the next day had come as a surprise to Gabriel and the thought of being part of a criminal conspiracy almost made him sick. The meeting with the nun had disturbed him deeply and no matter how much he wanted to know what was said between her and Charlotte, he could never gain the courage to bring it up.

"Did grandfather mention gold in his note?" asked Charlotte.

"No mention of gold, I suspect he knew nothing about it", replied Gabriel.

"I bet its payment for all those services rendered on behalf of the child recruiting agency", said Charlotte as she reached out with her hand to catch the tiny droplets of rain that were now beginning to fall.

"They will never see that gold", replied Gabriel as he lifted the lamp from the ground and began to walk indoors.

"Don't do anything stupid", replied Charlotte as she followed him inside and closed the door, "any blunder from you and those children die".

"I just can't see myself going against every grain in my body and soul", said Gabriel as he sat down on the rock hard bed.

"Sometimes in order to fight evil we must become evil ourselves", replied Charlotte as she divided a small loaf of bread and handed Gabriel half".

"This reminds me of someone else who broke bread, I hope this is not going to be our last supper", said Gabriel after thanking Charlotte.

At the closing of these words Gabriel noticed Charlotte's head turn away as she placed her hand on her forehead. He wanted to apologize for frightening her and tell her that everything would be ok, but three loud knocks on the door drew his attention away from her and onto the luger in his pocket.

"Stay where you are", said Gabriel as he drew the pistol and slowly walked to the door.

"Are you going to shoot me with my own gun?" said Hans as Gabriel opened the door.

"My God" shouted Charlotte, as she smiled in Hans' direction, "where did you come from?"

"I mean you no harm my friends", said Hans, "please put my gun away".

Gabriel returned the luger to his pocket and beckoned Hans to take one of the chairs beside the table. The sight of Hans at the door had temporary frightened him but he quickly arrived at the conclusion that the German had no reason to hate them.

"How did you know we were here?" asked Charlotte as she sat down on the last chair.

"Young lady", said Hans as he offered her a wide grin, "I did not receive the title of Master of Spies for nothing".

"So you know why we are here", replied Charlotte.

"Indeed, and I have come to offer you my help", said Hans.

"Why should we trust you", replied Gabriel as he sat down on the rock bed, "didn't you work for Bishop?"

"First let me answer why you should trust me", said Hans as he produced a photograph from his wallet, "this here is my youngest son; I arrived home just in time for his birth".

"He's beautiful", replied Charlotte as she looked at the photograph of the baby, "he looks just like you".

Gabriel watched the look of pride sweep across the German's face as Charlotte commented on the resemblance, and realized with that look alone, Hans had convinced him of his sincerity.

"And second", said Hans as he put the photo back into his wallet, "I did not work for Bishop, I work for Germany".

"Ok I believe you", replied Gabriel, "how can you help us?"

"On Christmas Eve night our side will instigate a massive attack on the British and French lines, I will exaggerate my reports to such an extent, that there is a good chance they will call it off. I need you to stop any attempt by the British and French to do likewise, use whatever means available to spread the festive spirit. We need to create an environment where it is possible to get those children out", said Hans.

"What about Bishop and General Arkwright?" asked Charlotte, "surely they will have something to say about all this".

"I need you to try and stop the gold shipment tomorrow", said Hans, "by fair means or foul you have got to make sure the gold is hid in General Arkwright's office. I am sending a letter to the British High Command implicating him in treason, the letter will contain some proof of this but the gold found in his person will seal his fate".

"And Bishop?" asked Gabriel.

"Bishop will be your responsibility", answered Hans, "I have nothing to implicate him; he covers his trail well by getting others to do the lion's share of his dirty work".

"Back home in London we have some people safely tucked away who will swear to Bishop's involvement, but it may not be enough", said Charlotte.

"Leave Bishop to me", replied Gabriel, "I will deal with Bishop on the night".

"You will stay away from Bishop on that night", shouted Charlotte as he stood up from the chair, "do you hear me Gabriel, in the name of God please stay away from him".

Both Hans and Gabriel were stunned by Charlotte's sudden outburst of anger and visible emotion. Gabriel could see tears forming in her eyes and as she walked towards the door he realized she was trying to hide much more than tears.

"Well my friends I must leave you to sort out your problems", said Hans as he made towards the door, "this Christmas is one I hope to remember for all the right reasons".

"How did you know about the gold?" asked Gabriel as Hans walked out the door.

"Master of Spies my friend, Master of Spies", replied Hans as he disappeared off into the cold wet night.

CHAPTER 22

The Motorcar signaled with its horn to remind Charlotte and Gabriel that General Arkwright does not like to be kept waiting. Gabriel had just woke up and when he saw the freshly made tea and toast gesturing to his growling stomach, he arrived at the very quick conclusion that the general could blow his horn all day if he so wished.

"I'm frightened", said Charlotte, as she looked across the table at Gabriel, "how on earth are we going to stop that gold?"

"I have no idea, but whatever course of action we take, under no circumstances does that gold reach its intended destination", replied Gabriel as he hungrily consumed the toasted bread.

In all honesty, Gabriel knew that under no circumstances meant that he may have to use his luger with lethal force. Hans had also stressed how important it was to use the gold as the general's bate, and he had no intention of letting anyone down.

"I guess we may depart this humble abode and ride forth to do our duty", said Gabriel as he buttoned up his coat and made for the door.

"I'm not so sure about duty", replied Charlotte, "if duty was going home and forgetting everything, I would be sorely tempted".

"Stop pretending", said Gabriel as they closed the door behind them and walked towards the car, "you love every minute of this noble adventure".

"I expected you to be on time", shouted the general as he signaled the driver to move off, "if you were under my command I'd have you whipped".

"Have you ever been removed from a moving Motorcar?" asked Gabriel as he looked hard into the general's face.

The general did not reply to Gabriel's question but turned his head and for the remainder of the journey, stared out through the window at the mixture of nature's assorted colors, garnished by wreck and ruin. At that very moment Gabriel knew he was capable of carrying out his violent suggestion, and the general had no doubt by the look on his face.

"Pull in here", said the general to his driver, "I see he is already waiting on us".

As the car pulled in to a clearing, an old army truck was parked up and waiting. Gabriel waited for the general to disembark before Charlotte and he stepped out of the motorcar and viewed the area around them for any sign of prying eyes, ears or hidden daggers.

"I'll fetch the gold", said the general as he opened the trunk of the car, "go and make sure he is genuine and then give me the nod".

Gabriel walked towards the truck and stopped beside the driver's window. As mud had splashed the door window, Gabriel knocked the window to inform the driver of his presence. As the door opened, Gabriel stepped back to allow the driver to depart from the cab.

He looked excitedly into the driver's face and very quickly reminded the driver that in order for the gold to be realized, he needed to know the password.

"To thread the needle of time", replied a smiling Tiny Tim.

Gabriel looked over at the general and nodded his head to reassure him that the receiver was genuine. The general approached the truck struggling with two leather cases weighed down with gold bars.

"I am sorry for the delay", said the general, "these two sleepy heads held me back".

"Don't be late the next time", said Tim in his best theatrical tone, "the next time I won't wait".

"Please don't mention anything to Bishop, you know how his temper can sometimes get the better of him", pleaded the general.

"I will have a think about it on the way back", replied Tim, "in the meantime I have a message from him for the young gentleman and his lady".

"Ok, yes?" said the general as he waited to hear the message.

"I said for the young gentleman and his lady", replied Tim as he raised his voice.

"Ok I'll wait in the car", said the general as he scurried off towards the Motorcar.

"Grandfather", said Charlotte in an excited tone of voice, "where, how did you know?"

"Keep your voice down my dear and I will fill you in later", replied Tim as he lifted the heavy bags into the cab of the truck, "I'll meet you back at your place in two hours for a cup of tea".

Charlotte and Gabriel waited until Tim was driving off before they made their way back to the general's car. By the look in Charlotte's face Gabriel could tell that she was both pleased and relieved to see her grandfather. Gabriel felt confident now that Tiny Tim was once again playing a part in their endeavors. He was expecting a serious confrontation at the gold drop off point, and felt a great weight being lifted off him when a friendly face was there to meet him.

"What did he say?" asked the general as they car moved off in the direction they came.

"That is none of your business", answered Gabriel.

"Is Bishop angry with me, am I to be chastised?" asked the general in a cowardly tone of voice.

"You are from this moment on probation", replied Gabriel as he threw a sideward glance at Charlotte, "If I feel you are not cooperating enough I must report it back to Bishop immediately".

"I have been good, I will be good, I will do anything you ask, oh please don't tell Bishop", mumbled the general as he reached out to grab Gabriel's hand.

"Don't touch me, don't ever touch me you sniffling excuse for a weasel", shouted Gabriel as he pushed the general's hand away as if it was riddled with an infectious disease.

"Ok, sorry, I'll do as you say", replied the general.

"Drop us back at that ramshackle of a billet you organized", said Gabriel as he turned away from the general to stare out the window.

"I'm sorry. It's all I could get", replied the general as he suddenly burst out crying, "don't let him chastise me oh please, please, I want my mummy".

As they made their way back to the barn, Gabriel knew by the general's reaction that his mental health was seriously in question. He also became aware in that short space of time that the general was not only a coward, but his paranoia was working overtime.

Getting General Arkwright out of his office for enough time to plant the gold was going to be a lot easier than he first thought.

"Don't worry my favorite niece", said Tim as Charlotte and Gabriel walked into their billet, "the truck is back where I borrowed it and the gold is in a safe place".

"We are glad to see you grandfather", replied Charlotte as she threw her arms around Tim's neck and kissed him on the cheek.

"My dear, ahh yes I assure you the feeling is mutual", mumbled Tim, "perhaps a cup of tea to cheer a weary soul".

"You are never weary grandfather", replied Charlotte as she skipped playfully to the small Woodburn stove, "you are truly forever young".

"Thank you my dear, for reminding me of my eternal ability to stay young", said Tim in a manner reflecting his own belief.

"We had a visit last night from Hans", said Gabriel as he sat down on the bed.

"What did he want?" asked Tim as he applied his finger nails to a nonexistent itch on his head.

"He is on our side grandfather", replied Charlotte, "I can trust him with my life.

Charlotte and Gabriel began to enlighten Tim about their meeting with Hans and how Hans would put himself at great risk to help them. They informed him of the plan to snare the general and reiterated Hans' suggestion that it was up to them to stop Bishop.

"Then if it's up to us to deal with Bishop we must deal him a losing hand", said Tim as he loudly sipped and sucked the welcome cup of tea.

"And the gold?" asked Gabriel.

"We need to get it planted somewhere safe in General Arkwright's office as soon as possible", answered Tim as he finished licking the remainder of his tea from the cup, "we don't know when Hans will strike".

"Gabriel, you can have the unsavory task of getting the general out of his office", said Charlotte, "and I will plant the evidence".

"And I will accompany you my dear in case you decide to run off with all that shiny metal", replied Tim as he turned and winked at Gabriel.

"You will not", said Charlotte as she finished tidying up the table, "no one knows you and you could draw attention".

"Not if I'm an officer who just happens to outrank all those who dare to ask too many questions", replied Tim.

"When Arkwright is down, that leaves Bishop", said Gabriel as he lay down on the rock hard bed.

No sooner had Gabriel spoke these words when the twirling, gnawing feeling began to arrive at the pit of his stomach. He knew what he had to do when that time arrived and he was not looking forward to the prospect. It was only three days until Christmas Eve and the childhood memories of peace and happiness were being slowly eroded by the mere thought of dying. Charlotte and Gabriel continued with their talk of plans, of ideas that may work and hopes of succeeding. But Gabriel never heard a single word, the disturbed sleep from the night before had finally caught up with him and convinced him of the need for a midday nap.

When Gabriel finally awoke, it was not due to a crowing rooster or Charlotte's soft welcoming voice. The realization that something was seriously wrong had dawned on him from the barrel of a Webley revolver hovering about four inches from his face, and the wide almost toothless grin of Jimbo.

"Well, well", said Jimbo as he indicated with the revolver for Gabriel to get off the bed, "this is indeed a very pleasant surprise".

Gabriel sat up on the bed and scanned the room for any sign of Charlotte or Tiny Tim. He had no idea what happened while he was sleeping and the sudden threatening nature that had returned him to reality, had left him scared and confused.

"What is going on?" asked Gabriel as he began to stir a plan of action inside his head.

"You tell me Mr. Tom Drennen", replied Jimbo as he moved back to lean against the table, while still pointing the gun in Gabriel's direction.

"I don't know what you are saying", replied Gabriel, "Who is Tom Drennen?"

"Now didn't I ask myself that very same question when our dear old General Arkwright informed me of someone by that very name staying in my billet and sleeping on my very bed", said Jimbo, "and didn't I say to myself, I don't know anyone by that name, and so I decided to make your acquaintance".

"Listen Jimbo", replied Gabriel as he tried to scratch a way out of his predicament, "the game's up, why don't you save yourself by putting that gun down".

"The game is certainly up my lad, for you that is", said Jimbo as he continued to threaten Gabriel with the army issue revolver.

"killing me, won't save you, at this very moment the

cogs of the law are turning and soon you will be staring up at the swinging rope hovering above your head", replied Gabriel as he still thought of ways to appeal to Jimbo's limited conscience.

Following this plead by Gabriel, Jimbo began to burst into a frenzy of laughter.

"You really don't know who you are dealing with", laughed Jimbo, "have you any idea how stupid and amateurish you sound?"

"Remember the well-known saying, thee who laughs last, laughs the loudest", replied Gabriel.

"Trust me lad", said Jimbo as he finished laughing, "it is I who will be laughing last and you who will never laugh again".

"You still have a chance to save yourself", replied Gabriel as he tried to buy time in the hope that something would turn up.

"Bishop is the law lad; no one touches him or any of his associates, not even the king himself", said Jimbo.

"No one is above the law", replied Gabriel.

"Where is your lady friend?" asked Jimbo, "gone out for a little stroll in the beautiful Belgian countryside".

On hearing this question Gabriel breathed an inward sigh of relief and realized that Charlotte and Tim must have indeed went for a stroll. If he could only keep Jimbo talking a little while longer Gabriel thought, perhaps they may be able to save his life.

"She left for England a few hours ago", lied Gabriel, "she apologizes for not being here to greet you but sincerely hopes that you can find the compassion within yourself to forgive her".

"I am sure both her and I will meet again, in fact I am convinced of it", said Jimbo as he flashed his grotesque smile, "who knows, perhaps we might get married and live happily ever after, which is more than I can say for you".

"She told me that even after considering your ogre smile and vagabond sense of dress", replied Gabriel as he fought bravely to ward off the emerging temper attacks now welling up inside him, "she could never see herself taking you out for a walk during the day, in case you frightened the children".

"Listen to me you little toe rag", shouted Jimbo as he lunged forward and held the gun to Gabriel's head, "I only wish you could live long enough to see frightened children, hear them cry for a mother they never knew and watch the pictures of terror flash before their very eyes".

By Jimbo's sudden burst of anger, Gabriel knew that he had won the battle of the minds. He understood that Jimbo was not going to kill him at this very moment, as he would have already done so while he was sleeping.

"Get up", shouted Jimbo as he directed Gabriel to the door, "I know someone who would like to ask you a few questions before, well you know".

Gabriel walked out through the door and was closely followed by the triumphant Jimbo. A motorcar was parked a few yards away from the entrance to the barn and Gabriel was pushed by the barrel of Jimbo's gun in its direction.

"Get in and drive", said Jimbo as he demanded that Gabriel open the door and climb in behind the steering wheel.

"I can't drive", replied Gabriel as he did what Jimbo ordered him to do.

"Don't try that one with me", said Jimbo as he swung the starting handle, and as the car fired into life he jumped in beside Gabriel and shut the door, "If you can't drive then you are about to get a speedy lesson". Gabriel moved the gear stick up and down making loud grinding noises as he tried to figure out what to do. He felt around at pedals at his feet and before long both Jimbo and himself were swerving and bouncing along the uneven Belgium road.

"Don't be trying any funny stuff", said Jimbo as he raised his voice and continued to point the gun in Gabriel's direction.

"I am in no mood to make you laugh at this very moment", replied Gabriel sarcastically, "but if I was you I would be getting a little worried about my driving".

Gabriel's mind was processing a thousand pieces of information a second, as he tried to figure out a way to stop Jimbo delivering him before the cowardly General Arkwright. Every idea and every plan of action concluded with the same question each time, how to stop someone who was pointing a loaded weapon in his direction? He thought of jumping out and letting the car run on, but he knew Jimbo could both stop it by himself and still have enough time to shoot him, or fire at him through the window. Either way, Gabriel had to think fast and fast is precisely what plan of action he chose to take.

"I told you no funny business", said Jimbo as he noticed Gabriel deliberately applying his foot to the petrol.

"I can't hear you", shouted Gabriel as the car sped down the steep hill bouncing and shaking in every direction.

"I said slow down now or I'm going to pull the trigger", shouted Jimbo in reply.

Gabriel noticed Jimbo's expression change from confident and victorious, to pure and present terror written beautifully across his face. He now knew that he had the superior weapon and Jimbo had no way of responding. As he saw the broad gable wall of the ruined church getting closer, Gabriel's heart began to ache for what his life might have been. He knew there was no other way but sacrifice his own being in order to stop Jimbo from blowing their mission wide open. He waved at his mother as she smiled at him from the open door of the house he was born in. His old school friends pulled funny faces as the car wheels sprayed dirty water over their Sunday outfits. And then there was Tiny Tim, standing upright and saluting the bravery of a fallen friend. With the wall almost upon them Gabriel knew there was someone missing, some person who crashed into his life like a golden ray of undiluted sunshine. A portrait that would stay etched on his heart far beyond the realms of eternity and a heavenly shadow that would be forever theirs.

"Goodbye my lovely", sighed Gabriel.

The car smashed hard into the wall with enough force to cause the occupants to die instantly. From the distance a farmer heard a loud explosion followed by a ball of flames reaching high into the air as the petrol tank ruptured and ignited.

"What did you say?" asked Charlotte as Gabriel opened his eyes and stared strangely in her direction.

"Like I said", continued Tim, "the gold must be hidden in such a way that the old weasel of a general doesn't trip over it".

"Floorboards are always a good hiding place", replied Charlotte as she turned again to look at the surprised look written plainly across Gabriel's face.

"So you have decided to join us my good man", said Tim as he threw a wide grin in Gabriel's direction.

"Wake up sleepy head we have villains to deal with", said Charlotte as she playfully shook Gabriel's leg.
Gabriel pushed himself up from the bed and sat on the edge to try and gather some of his remaining faculties together. He could hardly believe his eyes when he awoke and discovered two of the people he cared for most, embracing normality like some wishful memory.

"What's happening?" asked Gabriel as he rubbed his hands across his forehead.

"While you were snoring your lazy head off, grandfather and I were discussing the finer points of fighting fire with fire", answered Charlotte.

"I do believe the chap needs a good strong cup of your finest brew my dear", said Tim as he tapped his own empty cup with his finger nails.

"A strong cup coming up", replied Charlotte as she arose from her chair and made her way to the stove,

"but you will not get the finest brew, I don't know what these leaves are but they are certainly not tealeaves".
As soon as Charlotte finished talking three loud knocks could be heard vibrating through the rugged room.

"A message for Mr. Tom Drennen", shouted a voice from the other side.
Gabriel staggered to the door and upon opening it a messenger handed him a brown envelope stating private and confidential. Before Gabriel had time to thank the messenger, he mounted his bicycle and rode off down the road.

"Please open it", said Gabriel as he handed the envelope to Tim and returned to his seat on the edge of the bed.

"Well?" asked Charlotte as she froze beside the stove awaiting the contents of the note.

"Excellent news my dears", answered Tim as he walked over to playfully slap Gabriel on the back,

"Our long and dearly unloved adversary Mr. Jimbo has somehow managed to be the occupant of a car when it crashed into the wall of an old ruined church, killing him instantly. The note also says that we must be on our guard as the driver who has escaped unharmed, may have smashed into the wall deliberately.

"If I had the driver here now", said Charlotte as she began to playfully dance around the room, "I would plant a very large kiss on his lips".

Gabriel reached his arm out and stopped Charlotte before she passed him by.

"I'm afraid you're going to have to kiss these lips", replied Gabriel as he stared up at the bewildered Charlotte, "I was the driver".

Charlotte stared at Gabriel for what felt like eternity before she spoke.

"That's impossible, you were lying here beside us sleeping", said Charlotte.

"Please my dear", replied Tim as he sat the note on the table, "I'm afraid he's right".

Charlotte walked over to the table and after kneeling down before it; she placed her head on the rough wood surface and began to cry.

"Oh no, please God, Dita please, please, it wasn't supposed to happen today", cried Charlotte, "Oh why, my heart is going to die?"

CHAPTER 23

"He was somewhat baffled when he heard someone had taken over his billet", said General Arkwright as he rubbed sweat from his brow with a dirty handkerchief.

"He came to see me and when I laid down the law of Bishop he took off like the charge of the light brigade", replied Gabriel as he stood before the general presenting his version of lies.

"I must say, he was behaving rather curious", said the general as he returned the well overdue a wash handkerchief to his breast pocket.

"In the meantime I need you to accompany me on a short reconnaissance", replied Gabriel as he opened the door of the general's office.

"Must I?" said the general, "I do have a slight cold coming on".

"The question you need to keep asking yourself sir", replied Gabriel as he directed a half smile towards the general, "did Jimbo die by accident, or did our good friend Bishop decide that he was a non-conformist".

The general quickly removed himself from behind the desk and followed Gabriel out of the building and into the waiting car. Gabriel needed to remove the general from his office for at least half an hour. This was the minimum time needed for Charlotte and Tim to carry out operation Boomerang, return the gold to whence it came and wait for Hans to fulfill his part of the bargain.

"I expect this was once a beautiful country before warmongers like you got their vile hands on it", said Gabriel as they moved off down the pothole peppered road.

"We do try our best", replied the general, just before he turned and sneezed in Gabriel's direction.

"Whatever germs that caused you to lack compassion for your fellow man, I would be grateful if you kept them to yourself", said Gabriel as he wiped away invisible germs with a much whiter handkerchief than the general's.

"Where is it we are going?" asked the general as he began to display a worried looking expression.

"Pull up here", Gabriel shouted at the driver.

As soon as the driver had brought the car to a standstill, Gabriel opened the door and stepped into a deep water filled pothole. He said nothing as he tried to shake some of the water from his shoe, pretending only that he must have took cramp from sitting in a small space.

"Now sir", said Gabriel as he looked out across at the town of Ypres, "show me where the church is in relation to the trenches".

"To the right of us about three miles back is the church where the assembly point will be", replied the general as he walked closer to Gabriel and stepped into the same puddle, "drat and damn it, now I am sure to go down with a blasted cold or worse".

"That is what's wrong with all you privileged, one iota of what millions put up with every day of their lives and you think you have been hit by a train", said Gabriel as he glowed inwardly at the sight of the general's misfortune.

"Stepping into icy cold water in winter is nothing to be taken lightly, privileged or peasant alike", replied the general as he sat down on the car's foot well to remove his shoe.

"Those men down there have to put up with a lot worse", said Gabriel as he pointed in the direction of the trenches, "they live in cold, wet and soul destroying conditions none of us can even begin to imagine, yet if you listen carefully you will not hear a sound".

"Where is this all leading us?" asked the general as he labored to squeeze the water from his sock.

"Why don't you ask Bishop the next time you see him", answered Gabriel as he removed his pocket watch to check the time.

Gabriel could only hope that before the next meeting with Bishop, the general would be well and truly bagged. Almost forty minutes had passed since they left the general's office, enough time for Charlotte and Tim to have carried out their plan.

"Let's get back and get you tucked warmly into bed", said Gabriel as he unsympathetically mocked the general's plight.

"As a matter of fact I was thinking about that very same idea", replied the general in earnest agreement.

"Who are you and what are you doing in my office?" asked the general as Gabriel and he walked into the room.

"This is Mr. Charles Dickenson", replied Charlotte, "he has been sent by Bishop to monitor the preparations".

"That does not give you the authority to enter my private office", said the general as he took his seat behind the desk, "why didn't you wait outside until my return?"

"I did not deem it approbate to keep Mr. Bishop's right hand man waiting outside", answered Charlotte.

While Charlotte made excuses for being in the general's office without permission, Gabriel had to rub his eyes several times to convince himself that what he was seeing was real. Unless Charlotte had eaten a gluttonous amount of pies over a long period of time without his knowledge, she looked pregnant. With the many trials and hardships that had taken over their lives these last few weeks, Gabriel hadn't noticed the bulging mass now clearly visible under the light bulb hovering above their heads. Gabriel suddenly felt a sharp piercing pain finding its way to his heart and a strong duo of anger and jealousy following closely behind. He could do little else but to turn around and without saying a word, walk out of the office and into the cold icy December air. He could not feel his legs as he somehow managed to make it through the gates and down the road that would lead him back to the billet. He stopped beside a large flat stone at the side of the road to catch his breath, and convinced himself that he needed to sit down. He took deep breaths as he tried to come to terms with Charlotte's terrible and unforgivable betrayal. He had always behaved as a perfect gentleman towards her, forever keeping his desires to himself and promising himself that every part of his mortal and immortal soul would be hers. He wanted to scream, he longed to face the sky and shout to the very heavens above in the hope that someone would show him even a tiny morsel of pity.

"Why did you leave in such a hurry?" asked Tim as he proceeded to empty large amounts of soil out of his socks.

"I am so relieved to get this dirt out of my dress", said Charlotte as she too began to off load the large quantities of soil onto the damp road below them.

"I wasn't feeling well", replied Gabriel as he began to laugh uncontrollably, "I think I have a touch of cold coming on".

Charlotte and Tim looked down at Gabriel sitting on the stone and began to worry about Gabriel's sanity.

"I don't find this one bit funny", said Charlotte trying to sound angry, "and I also don't care to be laughed at by a crazy man".

"She is a tot right you know", said Tiny Tim, as he returned his socks to his feet, "you do look as if you have several marbles rolling around in your head ".

"And when we pulled the floor boards up there was nothing there but soil", said Tiny Tim as he stretched out on top of Gabriel's bed.

"We had to start digging and stuffing the soil into places we never thought possible", laughed Charlotte, "I could be doing with a really good hot bath".

Gabriel laughed loudly as Charlotte and Tim relayed their story and how the general's return almost caught them off guard. He laughed so hard that his sides and cheeks were hurting and tears began to be visible flowing down his face. In normal circumstances Gabriel would have found the story only moderately amusing, but these were by no means moderate circumstances. He was happy that the general stepped in the puddle and moaned like a spoiled child. He was glad that Jimbo would not be taking part in any future proceedings, and most of all he was elated that Charlotte's stomach had now returned to its former glory.

"You didn't think I was pregnant?" asked Charlotte as she suddenly turned and looked Gabriel in the face.

"Of course not", lied Gabriel, "what brought that idea into your head?"

"I just had a funny feeling that you as a man would allow something so ridicules to cross your narrow mind", answered Charlotte as she walked over beside Gabriel sitting at the table.

"Now, now my dear", said Tim as he stretched out on the bed and yawned, "don't be cruel, I'm quite sure nothing of the sort crossed his narrow mind".

"Here", said Charlotte as she took Gabriel's hands and placed them on her stomach, "does that feel pregnant?"

Gabriel's face began to burn red with embarrassment as the door leading to his inner thoughts was suddenly flung open before him.

"No, noo, ahh certainly not", Gabriel stuttered as he pulled his hands away.

"How could you think such a thing, I am really disappointed in you Gabriel Shivers", shouted Charlotte as she ran for the door and disappeared outside.

"Better go after her old boy", said Tim as he closed his eyes as if to catch a nap, "she might betray us to the enemy".

Gabriel arose from the chair and ran outside, he noticed Charlotte sitting on a stone with her head bent over and resting on the palms of her hands. He noticed her shaking as if her emotions had boiled over and were now flowing in absolute despair.

"Charlotte, please my love I didn't think any, well perhaps for a brief moment", said Gabriel apologetically, "you were right I am narrow minded and wrongly come to swift conclusions without ever considering the facts first".

At the closing of Gabriel's apology Charlotte's visible quivering seemed to be more frequent and apart from what he had just told her, he struggled to finds any more words of appeasement.

"Would you like a cup of tea?" asked Gabriel.

"Gabriel Shivers", said Charlotte as she lifted her head to look up at him humbly before her, "you are so innocent and naïve I often wonder if it's safe at all to allow you out on your own".

Gabriel looked at Charlotte and realized there and then that she had pulled the wool over his eyes. She continued to laugh as he sat down on the stone beside her and as Charlotte reached out and took his hand, Gabriel felt a perfect peace flow through his heart.

"You called me your love", said Charlotte.

"Can we see your papers?" asked the military policeman standing at the door.

"Certainly, my good man", replied Tim as he reached into a bag hanging on a makeshift hook behind the door.

"And what is your purpose in Belgium? asked the policeman as he looked through their papers.

"We are war correspondents for the News of the World", answered Tim as he smiled broadly at the policeman.

"Have you had any relationship with a General Arkwright?" asked the policeman as he handed Tim their papers back.

"I have never heard of the man", replied Tim "is there anything we need to know, or may I say the general public back home in England?"

"Good day sir", said the policeman as he made his way towards his bicycle.

Tiny Tim followed the policeman outside and a few minutes later he returned with a look of extreme happiness written across his face.

"Our number two foe the general has been arrested and following a search by the Military Police, a valuable stash of German gold has been found hidden under the floorboards in his office", said Tim in a triumphant tone of voice.

"My God", replied Charlotte as she leaned against the wall beside the stove, "Hans has followed through with his promise".

"Did they mention what he is being charged with?" asked Gabriel

"He did mention a charge of treason which no doubt will have him crying for his mother", answered Tim.

"Now for Mr. Bishop", said Charlotte as she looked towards Gabriel, "and you stay away from him, do not dare to defy me on this one Gabriel Shivers".

"I have every confidence in the general's ability to sing a jolly tune my dear", said Tim, "sooner if not later he will implicate Bishop and all his merry rogues".

"You stay clear of him I tell you" said Charlotte as her voice began to quiver with emotion, "do not challenge him, do not try to stop him if you think he's getting away".

"Bishop is a coward like all the rest, one look at the barrel of the luger and he'll crawl at my feet for mercy", replied Gabriel in an air of bravado.

"If you do not listen to my plea and go against me

Gabriel, I swear to almighty God we will never cross paths again in this life or the next", said Charlotte as she reached to fill the kettle with water.

Gabriel was unsure how to respond to Charlotte's almost fanatical request and chose to remain silent. He had no idea of where or when their paths would cross, but Gabriel was conscious of the dangers that lay before them and had no intention of allowing Bishop to walk quietly into the night.

"Let's say we leave the subject of Bishop until we have cause to resurrect it", said Tim as he continued to stretch out on the bed, "In the meantime, according to the last mirror I looked in, I'm the only one around here who needs beauty sleep, wake me up in an hour".

"Forget the tea", said Charlotte as she walked towards the door, "I'm going outside to enjoy some female company with myself.

As soon as Charlotte closed the door behind her, Gabriel noticed Tim's eyes open wide. He didn't think the door slamming was enough to cause the interruption and knew that something was stirring when he turned around and looked at Gabriel.

"Is she beyond earshot?" asked Tim.

Gabriel walked to the small dust-stained window and on looking out he reassured Tim that she was.

"I wasn't quite generous with the truth", said Tim, "the policeman told me that General Arkwright had indeed been arrested but escaped a short time after".

Gabriel felt his heart begin to sink into the depths of disappointment and cursed the many contacts who were being influenced by Bishop's gold.

"Why did you not tell Charlotte?" asked Gabriel as he walked over to be closer to Tim.

"I'm beginning to notice small cracks appearing in

her character, for example, the dressing down she just administered to you, and I am of the firm belief her sanity is teetering at the cliff edge", answered Tim.

"I have noticed a change in her these last few days", said Gabriel.

"She cares deeply for both of us, a little too much for her own good", replied Tim as he pulled himself up and sat on the side of the bed.

"It means we have to catch the general all over again and this time rather more discreetly", said Gabriel.

"Indeed my fine fellow, I will need to slip out tonight while you are sleeping and make some inquiries of my own", replied Tim as he once again lay down on Gabriel's bed, "that's why I need to fall asleep right now".

"Ok, I'll go out and see how's she holding up", said Gabriel as he made his way to the door.

"Look after her my boy", said Tim as he closed his eyes, "If anything happens to me you are all she's got.

"What about her mother?" asked Gabriel as he stopped half way across the room.

"You might have heard her mention her mother, but the woman she is referring to was her nanny and house keeper", answered Tim as he opened his eyes to look at Gabriel.

"And her real mother?" asked Gabriel as he remained frozen between Tim and the door.

"Her mother, my daughter died in a coach crash along with her husband when Charlotte was only five years old. My dear wife bless her, tried to bring Charlotte up as best she could, but she too died a few years later from what doctors called an absence of the will to live", answered Tim.

"I'm so, so sorry for you both", said Gabriel as he

stood stunned with emotion.

"My granddaughter has met tragedy after tragedy, and all those she dearly loved have been taken away from her. I have been her shoulder to cry upon, but someday I too will hear my name called and like all those before me, walk into the fog of death. When that time comes, I trust no one else but you my good friend to take my place," replied Tim.

Gabriel wanted to ask Tim why he chose him, to look into the eyes of the greatest friend he had ever known to find answers. But Tim was asleep and it was some time before Gabriel could cloak his feelings well enough to face Charlotte.

"This is the only night of my entire life that I hate the stars", said Charlotte as Gabriel approached.

"What have the poor stars done this time?" asked Gabriel as he sat next to Charlotte on the stone.

"Their presence means it's going to freeze", replied Charlotte as she looked up into the sky, "and all those soldiers are going to be shivering in their trenches".

If it had have been any other time or place, Gabriel would have happily commented on both stars and shiver and laughed the while away. But tonight Gabriel knew that both their comical names would have to be set aside to make way for the critical reality that rested below that December sky.

"Someone told me that the mud in the trenches freezes and allows for a more sturdy footing", said Gabriel as he followed Charlotte's gaze at the heavens above them, "at least their bed will be dry".

"And cold, very cold", replied Charlotte as she suddenly looked across to her right at the town of Ypres, "why do men cause so much suffering?"

"I wish I could answer that", replied Gabriel as he

felt the pain of her words, "but maybe someday the suffering will stop and the world will realize for the first time how futile the madness had been".

"Is grandfather sleeping?" asked Charlotte.

"Yes, he decided to have an early night", replied Gabriel as he noticed Charlotte shivering with cold, "Perhaps you should come inside, it's a little warmer".

"Fetch me the blanket on my bed", said Charlotte. Gabriel made his way into the building and in a short time returned with Charlotte's thick grey army blanket.

"I tried to grab mine but your grandfather threatened me", said Gabriel as he handed Charlotte the horse hair cover.

"You can share mine", said Charlotte as she got closer to Gabriel, "it will not be the first time we shared a bed cover and it certainly won't be the last".

Gabriel happily accepted Charlotte's offer of mutual nearness and despite the cold crisp air around them, he felt warmer than he had ever felt before. As they looked up at the sky again Gabriel saw the bright stream of a shooting star and made a wish that even he would never know.

"Time to make a wish", said Gabriel as he pointed at the heavens.

Charlotte looked at the long bright light as it entered the earth's atmosphere and smiled for the first time since Gabriel arrived to accompany her outside. Gabriel watched her close her eyes and mumble something he could not understand, yet he knew that it was something so important that a star was sent for that very purpose. As he remembered what Tiny Tim has told him, he could see the five year old child in Charlotte's eyes as she looked through the window of time, patiently awaiting the arrival of a beautiful dawn.

"When I was a child my grandfather and I used to sit up for hours on clear nights, staring into his telescope in search of other forms of life", said Charlotte as she focused her attention towards Gabriel.

"When I was a child I used to steal out of the house on clear nights with one purpose only, to relieve a local farmer of some of his juiciest apples", replied Gabriel.

"Once a rascal, always a rascal my dear", said Charlotte as she lay her head on Gabriel's shoulder. Gabriel put his arm around Charlotte as he felt her warm breath rise to tread lightly on his cheek. Within that peaceful silence he wanted to translate the pangs in his heart to words and lay them out before her like long lines of neatly formed handwriting. He wanted to pause the night and dare the spirits of harm to cross their paths. He yearned to return through the shadows of time and save Charlotte from a river of undeserving tears. But Gabriel knew that Charlotte's past belonged to her and her alone, and all he could hope for was the shared moment and the flicker of an eternal light.

"Gabriel", said Charlotte as her breathing became heavier.

"Yes, my dear", replied Gabriel.

"I wonder what our children will look like", said Charlotte as she slipped off into a peaceful sleep.

CHAPTER 24

"Press down hard and don't move until I get some bandages", said Charlotte as Gabriel quickly followed her instructions.

"I don't know what all the fuss is about; I have lost more blood picking gooseberries", said Tim as he stood over the wounded Hans.

"You're lucky it's not serious", said Charlotte as she took over from Gabriel.

"What happened?" asked Gabriel.

"Had a run in with our dear friend General Arkwright and a few of his scallywags", replied Hans as he allowed Charlotte to treat his wound without complaining.

"General Arkwright, you must be mistaken", said Charlotte, our so called general is locked up neatly behind solid iron bars".

"I'm afraid not my dear", replied Tim as he walked towards her like a child who had done something wrong, "I didn't want to alarm you but shortly after his arrest, the general managed to slip the guards".

"That is all we need, just when I thought it was coming to an end", said Charlotte as she continued to treat Hans' wound.

"I did succeed in preventing him from boarding a ship for England", replied Hans.

"And how did you manage that my friend?" asked Tim as he began to pace back and forth.

"I put a bullet in each of his legs and one in the arm to be getting along with", answered Hans as he sat up with his arm in a sling, "thank you my dear you have the hands of a saint".

"I suppose he took it like a man and limped off in the opposite direction", said Gabriel as he helped Charlotte clean up.

"Quite the opposite, he cried like a baby and had to be taken away by two of his bodyguards", replied Hans.

Gabriel could sense that something was wrong when he was awakened by three taps on the door. They had just settled down for the night and Tiny Tim was waiting his chance to slip off into the dark. Hans was a seasoned soldier and a highly trained spy, yet his confrontation with the general had spilled his own blood. Bishop was a more dangerous adversary and as the hours quickly passed, Gabriel knew that soon he would have to face him with little experience and a gun with only one bullet left.

"Have you any idea where he might have escaped to?" asked Tim as he paced back and forth.

"I know exactly where he is holed up", answered Hans, "you don't believe I walked all the way back here just to lick my wounds".

"So where is he then?" asked Tim as he stood like a statue in the middle of the floor.

"About four miles east of here curled up inside a hayshed crying for his mother", replied Hans.

"Let him cry then", said Gabriel as he handed Hans

a cup of tea, "I don't believe he ever had a mother".

"One of his bodyguards, the one who give me this nick on the arm, sent a message informing me that the general wants to turn King's evidence" continued Hans.

"He has most definitely lost his mind", said Charlotte as she thanked Gabriel for the tea.

"The message I received was, he is willing to make a statement against Bishop and divulge all his illegal activities for the price of a pardon", said Hans.

"Absolutely no way, let him cry his black heart out", replied Charlotte with anger clearly projecting from her voice.

"Let's see what he has to bargain with", said Tim as he reached for his coat, "you two stay here and I will be back in a few hours".

"I'm coming with you", said Gabriel as he made to reach for his coat.

"If you go then I won't leave my granddaughter on her own, and if we take her with us she will be exposed to unnecessary danger", replied Tim as he reached to open the door.

"Please be careful", said Charlotte as she secretly slipped a small piece of paper into Hans' hand on his way out.

"Don't worry, he will be back safe and well before long", replied Hans as he followed Tim through the door and out into the frost smitten night.

Gabriel was slightly disappointed that Tim did not take him along, but in his own heart he knew that exposing Charlotte to any more danger than was deemed necessary was clearly beyond a question or an answer. After securing the door and turning down the oil lamp, Gabriel lay down on the space left for him beside

Charlotte and quietly prayed for Tim's safe return.

"The whole episode has been written, read out loud and signed off", said Tim as Charlotte sat the steaming cup of hot tea on the table before him.

"I don't believe it grandfather", said Charlotte as she joined Tim at the table, "what possessed you to negotiate a pardon for that monster".

"I believe that it will strengthen our case against Bishop", replied Tim as he sucked thirstily on the cup.

"So what you are saying", said Gabriel while he still remained under the bed cover, "is that in a few short hours you have negotiated with the King, the government and all the other justice departments to convince them to grant a pardon".

"Grandfather is a genius, he moves in fast and mysterious ways", replied Charlotte as she reached out to touch Tim's hand.

"Fast and mysterious he may be my dear", said Gabriel as he sat up on the bed still wrapped in the bed cover, "but to travel to England and back again before we woke up is an unquestionable impossibility".

"I'm not the least bit ashamed to admit that I may have presented the general with a document that stated less than the truth", said Tim as he forced a smile in Charlotte's direction.

"My God grandfather, you didn't, I mean you got away with it", replied Charlotte as she returned Tim's smile.

"My dear, it was rather easier than I thought and at this very moment the general is boarding a ship for England sporting his useless piece of paper", said Tim as he begged for a second cup of tea.

"Tim", said Gabriel as he arose from the bed still

wrapped in the blanket and commandeered Charlotte's chair, "you have the purest, well-polished and finely fashioned brass neck I have ever seen".

"Thank you my old friend, but there is something else you need to know", replied Tim, "we need to leave here today and find alternative lodgings, Bishop will be arriving shortly and take one guess where he's going to make an unfriendly stop".

"Where will we find accommodation at such short notice?" asked Charlotte as she began to quickly pack her few belongings into a carpet bag.

"Hans told me about a place not far from here who will gladly put us up if we pay over the going rate", said Tim.

"Greed always finds a way to raise its ugly head, especially when they have you over a needy barrel", replied Gabriel as he hurried to get dressed.

"Greed and the firm belief in all things Godly", said Tim as he too began to pack, "the couple who own it are deeply religious and expect all those who enter there to abandon all the fineries of modern living".

"I can't even remember the last time I slept in a soft bed, never mind anything else", replied Charlotte as she made her way towards the door, "let's get going before Bishop raises his ugly head.

Gabriel walked alongside Charlotte as they followed Tiny Tim down the frost baked rugged road. The night of nights was fast approaching and the never-ending cycle of hardships and fear were slowing down and preparing to stop. As he reached over to carry Charlotte's bag, the sound of gunfire could be heard from the distance, sending them a ghastly reminder that violence was never far away.

"Good Morning sir", said Tim as a tall scrawny bald head man answered the door, "I wonder if you would be kind enough to offer accommodation to a family of weary travelers".

"I have one room left", replied the man in a polite English accent, "it will cost you five pounds a day".

"My God", said Charlotte as she stood before the man, "I could get a whole month for that in London".

"I will not have blasphemy on my property", said the man angrily, "if you don't want it at that price then I suggest you go back to London".

"The price is fair my good man", said Tim as he quickly intervened to prevent their speedy expulsion, "and I do sincerely apologize for my daughter's lack of Christian gratitude".

"How long will you be staying?" asked the man as he cast a suspicious eye over Charlotte and Gabriel.

"No more than three days and nights", replied Tim, "Trusting in God's good and infinite mercy we will be back home by then".

"What is your business here?" asked the man as he continued to eye them with suspicion.

"I don't believe that our business is any of your business", replied Gabriel as he desperately tried to keep his temper at bay.

"It is required by law that all landlords report anyone they suspect of being spies, are you spies?" said the man as he proceeded to feast on the flowing contents of his nostrils.

"My son, their brother who is a soldier was reported missing, presumed dead", replied Tim as he removed a bundle of white five pound notes from his pocket,

"We arrived here in the hope that we might find him alive and if dead make sure his body is returned home to be buried in the family cemetery".

"Three days and nights you say", said the man as he licked his lips at the glorious and heavenly sight of money, "I will have to charge you a longer stay fee, let's make it an even twenty".

"An even twenty it is", replied Tim as he placed the notes into the man's open palm, "and here's an extra ten for being so kind at such a short notice".

"Follow the stone path over there to the right", said the man as he greedily pocketed the money, "you will find your room at the very end, here's the key".

As Charlotte, Tim and Gabriel took leave from the landlord and followed the path; Gabriel came to a swift conclusion that the only God the man cared for was a golden one.

"My God", said Charlotte as she stood facing the hastily put together tin shack before them, "I'm going to get our money back".

"No, no my dear", said Tim as he put his arm around his granddaughter, "Beggars can't make their own choices and besides, we are going to find it extremely difficult if not impossible to get anything else".

"Let's get settled in", said Gabriel as he smiled at Charlotte and opened the door.

The smell of damp and unwashed bedclothes greeted them as they made their way inside. In the middle of the floor stood a solitary bucket of frozen water to catch the leaky roof. Under a filth stained window a make shift bed consisting of moldy hay and grey bedcovers shadowed three chairs and an overturned oil drum to act as a table.

"This is getting worse", said Charlotte as she stared around the room in disbelief, "we are not surely going to let that beast away with this".

"It can't be any worse than those poor men in the trenches", replied Gabriel as he sat their bags down beside the hay bed.

"You see my dear, a voice of reason and acceptance", said Tim as he sat down on a chair, "it won't be for long, I hope".

"We should put a match to this monstrosity before we leave", said Charlotte as she continued to shake her head in disbelief, "and he has the tenacity to charge a great deal of money for this".

"Don't worry my dear, I paid him with the other stuff", replied Tim while trying to thwart an insect he had never saw before from crawling up his arm.

"Other stuff?" asked Charlotte as she passed a look of confusion in Tim's direction.

"You know, the stuff we use to pay scallywags and conmen", replied Tim as he continued to do battle with the bug.

"So what you are saying is the money you paid the conman just now, was counterfeit?" asked Gabriel.

"Precisely Mr. Shivers, always be prepared to fight fire with fire", answered Tim, "trust me my boy, you will sleep all the better for it".

"Ok, I feel much better grandfather", said Charlotte as she took a chair beside Tim, "don't you feel a lot better Gabriel?"

"I feel a whole lot better", replied Gabriel as he sat down on the third chair and came crashing to the ground.

"Heathens, Sinners cheating their fellow man who was only trying to earn an honest crust", roared the landlord as he fired the first barrel of the shotgun through the rust eroded tin door.

Gabriel grabbed one of the two remaining chairs and began to thump an escape route through the gable end. He never expected Tim's not so real currency to be discovered so easily and upon realizing that his luck was false, Gabriel became dangerously aware that hell hath no fury than a miser scorned.

"Quick", said Gabriel as he managed to kick a hole in the gable wall, "we need to get out of here in a hurry".

"Sorry about that dear chap", said Tim as he followed Charlotte through the gaping hole.

Neither Charlotte, Tim or Gabriel said a word until they were far enough away from the screaming landlord. They had lost their only chance of a roof over their heads and as Gabriel slowed his pace to catch his breath, Charlotte decided that something needed to be said.

"Thank you so very much grandfather", said Charlotte as she turned her bright red face towards Tim, "you might have chosen someone else with a lesser tendency to violence".

"My dear", replied Tim as he skipped briskly alongside his unfit and weary accomplices, "there is nothing like a good chase to keep us on our toes, what".

"I am tired, I feel dirty and I probably smell to high heaven, do you not think I've been kept on my toes for long enough", said Charlotte as she struggled to keep up with Tim.

"Let's look on the sunny side", said Gabriel as he too had difficulty with Tim's pace, "we all escaped in one piece".

"I don't believe I can agree with you Mr. Shivers, I think I may have left my head behind", replied

Charlotte as she rubbed a handkerchief across her forehead.

Tiny Tim's preparedness for fighting fire with fire had left them out in the cold, but Gabriel was not the least bit angry with the old gentleman. He knew that their chances of finding somewhere else to stay were as minus as the weather they would have to sleep out in. He began to search his surroundings for any sign of shelter, a barn, stable or anything with a roof or at least half. He knew they needed to get off the road as soon as possible, as a lot of disgruntled characters would only be too pleased to make their acquaintance.

"I don't believe it, no I still don't believe it and I say again if I didn't see it with my very own eyes, I would simply walk straight by and still not believe it", said Tim as he stood facing a house with a rooms for let sign outside.

"Where in God's name has that come from?" asked Charlotte as she too was baffled by its very presence.

"The fog my dears", replied Tim as he leaned against the stone wall that surrounded the clean white two story house, "we walked straight by it while it was hidden by the density of the fog".

Gabriel could also see the beautiful and inviting house before them, yet he too had to look twice in case his eyes were playing tricks. The dark wood sign clearly announced in staggered white letters that rooms were there for the asking and all they needed to do was to ask.

"Excuse me dear", said Tim as a middle age woman walked out through the door and smiled in their direction, "the sign says you have rooms to let?"

"We most certainly have, one single and I believe, yes and one double left", replied the lady.

"It would be an understatement my dear if we said we were delighted", said Tim as he walked closer to the lady, "weary and cold and greatly longing for a hot cup of tea".

"Please follow me, I have a nice blazing fire ready", replied the lady as she led the trio through the door and into the warmth of the kitchen.

Gabriel could sense by the cheerful atmosphere and the hot cup of steaming tea, that the landlady was indeed a genuine and caring person. A few moments before they faced the cold and discomfort of homelessness but almost as if by some divine arbitration, they would sleep in a warm dry comfortable bed.

"Could you please tell me your rates?" asked Tim as he sucked on his teacup much to the amusement of the landlady.

"How long are you hoping to stay for sir?" asked the landlady.

"Three days and nights my dear", replied Tim before continuing to suck on his tea cup.

"Four pounds and ten shillings", said the landlady as she poured more tea into Tim's pleading cup, "If you make it an even fiver I will throw in your breakfast".

"Bless you my angel", replied Tim as he reached into his pocket to pay the bill.

"It's ok sir, you can pay me on the day you leave", said the landlady as she proceeded to show them the rooms. As Tiny Tim consumed several cups of tea while negotiating business, Gabriel noticed Charlotte stare at the two pink and white porcelain candlesticks, perched at the top of the fireplace. As they arose from their chairs to be shown to their rooms, Charlotte still stared and as they were leaving the kitchen, she turned around to look at them again.

"You can sort it out among yourselves who sleeps where", said the landlady, "I will leave you to it then". All three thanked the landlady sincerely and walked into the double room, before closing the door gently behind them.

"A fine lady I must say", said Tim as he tested the bedsprings for comfort, "although she does remind me of someone".

"Now that you mentioned it, she does look familiar", replied Gabriel as he too tested the quality of the mattress.

"Did you see those candlesticks, the ones perched on top of the fireplace?" asked Charlotte as she sat down on a soft chair by the window.

"You certainly didn't miss them", said Gabriel, "you looked at them as if you saw a ghost".

"I have two the exact same, I was led to believe they were the only pair", replied Charlotte in a soft faraway tone of voice.

"I guess Tim and my good self will share this room", said Gabriel as he stood up to look around the room.

"With all due respect my good man", replied Tim as he made his way to the door, "I not only prefer to sleep alone, but I also prefer to sleep".

Gabriel watched Tim leave the bedroom and heard him rattle around next door like a lion let loose in a China shop.

"Are you ok Charlotte?" asked Gabriel as he noticed her silence.

"I can't really complain, just a blast from the past that almost swept me off my feet", replied Charlotte.

"Did those candlesticks stir something?" asked Gabriel.

"The pair I have the same were given to me by my mother, they were commissioned and are unique", replied Charlotte as she sat down beside Gabriel on the edge of the bed.

"Perhaps they were designed and crafted by the same person", said Gabriel as he tried to find a suitable answer.

As soon as Gabriel finished the last word, Charlotte threw her arms around him and began crying.

"Oh God, I miss my mother so much, why Gabriel, why did it have to be my mother?" cried Charlotte.

CHAPTER 25

The stars hovered high above Gabriel's head like a million flickering candles as the man he had grown to hate so much stood before him. He could still hear Charlotte's words pounding within his skull not to approach him, and the very threat of their friendship now hang from Gabriel's outstretched arm. He placed his finger firmly on the trigger and with everything that ever dwelled within his body and soul; he wanted to pull the trigger so much. He felt his arm drop slowly to his side and almost simultaneously a shot rang out from someone he trusted with his very being. He could feel the wrenching pain pull at the strings of his life as the warm flow of blood gathered pace to hurry an expected death. Charlotte appeared at Bishop's side smiling with the smoking gun still pointed in his direction.

"You didn't believe I would ever have married a runt like you", said Charlotte as she fired another shot at Gabriel.

"One of the biggest fools I have ever had the misfortune to meet in my entire life", said Tiny Tim as he too appeared beside Bishop.

"In Germany we would have him earmarked as the village idiot", said Hans who poked his head up from behind a ruined wall.

"Charlotte, Charlotte, why?" asked Gabriel as he began to fall to the ground.

"Because you lack the necessary skills to make a decent cup of tea", replied Charlotte.

"What in the name of God is wrong with you Gabriel and why are you lying on the floor", asked Charlotte as she bent down to help Gabriel up off the clean polished wood floor.

Gabriel unsteadily gathered himself off the floor and sat down on the edge of the bed. He could hear Charlotte's words mumbling something about dreaming but his mind had still to recover from the onslaught of a terrible nightmare.

"Charlotte do you really believe I am a runt, a fool and an idiot?" asked Gabriel as he began to rub his forehead with the palm of his hand.

"You most certainly looked like one lying there on the floor mumbling my name", answered Charlotte, "get back into bed I need your body heat I'm freezing". Gabriel rolled back into bed beside Charlotte and felt her soft body snuggling up beside him. The dream had disturbed him and like all nightmares he knew the new day would either wash them away, or soil him with a completely new one.

"Dreams are contrary", said Charlotte as she slipped off to sleep.

"I have no idea how Bishop is going to bring all those children into the trenches, without attracting the attention of hundreds of thousands of soldiers", said

Tim as they walked through the desolated town of Ypres.

"General Arkwright did say they had certain soldiers on their side", said Gabriel as they walked past the remains of a ruined church.

"Certain soldiers wouldn't be enough my good man", replied Tim, "Bishop would need all the Gold in England to pay off all those men".

"We could always go to St Dita's and either stop it before it starts, or follow them to their destination", said Charlotte.

"I am very much betting on the odds that the general's capture has derailed Bishop's plans, but I have no doubt he has a plan B crawling up his sleeve", replied Tim as he stopped to stare at an old man laughing to himself beside a bomb crater.

"That is the first civilian I have seen since we walked into this town", said Gabriel.

Gabriel stared at the old man and wondered if some day he too might take leave of his limited senses and follow in the man's footsteps. As he looked around him, thousands of weary and mud soaked soldiers walked along Menin Road towards the front line like walking lines of dead. The roofs, the walls, the glass windows of every shape and size were now remnants of what once was a better time. The eeriness of the fog and the crisp cold give way to allow the dismal grey reality to take its place. Gabriel wept inwardly for the young and old, the fathers and uncles, the husbands and brothers and all those who were cursed with being born into this murderous time. He reminded himself that he too was fighting a war and every battle however small was a victory for humanity.

"I saw him once before staring into the same crater",

replied Tim, "one of the soldiers told me he was the village idiot who can't seem to accept the grave changes around him".

"I bet he is the happiest person alive", said Charlotte. Gabriel didn't hear what Charlotte said, if she had spoken again her words would have fell on nothing. For all Gabriel could hear were the words village idiot thumping the walls of his mind like thunder. He walked towards the village idiot and as he got closer, the man suddenly stopped smiling and ran towards the ruined church. Gabriel was quickly followed by Charlotte and Tim as they pursued the frightened idiot as he jumped over a wall and disappeared.

"God bless the village idiot", said Gabriel as he stopped beside the wall to catch his breath.

"What has come over you Gabriel?" asked Charlotte as she too came to a breathless stop.

"I believe my dear granddaughter, our Mr. Shivers has hit upon a most brilliant observation", replied Tiny Tim who looked no worse for wear from their brief sprint.

"The village idiot sees everything yet remains invisible", said Gabriel as he proceeded to climb the wall.

"What is this child raving about grandfather?" asked Charlotte as she turned around to Tim.

"Wait and see my dear, just follow the man of the hour", answered Tim as he followed Gabriel over the wall.

"He must have disappeared somewhere around here", said Gabriel as he pulled aside pieces of broken pews and decorative wood.

Gabriel could feel a metal handle and on lifting it with surprising ease; he looked at the stone steps that led down into the darkness below.

"Has anyone got matches?" asked Gabriel.

"Wait one minute my remarkable boy, my intelligent boy", replied Tim as he ran off towards some soldiers.

"What do you expect to find down there?" asked Charlotte as she annoyingly brushed the dust from her coat and skirt.

"Either a nest of village idiots or a wonderful discovery", answered Gabriel as he awaited Tim's return.

"Why don't we settle for a wonderful discovery of village idiots", said Charlotte in a tone of annoyance.

"Let there be light", said Tim as he returned with a hurricane lamp complete with wick, globe and paraffin oil.

"Do I dare ask how you managed to get your hands on that", said Charlotte.

"Remind me to fill you in on the details at a later date", replied Tim as he handed the lamp to Gabriel and then followed him down the stone cold steps.

As they made their way through the narrow tunnel, the lack of confrontation with spiders' webs convinced Gabriel that the tunnel had been used several times in the present. As the tunnel widened Charlotte jumped as her own shadow grew bigger and Gabriel stopped as the outside light appeared before them.

"Let's not make a second guess as to where that leads us", said Tim as he removed Charlotte's vice grip hand from his arm.

"Let me go take a look", replied Charlotte as she moved towards the opening, "I am not afraid of the light".

"If that is what we believe it to be my dear, your presence will result in not only several thousand proposals of marriage, but will raise a thick air of suspicion", said Tim as he reached to pull her back.

"I will go take a look", said Gabriel.

"No my young man, you are not leaving me all alone with this vixen", replied Tim as he made his way towards the opening.

"You don't surely believe this will lead to the trenches?" asked Charlotte as she hooked her hand around Gabriel's hand.

"I am confident that it will", answered Gabriel, "this may be Bishop's route to plan B".

"Several thousand proposals of marriage sounds exciting", said Charlotte as she squeezed Gabriel arm lightly, "I could be courted by each and every one and treated like a princess, but then the hard part would be choosing one and breaking all those gorgeous hearts". Gabriel could sense that Charlotte was attempting to draw him out in the open, and force him to draw the sword of jealousy. He knew she wanted him to say something, to make a comment denouncing her choice of husbands and make his own claim of honor and love. But Gabriel clinched the fists of his heart and bit his tongue of longing and stood firm at the sentry of his deepest desires.

"Gabriel Shivers", said Charlotte as she caught Gabriel by surprise, "when in God's name are you going to ask me to maaaa".

"Your instincts were right my old friend", said Tim as his sudden return stopped Charlotte from finishing her sentence, "there is a feeder trench that leads to all the ones stretching out to the right and left and facing the Germans on the other side".

"So this is where Bishop will bring the children on Christmas Eve", replied Gabriel as he handed the lamp to Tim.

"And this is where we will stop them my fine children", said Tim as he lead the way back down the tunnel.

"You were saying before we were so rudely interrupted?" asked Gabriel.

"I believe it was you who was interrupted", replied Charlotte in a tone of denial.

"No my dear, I distinctly remember you were trying to ask me something, or was it trying to tell me something", returned Gabriel.

"I most certainly was not trying to ask you anything, it was you who wanted to ask me something", replied Charlotte as the climbed the steps and stepped back into the light within the darkness.

"When I was a boy my father used to set me on his shoulder and carry me home on his way back from work", said Tim as he sucked on his cup of welcoming tea at the kitchen table.

"Excuse me sir", interrupted Gabriel as he smiled in Tim's direction, "but where have I heard that before, oh that's right, a book by Charles Dickens".

"Where is your manners Gabriel Shivers?" replied Charlotte as she slightly raised her voice, "why don't you let him finish his story".

"Certainly my dearest Charlotte Starrs", said Gabriel as he tried to mirror Charlotte's annoyance, "let him finish, the Story".

"My dears", replied Tim in an apologetic voice, "it's not important I was just reminiscing".

Gabriel suddenly felt guilty and a deep sense of shame began to creep over his conscience. He had no business mocking the old gentleman and he most certainly had no reason whatsoever to doubt his sincerity and honesty.

"I am truly sorry Tim", said Gabriel as he first looked at Tim and then turned to Charlotte, "and you too my dear, please forgive me both of you".

"It's ok old friend and like I said, just recalling a few childhood memories", replied Tim.

"Did I hear you call someone Charlotte?" asked the landlady as she sat a plate of jam buns on the table before them.

"Indeed you have my dear", replied Tim as he reached for the buns like a hungry child, "my beautiful granddaughter here has been blessed with that very name".

"It's nice to have another Charlotte in the house", said the landlady before returning to the kitchen.

Gabriel reached for the plate of buns and without pausing he consumed one without lifting his head. Just as he finished he looked over at Charlotte and was surprised to find her quiet in her own thoughts.

"Would you like a bun?" asked Gabriel as he pushed the plate in her direction.

Charlotte slowly reached for the plate and then pulled her hand quickly away as if she discovered they were poisoned.

"Grandfather", asked Charlotte in a quiet voice, "you know when you said the landlady reminded you of someone, who was it?"

"I'm not quite sure my dear", replied Tim as he reached for his third bun, "come to think of it she reminded me a little of your dear mother".

"Have you noticed something else about this house?" asked Charlotte as she continued to talk in a loud whisper.

"Not really", replied Tim as he swept his eyes around the kitchen, "looks like any other house to me".

"What do you mean like any other house, do you mean a house in England or Belgium?" asked Charlotte.

"My dear, why are you so interested in what a house looks like?" replied Tim, "most houses are homes whether they are in England or Belgium".

"We are in Belgium and you would expect houses to look different", said Charlotte as she battled to prove her point.

"My dear we are not on the other side of the world, this is a European country with European influences so you would expect them to be similar", replied Tim as he hurried to bag the last bun.

"Charlotte", said Gabriel as he edged into the conversation, "your grandfather has travelled a lot more than us; I believe he knows what he is talking about".

"You stupid idiotic men", replied Charlotte as she slightly raised her voice, "take a look at the photograph hanging above the vase".

When Gabriel first looked at the photograph he smiled before applying his fingers to a nonexistent itch on the top of his head. The second time he looked he could barely believe what he was seeing.

"My God Tim it's you", said Gabriel as he continued to stare at the photograph in a trance like state.

"Is there something you are not telling us grandfather?" asked Charlotte as she threw Tim a solid non shifting look.

"Ahh, well my dear, I'm not sure, quite sure what you are talking about", mumbled Tim as he continued to focus on the photograph.

"Not sure what I'm talking about?" asked Charlotte as she pointed in the direction of the photo, "that is what I'm talking about".

"I don't really know what to say my dear and I can't deny that it is my very portrait", replied Tim, visibly confused by what he saw.

"Then what is it doing on that wall, in this house?" asked Charlotte in a continued whisper.

"I don't know, yes it does look like me, but it may not be me", answered Tiny Tim as he still couldn't believe what he saw.

"Well let's find out from the lady herself shall we?" asked Charlotte just before the landlady entered the kitchen.

"I like the photograph", said Gabriel as the landlady walked into the room, "who is it?"

"That's my grandfather", replied the landlady as she lifted the empty plate from the table, "It was taken just after the war".

Gabriel wanted to ask her his name and which war was she talking about, the first Boer war or second, but no sooner had she appeared than she was gone again.

"The hairs on the back of my neck are beginning to stand up sprightly", said Charlotte as she pushed back her chair and stood up, "I'm going up to my room to think".

"And I'm going outside to think", replied Tim as he made his way towards the front door.

Gabriel was left alone in the kitchen to stare once again at the portrait of Tiny Tim. He tried to doubt the similarities several times but kept returning to Tim's likeness beyond any shadow of a doubt. He could only assume that Tim was keeping one of his not so little secrets from them and laid bare the possibility that Tim had been here before.

"What fascinates you about the photograph?" asked the landlady as she quietly entered the kitchen and took a seat beside him.

"Ahh, well I suppose the likeness of my friend Tim", muttered Gabriel as he was caught off guard by her stealing presence.

"A little bit more than a likeness", replied the landlady as she deliberately kept her voice low.

"Are you trying to suggest it is Tim?" asked Gabriel as he tried to avoid meeting the landlady's eye.

"I am suggesting just that", replied the landlady, "why must you keep doubting your own senses Gabriel?"

Gabriel at first wondered how she knew his name but floated on the idea that she must have heard it from their conversation at the table.

"My senses can sometimes be affected by the environment around me, a motorcar passing by, a dog barking or even the smell of a woman's perfume", answered Gabriel.

"Do you know who I am?" asked the landlady as she continued to fix her stare on Gabriel.

"I know you're the landlady of this house", replied Gabriel as he too began to feel the hairs on the back of his neck begin to rise.

"I want you to stay calm because I am going to tell you who I am", said the landlady, "whatever happens between us in the next few minutes, for all our sakes it is important that you remain strong".

Gabriel wanted to push his chair backwards and run wildly from the house. He yearned to call out for Charlotte and Tim to come to his aid, but neither his legs nor voice wished to do anything other than remain as he was.

"In the name of God who are you?" asked Gabriel in a frightened voice.

"I am her and she is me, I am your Charlotte", replied the landlady.

Charlotte's mention of the candlesticks suddenly flashed up in his memory and within that short space of time, Gabriel knew the landlady was telling the truth.

"How, what on earth, how did you get here?" asked Gabriel as he fought to remain sane.

"That is not important at this very moment in time, but what is important is that you all fulfill your destiny", replied the landlady.

Gabriel gathered enough courage and looked into the landlady's face, he could see the resemblance almost immediately and the smile that reassured him had not changed despite the few wrinkles on each side of her mouth.

"Please spare me the pain of not knowing", said Gabriel, "tell me how this all ends".

"I am neither a mirror nor a book and in your case the end is for me only to know and you yet to find out", replied the landlady.

"Then what is your purpose here, I can see you are not of our time?" asked Gabriel.

"My purpose is to keep you from the clutches of evil long enough for you to stir the pot of humanity", answered the landlady, "I remember this time so well and to divulge it to you would be against the ethics of time".

"I am still confused by your purpose; you say to keep us from the clutches of evil, how will you do that?" asked Gabriel as he wiped the cold sweat from his brow.

"At this very moment all the guesthouses around us are being searched for spies, we both know who is behind that", answered the landlady, "It is my task to provide you with an unseen bed to sleep on and a table that does not exist.

"And will we meet again?" asked Gabriel as the landlady arose from her chair.

"Tomorrow the trumpets of man will announce the eve of a Christmas never to be forgot, only on that day you will find your answer", replied the landlady as her feet shuffled a soft goodbye.

When Gabriel stepped outside to embrace the cold breeze a single bright sparkling star made itself visible in a distant sky. The darkness of night had yet to arrive to give it residence but Gabriel knew by its very presence, a powerful beauty was about to be born.

CHAPTER 26

"What's wrong my dear?" asked Tiny Tim as they left behind the comfort of the landlady's hospitality.

"There's is something wrong with that house", replied Charlotte just before the landlady rode by on her bicycle.

"Goodbye all", said the landlady as she cycled past, "I'm off to Scarborough to meet my husband getting off the train".

"Over four hundred miles on a bicycle and the last time I checked, bicycles could not cross the channel on their own", said Charlotte as she stared after the landlady, "either that lady has lost her sense of direction or I was right in thinking that something was not quite right about that house".

"I'm afraid you are right my dear, take a look at the house", replied Tim as Gabriel and he stared at the empty space where the house used to be.

"My God it's disappeared, but why, what is going on?" asked Charlotte as she stood looking at a green field.

"Whatever happened my dear, it was all for the good", replied Tim as he continued on his way.

Gabriel wanted to tell Charlotte the truth, to explain that it was her who had provided them with shelter but decided that some things were better left behind. As they walked in the direction of St Dita's church, Gabriel thanked God for the curtain of fog that had arrived to keep them from dangerous prying eyes.

"There are two soldiers standing guard outside", said Tim as he came rushing back to Charlotte and Gabriel.

"What are they doing there, are they Bishop's men?" replied Charlotte as all three hid behind a grey stone wall.

"My presumption of the general employing his best singing voice to save his own skin could be right and the soldiers are there to stop Bishop from using the church", said Tim.

"Put your hands in the air", said the soldier pointing the rifle in their direction, "come on get up".

Gabriel had been taken completely by surprise by the soldier and as all three obeyed the soldier's command, he could not bring himself to believe that their great journey was about to end in this way.

"Who are you and what are you doing snooping around the church?" asked the soldier.

"My dear fellow", replied Tim as he prepared himself for another great and noble lie, "We thought you were Germans".

"I asked you a question", said the soldier as he raised his voice.

"We come here every year on Christmas Eve to honor our patron saint Dita, and when we saw soldiers guarding the entrance, we thought you were Germans", replied Tim.

"Let's pay saint Dita a visit then, go on keep walking

towards the church and keep your hands where I can see them", said the soldier as he walked behind all three with his rifle at the ready.

As all three were forced in the direction of the church, Gabriel's heart began to beat wildly. The two sentries were still standing at the entrance and to the right two more stood idling around. Without pausing to question either his motives or the madness that came with his actions, Gabriel turned quickly to the left and ran as fast as his body and soul would allow him. He heard Charlotte shout 'No' as she tried to stop the soldier from firing at Gabriel's disappearing body and heard the roar of Tiny Tim telling him to 'Run my boy, run'. The fog had once again been called upon to hide his tracks, yet Gabriel still heard the bullets passing over his head like whining arrows of death. He ran and ran, he jumped fences and waded through rivers, he passed over both hard and soggy ground until his body could move no more and he collapsed exhausted, cold and wet on a place he knew not where.

Gabriel hadn't realized he had either passed out or simply fell asleep. When he gathered himself up from the grass he could not believe his eyes. Hundreds and hundreds of small white crosses in neat lines painted the freshly cut green grass. On one cross it read, here lies a child of war, another read, sleep in peace dear child and another bore three words that pierced Gabriel's heart like a bolt of lightning, suffer little children.

"Not a pretty sight", said the lady wearing a long flowing purple dress.

"No", replied Gabriel as he wiped the tears from his eyes, "I failed didn't I?"

"Underneath this ground there are many failures", answered the lady as she knelt down to etch more words on a freshly painted cross, "these failures are as much mine as they are yours, and all those who join their heart to no one".

"I tried, I truly tried", said Gabriel as he wiped more tears from his ever filling eyes.

"On this day nineteen hundred and fourteen years ago a child like these was born to make lame men walk and blind men see, before he came along I am certain they too tried, tried to walk and tried to see", replied the lady.

"If I too, only had that miracle for one day, I would gladly give all my tomorrows", said Gabriel.

"One single day in exchange for years full of happiness and chance?" asked the lady as she stopped and looked up at Gabriel with two piercing green eyes.

"If a cross with my name on it replaced only one of the crosses here, then I would consider it a fair exchange", answered Gabriel as he wiped more tears from his eyes.

"A certain young lady of your acquaintance would not consider it a fair exchange", said the lady as she got back onto her feet.

"That young lady would not expect anything less of me", replied Gabriel.

"Would she also give up all her tomorrows for one day?" asked the lady as she began to walk towards Gabriel.

"That I have no doubt", replied Gabriel as he suddenly felt the tears stop flowing from his eyes.

"Then by that revelation alone, you both truly deserve each other", said the lady as a piercing green light from her eyes surrounded him in a fantastic glowing bubble and sent him spinning through the air.

When Gabriel awoke, the wet soggy ground had soaked through his clothes sending shivers throughout his whole body. He gathered himself up off the ground and scanned the area around him three hundred and sixty degrees to try and find his bearings. The familiar sight of Ypres cast a faint picture through the thin fog and with the heavy slush of his sodden feet; Gabriel pushed his way onwards to an end yet to be determined.

"Toy soldiers, toy soldiers, toy soldiers", shouted the village idiot as Gabriel made his way to the front of the ruined church.

"Where are the toy soldiers?" asked Gabriel as he sat down on a bundle of rubble to try and regain some of his inner and outer strength.

"Toy soldiers, toy man, moley holey", replied the idiot as he eyed Gabriel up from head to toe.

"Did you see any children dressed in soldiers' uniforms pass this way?" asked Gabriel as he tried to reason some sense from the man who had little cares. Suddenly the two words moley holey entered the sponge part of Gabriel's brain and were quickly absorbed to mean that the children had already passed through the tunnel. The time it took Gabriel to reach Ypres turned out to be longer than he thought and the night sky had caught him by surprise. The speckle of stars dotted the heavens as if they had just arrived to bear witness to something brighter than they. Gabriel made his way towards the entrance of the tunnel while at the same time wishing he had something to guide his way. He tripped over a bundle of wood and stones and landed on top of the door into the tunnel. He could feel his heart pound as he lifted the door and crawled on his hands and knees down the cold stone steps. He paused to call on his reserves of strength and soon found himself back on his feet and staggering down a blacker than black narrow tunnel. At each step forward into the unknown, Gabriel could not stop thinking of Charlotte and Tim and how they would struggle to convince the authorities that they meant no harm. The tunnel felt longer as Gabriel struggled with the cold and the dampness of his clothes and longing for the bitter end to a ring of blackness. The bright light came upon him like a hurried dawn and as he approached the end of the tunnel he could see the brightness swallow up the ground before him and replace it with a yellow and white carpet of peace. As Gabriel stepped out of the tunnel he looked up into the sky and beheld a star more beautiful than a spring morning and clearer than a summer sky.

"So you decided to follow me all the way here", said Bishop as he tried to reach for something inside his pocket.

Gabriel pulled the luger from his pocket and pointed it straight at Bishop.

"You want to know why I followed you all the way here?" asked Gabriel as his hand shook with both tiredness and emotion.

"To be a partner in my wonderful and prosperous plan", replied Bishop as he waited for Gabriel to drop his guard.

"To kill you and erase your name from existence", said Gabriel as he tried hard to hold the gun straight.

"Any minute now you are going to collapse and I promise you, you will be dead before you hit the ground", replied Bishop as his fingers very slowly crawled to reach his inside pocket.

Gabriel could feel the luger getting heavier and heavier as he fought hard to keep on his feet. His legs began to shake, first slowly then faster and the face of Bishop began to blur before his eyes. His finger pulled the trigger with every last ounce of strength in his body and one second later he felt Bishop's bullet tear into his arm with as much ferocity as evil could muster. Gabriel felt his body crash to the ground while his luger took leave of his grip and surrendered itself to the wet mud beside him. As Bishop walked towards him with a cold expression scrolled across his face, Gabriel could hear Charlotte's words echoing inside his head, pleading, warning, and praying that he did not try to confront Bishop. He made no promises, he give her no cause to believe he would do nothing less, yet Gabriel knew as his life was about to come to an end, she would both hate him and love him all the lonely days of her life. From the corner of his eye he could see thousands of child soldiers herded into a great wide open space, the light of the great star above them reflecting the terror in their eyes. If only the ghost that had entered his room would return and spare him five more minutes, or the wall would whisper some great and miraculous plan. He prayed for Saint Dita, The Lady of the Crosses and he prayed for Ebenezer Scrooge that they might turn the page backwards and give him a second chance. From some distant place he could hear the bells ringing, calling out to friend and foe, to child and adult that Christmas had arrived to remind mankind that the words peace and goodwill meant much, much more than words. And all who dwell in this place of pain and suffering, of terror and death, need not hate their fellow man.

"I thought you might allow me the very great pleasure of seeing you crawl at my feet and beg for your worthless life", said Bishop as he pointed the gun at Gabriel's head, "you really have disappointed me".

As the shot rang out Gabriel braced himself for a great thunder of pain, followed by the acceptance that the curtains of his life must be closed. He heard Bishop gasp and saw him turn his head around to see the perpetrator who cheated him of his final triumph. Behind the smoking gun stood the blurred figure of someone he thought he knew, and before Gabriel could breathe a long sigh of relief, that very person had disappeared into the light, leaving behind a shadow that would forever reflect on the wall of friendship.

"No, noooo, you stupid man, what have you done?" shouted Charlotte as she dropped down on her knees beside Gabriel on the ground.

"It's ok, I just took a bullet in the arm", replied Gabriel as his heart almost shone brighter than the star, at seeing Charlotte.

"I've cut myself worse having a shave", said Tiny Tim as he ripped Gabriel's coat sleeve to stop the flow of blood with a well-used handkerchief, "the bullet passed through".

"You can't use that grandfather", said Charlotte as she reached into her pocket and produced a length of bed sheet.

"I have been using that to stop blood for over forty years and I didn't even have to wash it", replied Tim as he suddenly stood up, "listen, do you hear that?"

Gabriel could hear singing, first in German, then English and followed by French. The words of Silent Night, 'Stille Nacht, Douce Nuit', flowed around the trenches like some great festive potion, three cultures singing with one voice. Gabriel was helped to his feet by Charlotte and as he looked across no man's land he could see thousands of candles, flickering to the voice of peace, all coming together to send a pulse to the living dead and giving life to poisoned hearts and minds.

"How did you manage to talk your way out of that church?" asked Gabriel.

"It took more time than it should have, we tried to convince the captain that Bishop would not be meeting at the church, but he wasn't having any of it", replied Tim.

"Grandfather eventually won him over by employing the mutual subject of football and exchanging his gold watch for a football signed by the regimental team", answered Charlotte as she wrapped her arm around Gabriel's waist.

"And where is the football now?" asked Gabriel.

"Right here my good man, or might I say my very good friend", answered Tim as he kicked the ball over the trench and into no man's land, "I never did like the game, I could never fathom why a bunch of intelligent human beings were so obsessed with chasing a round leather object".

"I owe my life to someone and I believe it to be Hans", said Gabriel, "how he managed to appear right on the edge of time I will never know".

"Do you remember when I stayed behind at the church to speak to the Nun?" asked Charlotte.

"I did find it rather strange but I decided I had more important things to worry about", replied Gabriel.

"I begged her for one miracle and on receiving it I asked that your life be saved. Your motorcar crash with Jimbo used it up and that was why I was so adamant that you did not confront Bishop", said Charlotte as she helped Gabriel sit down on an old tea chest.

"So where did Hans come into it?" asked Gabriel.

"I knew you wouldn't listen, so the last night we talked to Hans, I slipped him a note explaining how head strong you were and in particular, that Bishop would without doubt kill you", replied Charlotte as she sat next to Gabriel.

"So, Hans must have been tracking Bishop to watch over me", said Gabriel.

"And it was a good thing that he did for all our sakes", replied Tim as he patted Gabriel on the back, "if anything had have happened to you there is no way I could have remained on the same planet as my granddaughter".

"Hello my friends", said Hans as he greeted the trio, "this is truly a wonderful night".

"Indeed my fine fellow", replied Tim as he reached out and shook Hans' hand.

"Made more so by your very hands", said Charlotte as she arose from the tea chest and give Hans a warm embrace, "thank you so much, we are forever indebted to you".

"No, my friends I am forever indebted to you, if you had have left me in that prison camp, this might never have happened", replied Hans.

"No matter", said Gabriel, "I cannot thank you enough; if you had have been delayed another second Bishop would have got me first".

Suddenly Hans went quiet and first looked at Gabriel, then at Tim and followed on by staring at Charlotte.

"I'm so sorry but I believe I may have missed

something", replied Hans as he looked confused.

"Bishop", said Charlotte, "you must have followed him".

"I'm afraid you have your wires crossed dear", replied Hans, "I left Bishop to your capable hands and I see you have done an excellent job".

"You read my note?" asked Charlotte as her voice now began to shake.

"I'm so sorry, I meant to read it later that night but I was forced to have a midnight swim fully clothed and by the time I fished it out of my pocket it was unreadable", replied Hans, "was there anything important you wanted to ask me?"

Charlotte sat down again next to Gabriel and wrapped her arm around his waist, holding on tighter than ever before. As Tim took his place beside them they could hear the children's voices joining in to add to the many thousands of voices singing a song they all knew so well. For that night at least the guns fell silent and the blind indifferences that grew in men's hearts lost their memory. And if you were one of the millions of rats and lice that thrived on the misery of humanity, then you too would have paused and paid homage to the wondrous earthly glow of three thousand Christmas candles.

And you the reader may ask, what became of Tiny Tim and did Charlotte ever get to hear those three forever lingering words? Even in stories, the magical words are left unspoken and the greatest stories are spoken words. When we close the page for the last time, are we turning off the light or just turning down the lamp? Do we say goodbye to a lesson taught or do we dry a tear and turn our back forever on the ripples in life's muddy stream? Mr. Scrooge may have done things different than the voice in the wall, and the lady of the crosses may have started again at the beginning. For those who choose to knock gently on a long lost door or share the whispers of a distant regret, then you too would share the glow of life's radiant treasure.

And as Tiny Tim would say, well that's another story.